A DOCTOR'S PRIDE

Sara said, "It's pneumonia, isn't it?"

Dr. Hasbrook's face turned a bright red. "I'll not tolerate being told how to do my job—especially by a young woman! This child has catarrh!" Hasbrook insisted. "I prescribed a purgative, and I suggest we all give it time to work." He looked at the girl's father. "Sir, I want you to take your daughter home. Keep her warm and see that she eats. She'll be better in a few days."

"She'll be dead in a few days!" Sara exclaimed. "You can't do this, Doctor! You can't sacrifice this child's life just because you're too proud to admit you made a mistake."

Hasbrook swung around toward her, his face a dark, mottled red. "You've been dismissed from my staff, young woman, and I can promise you that none of the other hospitals in Boston will make the mistake of allowing you to practice there. Now, if you don't leave this building and stop interfering, I'll summon a constable and have you arrested!"

"Go ahead, damn you!" Sara shouted. "Go ahead and have me thrown in jail! But get that little girl the attention she needs, otherwise she's going to die!"

HEALER'S CALLING
by J. L. Reasoner, author of *The Healer's Road*

HEALER'S CALLING

J. L. REASONER

Roger E. Miller
1885 Lawhead Lane
Zanesville, Ohio 43701

BERKLEY BOOKS, NEW YORK

HEALER'S CALLING

A Berkley Book / published by arrangement with
the authors

PRINTING HISTORY
Berkley edition / June 1996

The Putnam Berkley World Wide Web site address is
http://www.berkley.com

ISBN: 0-425-15487-4

BERKLEY®
Berkley Books are published by The Berkley Publishing Group,
200 Madison Avenue, New York, New York 10016.
BERKLEY and the "B" design
are trademarks belonging to Berkley Publishing Corporation.

PRINTED IN THE UNITED STATES OF AMERICA

10 9 8 7 6 5 4 3 2 1

For Bruce Washburn,
without whom this writing team
might not have ever gotten together.

Special thanks, as always, to
Leslie Gelbman and Gary Goldstein
of The Berkley Publishing Group,
and to Barbara Puechner,
the world's best agent.

PROLOGUE

The woman rocking slowly back and forth in the chair was undeniably beautiful. At least, Dr. Thomas Black thought so as he sat at his desk and watched her. True, there was more silver than lustrous brown in the thick hair, and the years had left their tracks on skin that had once been so smooth and fair. Her eyes, which had sparkled with wit and vitality, were for the most part empty these days. But no matter. To Thomas, Clarissa was still every bit as lovely as she had been the day he married her thirty-eight years ago. Or the day he had met her there on Boston Common, when he had been a clumsy young medical student who had almost stepped right in the middle of the picnic she was having with some friends.

Such a long time ago, Thomas thought with a sigh, and so much had happened. And yet, it seemed in so many ways as if it had been just yesterday . . .

No point in dwelling on that, he told himself. He looked at his wife and said, "I'm writing a letter to Sara, Clarissa. Is there anything you want me to tell her?"

He didn't expect an answer, of course. Clarissa's

mind was long past the point where she could think clearly and rationally. He doubted that she even recognized him anymore, and the name of their daughter was meaningless to her. Still, it made Thomas feel better to have these conversations with her. They reminded him of the times when they had sat together like this in his study at the end of each day, and as he was writing up his notes on the day's cases he would tell her about the patients he had seen. They would talk of other things, too—family and friends, current events, even the local gossip—and there was always plenty of that in a small town like Handley's Mill. The town had grown considerably from the tiny hamlet in the Berkshire Mountains of western Massachusetts it had been when Thomas was a boy, but the feeling of community was still there, and Thomas hoped it always would be.

He paused only for a moment, and when Clarissa didn't say anything, he went on talking, telling her all the things he was writing in the letter to Sara. It was all rather mundane, of course; Thomas's life was long past the point where it contained any real excitement. But he still took considerable pleasure just in being able to convey the details of everyday life to his daughter. There had been a time, during the awful war that had ended eight years earlier, when he and Clarissa had believed that Sara was lost to them forever. She had spent long months as the captive of a band of Confederate raiders while her family had been convinced she was dead, killed when the field hospital in which she was working as a nurse had been overrun by Rebel troops during the Battle of Chickamauga. Fate had led her brother John to find her the very day the war ended, and her safe return to her family had seemed nothing less than a miracle. Despite everything that had happened since that time—some good, some bad—Thomas was still fervently thankful that Sara was alive and well.

A man could tolerate almost anything, he thought, as long as he knew that his children were all right.

"I believe I'll tell Sara about that dance last month," he said to Clarissa. "It was quite a scandal, you know. I'm told Margaret Bleeker danced with every man there—except her husband."

Thomas's fingers, gnarled and knobby but still strong, dipped the pen in the inkwell, and the tip began to scratch against the paper again as he wrote. He bent his head over the missive, and the light from the lamp on the desk shone on thinning, snow-white hair that had once been thick and red. Concentrating as he was on the letter to Sara, it was several moments before Thomas noticed what his wife was doing.

Dancing . . . she remembered dancing. Whirling around the floor with her tall, handsome husband as the musicians played and everyone watched. Thomas's strong arms were around her, holding her, protecting her, swooping her with effortless ease through the steps of the waltz. She wished she could dance like that with him again.

And why not? she suddenly thought. There he was, sitting right across the room. Her breath caught in her throat as she was struck by the power of her love for him. His hair was thick and red, and she always enjoyed running her fingers through it after they made love. She felt herself blushing at the thought, but there was no denying it. Thomas Black was the most attractive man in all of Boston. Soon they would be leaving here, going back to the village where he had grown up, where he would begin his practice of medicine.

Tonight, though, he was not Dr. Black. He was just Thomas, her beloved husband, and she wanted to dance with him and dance and dance until she was too tired to do anything except laugh and rest her head against his chest as he lifted her in his strong arms and carried her upstairs to bed. She wanted to dance . . . she wanted to dance . . .

Then she was on her feet, holding her hands out to him, smiling coquettishly as she spoke his name. The music swelled up, the lush notes enfolding her like the warm embrace of a lover, but he must have heard her anyway. He looked up, and a smile appeared on his handsome face, and as she spoke his name again he stood and reached out to her, taking her hands in his. He moved from side to side and she followed, and the music grew louder and louder until she could hear nothing else, could see his lips moving but could not hear the words, and she threw her head back and laughed.

And she danced, and was young again. She danced . . .

The steps were awkward, and his tired old bones didn't want to do them, but when he had looked up and seen her shuffling toward him, croaking his name, he had not hesitated. She said hoarsely, "Dance," and he began to move with her, even though there was no music, no sound in the room except the whisper of their feet on the rug and their labored breathing.

But as he took her in his arms, he thought he heard something. The first faint strains of a melody, soft and lilting, brushing across his senses like the touch of a warm breeze in springtime. The music grew louder as they danced, and muscles that had been weary became lively again, and for Thomas, too, the past was once more alive, the days long gone but still etched deeply in his soul, where he had could reach down and touch them at moments like this. He felt tears in his eyes, felt the moisture trickling down his leathery cheeks, felt the soft warmth of the woman in his arms.

And suddenly he felt the pain, deep inside him, deeper than the memories. It grew and blossomed like a flower, filling him, washing him away like a tide sweeping across a beach.

He barely noticed it.

Because the music was so loud, and so beautiful, and he had Clarissa in his arms. He wished he never had to let go, wished the music would never stop playing.

BOOK ONE

The heart has its arguments, with which the understanding is not acquainted.
—RALPH WALDO EMERSON

Let us, then, be up and doing, with a heart for any fate.
—HENRY WADSWORTH LONGFELLOW

ONE

Handley's Mill, Massachusetts, 1867

The music never failed to move Thomas Black. He considered himself a patriot, and as he listened to the stirring strains, he was thankful all over again that the Union had survived the horrible war that had threatened to split it apart.

But not without a cost. As he looked around the village green at the citizens of Handley's Mill who had gathered there to listen to the music and speeches of this Independence Day celebration, the faces of those who were missing haunted Thomas. He could see them as they had been six years earlier: young, eager, full of excitement and anticipation as they marched off to fight the Rebels. His son John had been among them, albeit somewhat belatedly due to Thomas's opposition to the war. So many of the young men had not come back. John had, thank God, but there were so many others who hadn't. So many . . .

Thomas gave a little shake of his head. That terrible conflict was over, had been over for more than two years, in fact, and brooding over the lives it had taken wouldn't bring back a single one of them. It was time to look to the future, and that was exactly what

Thomas resolved to do. As the song came to its end, he applauded along with everyone else for the musicians on the bandstand at this end of the green.

He glanced over at his wife Clarissa, who stood beside him swaying a little, as if in time to music that was no longer there. Thomas was accustomed to that; Clarissa had been in a world of her own for quite some time now, ever since that young private had killed himself in the hospital ward in Washington. Even before that, Clarissa's mind had not been what it once was, but the strain of the long, gruesome months working alongside Thomas in the military hospital had sapped even more of her mental strength, and the death of Private Hawkins had been all that was needed to push her over the edge. Since then she had lived in a sort of shadowland, coming out into the sunlight ever more rarely.

It was difficult for Thomas to see her like this, but she was healthy in every other way, as healthy as a woman of her years could be expected to be, and he was not so arrogant as to assume that she was unhappy. Indeed, he believed that the way she was now was perhaps her only hope for any semblance of happiness.

"I don't think I can listen to this," Sara said.

Thomas turned his attention from his wife and looked over at his daughter, who stood on his other side. Sara's thick red hair, which had been cropped off almost as short as a boy's when she returned to Handley's Mill after the war, had finally grown out to its previous length. Instead of braiding it and wrapping the braids around her head, Sara let her hair hang far down her back. She was striking looking, no doubt about that, although few would consider her beautiful.

Tall, slender, still coltish despite the fact that she was a young woman and no longer a girl, the main things that had changed about Sara were her eyes—gray-green eyes that had seen too much, had witnessed enough bloodshed and horror for ten normal lifetimes. Thomas sometimes wondered if he would handle it as well if he had gone through everything she had endured.

Now she was looking at the bandstand, where the musicians had sat down and a man in a conservative suit and a straw hat had taken their place. Judd Farnsworth was the mayor of Handley's Mill, and everyone knew he was about to make a speech. He never missed an opportunity to do just that.

"Thank you, thank you, ladies and gentlemen, and allow me the privilege and honor of welcoming you to the first annual Handley's Mill Independence Day celebration!" The politician's voice rang out across the green, carrying easily even to those standing at the other end of the long, open space. "This is a special day indeed, as we give thanks for our country's freedom and praise the Lord for giving us the strength to save our great nation from the evil forces which lately endeavored to rip it asunder!"

Sara's mouth was a tight line across her face. "I *won't* listen to this," she said through clenched teeth. She turned away, started toward the back of the crowd.

Thomas's first impulse was to go after her, but he knew he could not do that. He couldn't leave Clarissa alone here in the midst of all these people, even though most of them were longtime friends of the Black family. There was never any knowing what Clarissa might take it into her head to do, and Thomas always stayed close to her whenever they were out of the house. His mouth pulling into a grimace under the thick mustache, he looked over his shoulder and watched his daughter making her way through the press of spectators listening to the mayor's speech. It was easy for a few moments to keep track of Sara's red hair, but then he lost sight of her. Thomas sighed. Sara could take care of herself, he knew. She always had.

But that didn't keep him from worrying about her, even now.

Thomas suspected he knew what was bothering her. Judd Farnsworth had been a fervent abolitionist and a staunch supporter of the Union during the war, just like everyone else in Handley's Mill. Even now, after more than two years, he was still talking in speeches like this one about the evil and the horror brought down on the nation by the Confederacy's attempt to secede from the Union. Judd would have been right at home down there in the South with all the other Reconstructionists who were trying to mold the shattered Confederacy into something more agreeable to their own views. Thomas had read about it in the newspapers, and at times he thought the war had not really ended at all; it had merely evolved into another kind of struggle, this time not for land but for the minds of men. Sometimes, unfortunately, the weapons were the same either way.

Sara didn't want to hear about the war, had no patience for the abuse that was still being heaped on the heads of the South by men such as Judd Farnsworth. Thomas suspected that her time with the Rebel patrol had changed her in more than one way. She had not become a believer in slavery, of course; Thomas knew his daughter too well to think that.

But perhaps her eyes had been opened to the fact

that despite the war, the Southerners were still *people,* human beings with all the frailties and failings and glorious successes common to the race. Thomas knew that, had always known that, but some in the victorious North didn't seem to, at least not these days.

So Thomas couldn't blame Sara for turning away, for not wanting to listen to what the mayor had to say. She had heard it all before.

Sara made her way through the crowd. It was quite warm, even for the middle of July, and she wanted to find a nice shady spot underneath one of the trees at the far end of the green.

Laughter rippled around her as the spectators reacted to something Mayor Farnsworth had said. Sara was no longer paying any attention to him. His words made no impact on her. It had been a mistake to come here today, she thought. She was uncomfortable being around this many people, and the music and the speeches were unpleasant reminders of the war. But her father had seemed to think that it would do her good to get out, and she didn't want to disappoint him.

A young man bumped into her, stepping back quickly to tip his hat and smile as he apologized. "I'm sorry, Miss Black," he said. "I should have been watching where I was going."

Sara forced herself to return the smile. "That's all right," she told the young man. "No harm done."

But there had been some harm done, because he was fairly handsome and had blond hair to go with that cocky smile. For an instant as she looked at him, his own features faded and were replaced by those of Carver Gresham. Carver, who had led the Confederate patrol that had captured her, who had made her their unofficial medical officer, who had been her lover for long months that had ended all too painfully . . .

Carver, who had died on the side of a dusty road in Virginia, when the war, the goddamned war, was already over.

A shudder went through Sara as she pushed past the grinning young man. She saw the trees just ahead of her and stepped gratefully into their shade. She went to one of them, leaned against the trunk, and closed her eyes, trying to will her mind far away from everything.

A friendly voice pulled her back. "Hello, Sara. Are your mother and father here?"

She opened her eyes and saw an older man in a black frock coat standing beside her. He had tightly curled gray hair under his bowler hat and a neatly trimmed mustache and goatee. A silver-headed walking stick was clutched in his left hand. Sara recognized him immediately and said, "Oh, hello, Dr. Rawlings. Mother and Father are up closer to the front, near the bandstand."

Dr. Vincent Rawlings nodded. He was about the same age as her father, Sara knew, but he looked several years younger than Thomas Black. He had been practicing medicine in the nearby town of Pittsfield for many years, was as much a fixture there, in fact, as Sara's father was in Handley's Mill.

"I believe I'll go say hello to them," Rawlings went on. "How *is* your lovely mother, Sara?"

Sara drew a deep breath. "About the same," she said. Rawlings nodded knowingly. He and Thomas had been friends for a long time; he was well aware of Clarissa's condition.

"I daresay Thomas probably hasn't slowed down

any," Rawlings said with another smile. "He's like an old carriage horse, always anxious to be in harness."

That comment drew a small laugh from Sara, and she was thankful to Rawlings for taking her mind off Mayor Farnsworth's speech and all the unpleasant memories his talk about the war had stirred up. She wasn't insulted by Rawlings comparing her father to a horse. Thomas Black was *exactly* like that.

"Father still has plenty of patients," she said. "More than he can really keep up with."

"He needs to take in a new young doctor to help him. That would take some of the strain off of him."

Sara nodded. "I've told him the same thing. I even know where he could find such a doctor."

Rawlings lifted an eyebrow and asked, "Oh? And where might that be?"

"Right in his own home," Sara declared.

Rawlings pretended not to understand—or perhaps he actually didn't, Sara wasn't sure. He said, "I thought John had several more years of medical school left down there at Harvard."

"Indeed he does, but I wasn't speaking of my brother."

A smile appeared on Rawlings's face as he said, "Ah, now I see. You were referring to yourself."

Sara's chin lifted. "Of course. I know more about medicine than John ever will."

"And you're modest, too," Rawlings said with a dry chuckle.

Sara flushed in embarrassment. She had always been plain-spoken, and she wasn't going to change now. She *did* know more about medicine than John. It was true that John had learned quite a bit during the two-and-a-half years he had spent as Dr. Matthias Borden's aide in a variety of Union field hospitals, but Sara had been preparing for a medical career ever since she had surreptitiously slipped her father's books down from the shelves and studied them as a young girl. That had been followed by a great deal of practical experience, first in the military hospitals of Washington, D.C., field hospitals in Tennessee and Georgia, and then her time with the Confederate patrol. She would venture to say that she was more experienced in patching up bullet wounds than most doctors.

Yet she knew she was lacking in exposure to the other areas of medicine. There was no war on now, no real need for doctors who specialized in repairing bodies torn and mangled by bullet or cannonball. But a few years of medical school would take care of that deficit . . .

Yet here she sat in Handley's Mill, while her brother John, who had never really wanted to be a doctor, was at Harvard.

"I should think after what you went through that you'd have no interest in medicine now," Rawlings continued, his expression becoming solemn. "Not that I want to dredge up any bad memories, you understand."

Sara shook her head. "That's all right, Doctor. Perhaps some people would react that way to such an ordeal, but I'm afraid it just made me want to become a doctor even more." She groped for the words to express the ideas that drove her. "There are so many bad things in the world . . . I've seen so much suffering . . . and I want to do whatever I can to make it better. You can see that, can't you?"

Rawlings nodded slowly and said, "Yes, I can, Sara. You're a remarkable young woman, my dear."

She felt her face growing warm again. She wasn't looking for praise. Some doctors, she was convinced, sought a medical career because they thought it would give them some sort of exalted position in the community. Such a possibility never entered her head. She was only interested in doing good works and helping people.

Or at least, that was what she had always thought. But she had to admit that the words of admiration from Vincent Rawlings made her feel good. Very good indeed.

Rawlings linked his arm with hers. "Let's find your parents, shall we?" he suggested.

Sara nodded, and together they made their way back toward the front of the crowd. Mayor Farnsworth was still speaking, which came as no surprise. Sara estimated that he had at least twenty minutes left before he would begin to run down. Perhaps she could persuade her father to skip the rest of the speech and they could all get some chilled lemonade from one of the vendors who for this celebration had set up their stands along the edge of the green. Her mother wouldn't care one way or the other, Sara knew.

She supposed she and Dr. Rawlings made a rather incongruous-looking couple as they strolled among the crowd. He was much older than she, old enough to be her father, of course, since he and Thomas Black were roughly the same age. Sara was an inch or so taller than him, too. Of course, it wasn't as if they were actually a couple, she thought. Rawlings was an old friend of the family, nothing more. The admiration in his eyes when he looked at her was purely avuncular.

Thomas Black greeted his friend and fellow physician with a hearty handshake when Sara and Rawlings

came up to him and Clarissa. Rawlings hugged
Clarissa briefly, bringing a pleasant smile to her face
even though she obviously had no idea who he really
was. She said, "Carlton! So good to see you again!"

Sara saw her father and Rawlings exchange a quick
glance, then Rawlings just smiled at Clarissa and said,
"How lovely you look today, my dear." Clarissa
blushed like a young girl at the compliment.

That was because right now, she *was* a young girl in
her mind, Sara thought. Clarissa had mistaken Rawlings for Carlton Danvers, the young man who had
been in medical school with Thomas and whom
Clarissa had almost married. That was all Sara knew
about Danvers, because Thomas Black seldom spoke
of him and even after all these years seemed to harbor
some sort of grudge against the man. But Thomas did
not correct his wife when she mistook Vincent Rawlings for Danvers. There would have been no point in
it.

For several minutes, the four of them stood there
and listened to Mayor Farnsworth, then Sara leaned
over to Thomas and said, "Father, why don't we go get
some lemonade?"

Thomas frowned slightly. "It would be rude to leave
before the mayor finishes his speech, wouldn't it?"

Sara glanced around and waved her hand to indicate
the other members of the crowd, who were drifting
away as she said, "We wouldn't be the only ones."

"No, I suppose not," Thomas admitted. "All right,
then. Come along, Clarissa."

His arm linked tightly with hers, Thomas led his
wife toward the edge of the crowd. Sara and Rawlings
followed, and Rawlings took Sara's arm again, surprising her somewhat. She was also surprised by the

fact that as he linked arms with her, the back of his hand brushed lightly against the side of her breast. Rawlings didn't seem to notice, however, so Sara was sure it had been an accident. She certainly wasn't going to say anything about it.

The four of them had almost reached the edge of the green when there was a sudden flurry of small crackling sounds. Sara flinched involuntarily, as a part of her brain mistook the sounds for small arms fire. She had heard so many volleys of pistol shots during the war that the sound was imprinted in her mind. She realized an instant later that the noise had been fireworks going off, not an attack of some sort.

"Are you all right, Sara?" asked Rawlings with a small frown. Obviously, he had felt her reaction to the fireworks.

"I'm fine," she said, summoning up a bright smile as she did so.

A moment later, the smile faded as she heard a terrified shriek. A shocked silence fell over the green following the scream, and even Judd Farnsworth was quiet, his mouth still halfway open. Another terrible cry ripped through the hot summer air.

"Help us!" a woman implored. "Oh, God, someone help my boy!"

Thomas turned quickly to Sara and snapped, "Watch your mother." Then he said to Rawlings, "Come with me, Vincent. Someone must be hurt."

It didn't take a brilliant intellect to figure that out, Sara thought angrily as her father and Rawlings pushed among the crowd, calling out that they were doctors and needed to be let through. The woman was still pleading for help at the top of her lungs, and other people were beginning to shout. Sara looked at her

mother and saw that Clarissa was blinking rapidly. An
expression of concern and fear had appeared on her
face. Clarissa wouldn't have the slightest idea what
was going on, but she could surely sense that something was wrong, and that frightened her. Sara took
hold of her arm, saying reassuringly, "It's all right,
Mother. Everything's fine."

But it wasn't. There was trouble over there on the
other side of the green. Sara had figured out by now
that was where the woman's imploring cries were
coming from.

I ought to be over there, too, Sara thought. *I could
do something to help.*

But her father had left her in charge of her mother,
and Sara knew she couldn't abandon Clarissa. The
noise and the press of people around them had already
frightened Clarissa, and if left by herself there was no
telling what she might do.

Suddenly, Sara caught sight of Libbie Daulton in the
crowd. Libbie was seventeen, blond and pretty if
somewhat frail, and Dr. Thomas Black had saved her
life seven years earlier by performing an emergency
appendectomy—with the assistance of his daughter
Sara. Libbie couldn't really be considered a friend; in
fact, her late grandfather, old Frank Daulton, had been
a bitter enemy of Thomas's. But she *did* owe her life to
the Black family, and Sara saw her appearance now as
provident.

"Libbie!" she called out. "Libbie, over here!"

The girl came over to Sara and Clarissa, smiling un-
certainly. "Hello, Mrs. Black," she said. "And good
day to you, Miss Black. What can I do for you,
ma'am?"

Sara decided to let that "ma'am" reference pass unchallenged, even though she was only twenty-six. To someone as young as Libbie, an unmarried woman of that age had to seem like an old maid—which was exactly what Sara thought she was turning into. But that was neither here nor there, because Sara had much more important things on her mind.

"Could you keep an eye on my mother, please, Libbie?" she asked. "I have to go help my father with whatever happened over there on the other side of the green."

Libbie frowned and said hesitantly, "Well, I don't know, Miss Black . . ."

"It will only be for a few minutes, I'm sure. Just don't let her wander off or hurt herself."

The girl looked at Clarissa, and Sara saw something like fear in her eyes. Everyone in town knew that Clarissa's mind was not what it had once been. Some of them probably even whispered behind their hands that she was insane, Sara thought bitterly, and everyone knew that lunatics were dangerous and not to be trusted.

"Look," Sara said, letting some of the exasperation she felt come through in her voice, "my mother won't hurt you. She's not crazy, Libbie."

"Oh, no, ma'am!" Libbie exclaimed. "I never thought—"

"Just watch her, all right? I'll be back in a few minutes." Sara turned to her mother and said, "Libbie is going to stay with you while I go see what Father is doing, Mother. Is that all right?"

"Libbie?" Clarissa repeated, obviously not understanding who Sara was talking about.

"She's right here," Sara said firmly. "You stay with her, Mother."

Clarissa looked over at Libbie and said, "Why, Sara, what happened to your beautiful red hair? It's blond now!"

Sara took her mother's hand and put it in Libbie's, who clasped it nervously. "I . . . I can change it back if you'd like," Libbie said.

"Oh, no, dear, that's fine. I think it's pretty. Can we walk under the trees?"

Sara nodded to Libbie, who said, "Of course." Then, as Libbie and Clarissa moved toward the trees along the edge of the green, Sara turned and hurried in the other direction, making her way through the crowd toward the spot where she had lost sight of her father and Vincent Rawlings. The screaming had stopped, but there was still a lot of excited muttering going on.

When Sara reached the front of the crowd, she saw that her father and Rawlings were kneeling on either side of a boy about ten years old who was thrashing around on the grass. Rawlings was holding his wrists tightly to keep him under control. His face appeared to have been rubbed with charcoal, and Sara didn't recognize him. Nearby, however, a woman stood trembling with hands clasped as if in prayer. Tears ran down her cheeks as she said, "Please, Dr. Black, you've got to save my boy!" Sara knew her; the woman's name was Alice Scott, which would likely make the boy on the ground her son, Andy.

"The lad's in no danger of dying, Mrs. Scott," Thomas said as he glanced up at the woman. "I'm concerned about his eyes, however. You say the powder from those fireworks went off right in his face?"

Alice Scott nodded shakily, and Thomas and Rawlings exchanged a grim look.

"Some of that burning powder must have gotten into

the boy's eyes," Rawlings said. "Have you had any experience with such a thing, Thomas?"

Thomas shook his head. "Not in all my years as a doctor."

The boy's mother began to moan. She brought her hands to her mouth in horror. "He's going to be blind!" she exclaimed.

Sara had heard enough. She stepped forward and went down on one knee next to her father. "I've seen injuries like this before," she said briskly. "One day, a musket misfired and threw burning powder into the eyes of one of the men in the patrol. We were near a creek, so I began washing out his eyes with cool water."

Thomas looked at her and asked, "To get rid of the unburned powder, you mean?"

"And to help heal the burns that were already there."

Thomas grunted. "It certainly can't hurt at a time like this." He looked up at the crowd pressing around them. "Someone bring a bucket of water and a cloth. Make sure the water is clear and cool."

"I'll run down to the creek," one of the bystanders volunteered.

"Clean water!" Thomas called after the man. "It's got to be clean water, and a clean bucket!"

Sara wasn't sure they would get either one of those things, but it was worth a try. She said to her father, "I bathed that man's eyes for several hours."

"Did he lose his sight?"

She glanced at Alice Scott, who was hanging on her every word, then said, "In one eye, he did. But the other recovered."

"One eye is better than none," Thomas said. "Let's

get this lad into the shade. It's not going to hurt him to
move him."

Andy was still whimpering and thrashing feebly.
Sara doubted if he even noticed what was going on as
several men from the crowd picked him up carefully
and carried him underneath the trees. The pain in his
eyes probably made him oblivious to everything else.
His mother followed along anxiously behind them.
Alice was a widow, Sara knew, and she had no other
children. Andy was all she had. Sara took a deep
breath as she felt a pang of sympathy for the woman.

The man who had gone for water came hurrying up
with a sloshing bucket in his hand. He set the bucket
on the ground beside the boy. No one had offered a
cloth, so Thomas took his own handkerchief from his
coat pocket, dipped it into the bucket, and let it soak
up as much water as it could. When he took it out, he
said, "Someone hold him down. This is liable to make
the pain worse for a moment before it begins to get
better."

Sara doubted that, recalling how the injured man
had reacted when she treated him during the war, but
she didn't say anything. Vincent Rawlings gripped
Andy's shoulders tightly and another man grasped his
hands to keep him from rubbing at his eyes. Thomas
held the dripping handkerchief over the boy's eyes and
wrung it out.

Water flooded down across Andy's eyes, and
Thomas took hold of his chin and tipped his head to
the side so that the water would have some place to
run off. Andy gasped loudly, but it was a sound of relief, not pain. Quickly, Thomas dipped the handkerchief in the bucket again and let more water drip from
it into Andy's eyes.

"We're going to need more water," Thomas said without looking up from his task. "I want a steady supply of it."

More of the townspeople hurried off to follow his orders. Sara moved over to Alice Scott, put her arm around the older woman's shoulders, and squeezed reassuringly. "Andy's going to be all right, Mrs. Scott," she said. "You can tell already that he's not in as much pain as before."

Alice nodded shakily. "Th-Thank you," she managed to say.

After several minutes, Thomas said, "Take over here for me a little while, Vincent, will you?"

"Certainly," Rawlings replied, taking the water-soaked handkerchief from him. "Now that the eyes have been flushed some, perhaps we should use a cup. I think the lad could stand more water."

Thomas nodded. "I agree. I'll see to it."

He stood up and told one of the citizens to bring a cup from the tearoom in a row of shops alongside the green. While that was being done, Thomas turned to Sara and said, "I thought I told you to see to your mother."

"I left her in good hands," Sara said. "I thought I might be able to help over here."

"And so you did," Thomas agreed grudgingly. "It just goes to prove that no matter how long someone practices medicine, there's always an injury or an ailment that he's never seen before. I likely would have washed the lad's eyes out anyway, though. It's only common sense to do such a thing."

"Common sense doesn't always work. I had first-hand experience."

"True. Who's looking after your mother?"

"Libbie Daulton."

Thomas's eyes widened. "Libbie Daulton?" he repeated in amazement. "She's a child, and not a particularly reliable one, at that."

"She's almost a grown woman," Sara said, "and she *does* owe a debt to our family, if you remember a night about seven years ago."

"I remember," Thomas said grimly. "You didn't do as I told you then, either."

"And it was a good thing I didn't. You took John along on the call to assist you, and he passed out cold on the floor!"

"There's no need to remind me," Thomas snapped. His tone softened a little as he went on, "You did a good job that night, Sara, just as your knowledge came in handy today." He shook his head. "It was a foolish thing to do, throwing a bunch of firecrackers in a boy's face that way. If I could get my hands on the little hellion who did it, I'd thrash him!"

"Who threw the fireworks?" Sara asked.

"No one seemed to know, and I didn't waste a lot of time trying to find out. There was an injured lad to care for."

"Well, I suppose I had better get back to Mother."

"Yes," Thomas said crisply. "That's exactly what you should do."

She couldn't stop herself from making one more comment. "If we were working together all the time," she said, "I could probably help you more than you'd ever think."

Thomas's mouth tightened into a stern line. "If you were a doctor, you mean?"

Sara met his eyes squarely and said, "I *am* a doctor, in everything but name."

Thomas snorted. "Hardly! Now go on and find your mother." He turned back to Andy Scott and knelt beside him again, joining Rawlings in the treatment of the injured boy.

Sara stood there for a moment, so angry she was trembling. *She* was the one who had known what to do in this emergency. If Andy Scott's eyesight were saved, she was the one who deserved the credit. And yet her father had just told her to run along back to her mother, as if she were still seven years old!

One of these days he would see, Sara vowed to herself. One of these days he would be forced to admit that she deserved the title of "Doctor." Because she was going to medical school, and when she did, she would be the best student there. She was more sure of it now than ever, more clear in her mind what she had to do.

No matter what it took, the goal was going to be hers.

TWO

Boston, 1867

Rockets streamed across the sky, leaving trails of glowing sparks behind them before they burst and showered even more brilliance down over the Charles River. Exclamations came from the people gathered on the second-floor balcony of the Beacon Hill mansion to watch the fireworks. It was Independence Day, the Fourth of July, a holiday that had even more meaning to the citizens of this town than any other, for it was here that the nation's liberty had been birthed more than ninety years earlier. Oh, the Declaration of Independence might have been *signed* in Philadelphia, but that was only a formality. Boston, with the Massacre of 1770, the Tea Party a few years after that, the Committees of Correspondence, the Sons of Liberty, the famous ride of Paul Revere, the shot heard round the world fired only a few miles away, down the road to Lexington—these things marked the true beginnings of the noble experiment that had become known as the United States of America.

Even on this night, however, history was one of the farthest things from the mind of John Black. He was much more interested in the future than he was in the past.

Especially if that future included Judith Faulkner, the daughter of his hosts.

The gathering in the Faulkner mansion was a large one. As one of the city's foremost bankers, Edward Faulkner knew a great many prominent people, including Congressman Reed, whose grandfather and great-uncle had been heroes of the early days of the Revolution. The congressman and his usual retinue were in attendance tonight, and he was holding forth loudly as the crowd watched the fireworks. John tried not to pay any attention to the man. As far as he was concerned, all politicians were blowhards whose sole function was to extract as much money from the general public as possible.

John turned to the lovely young woman beside him and said, "Why don't we go for a walk in the garden? I think we could see the fireworks just as well from there without all the, ah, distractions."

Judith Faulkner smiled and tossed her head slightly, making the blond curls bounce on her shoulders. "Why, John Black," she said with mock severity. "If I didn't know better, I'd think you might have some ulterior motive for wanting to get an innocent young girl like me alone in the garden."

With a chuckle, he said, "Indeed I do."

"Well, I must admit . . ." Judith lowered her voice slightly. "The Congressman *can* be a bit overbearing. Why don't you slip downstairs first, and then I'll join you in a few minutes?"

John nodded quickly, trying not to appear too eager. "That's a good idea. But don't be too long. I'll be waiting for you."

She gave him another smile and squeezed his hand, and John moved toward the French doors that opened onto the large balcony.

When he was inside, he strolled through the second-floor sitting room and then went downstairs. As he reached the first-floor landing, another young man with sleek brown hair appeared from a nearby doorway. Jeremy Haverford was smoking a cigar, and he gave John a cocky grin. "Where are you off to, Black?" he asked. "I thought you'd be upstairs enjoying the fireworks."

"I imagine I'm down here for the same reason you are," John replied, thinking quickly. He certainly didn't want to tell Jeremy that he was planning to meet Judith in the garden. Jeremy was one of her suitors, too, although Judith insisted there was nothing serious between them. She had told John several times that she tolerated Jeremy only because her father thought highly of him. That, and the fact that Jeremy's father was a wealthy businessman who kept a large account in Edward Faulkner's bank, was enough to keep Jeremy in the good graces of the Faulkner family.

Jeremy inclined his head toward the door where he had just emerged. "The facilities are down that hall and then to the right," he said. "You can't miss them. Although, I suppose that coming from that little mountain hamlet of yours, the idea of indoor plumbing is a bit foreign to you, eh, Black?"

John bit back the angry reply that threatened to come to his lips. Jeremy Haverford was an arrogant ass, no doubt about that, but there was also some truth to what he said. The dwellings in Handley's Mill all had outhouses; John had never even known anything else existed until his first visit with the Faulkner family the year before. The mansion was one of the first in Boston to be equipped with a water closet.

"I'm sure I can find what I'm looking for," he said tightly to Jeremy now. "Are you going back upstairs?"

"Of course. Wouldn't want to miss anything."

John hoped he didn't run into Judith coming down the stairs. Jeremy would be certain to ask her where *she* was going, and the entire evening could turn out to be embarrassing. Not to mention frustrating.

He turned away and went through the door Jeremy had indicated, then paused, just out of sight. He listened closely and heard Jeremy's footsteps ascending the stairs. As the steps faded away, John eased the door open again and peered out. No one was on the staircase. It looked as if there was a good chance Jeremy hadn't encountered Judith.

Moving quickly but quietly, John left the little hallway that led to the water closet and hurried toward the rear entrance of the house. He slipped outside, finding himself on the edge of the extensive garden behind the mansion. The place was a veritable maze of hedges and shrubbery, and he didn't trust himself to find his way around in it during daylight hours, let alone in the darkness of night. He decided to wait right where he was, just outside the door, for Judith.

The wait was not a long one. Less than five minutes had passed when the door opened slowly and carefully, so that the hinges would not squeak—although it was doubtful that such a noise could have been heard over the bursting of the rockets that were still arching redly over the Charles.

A figure stepped out, a blur in the deep shadows behind the house, and John put his arms around the shape, bending his head for a kiss. For a fraction of a second, the horrible thought that he might be mistaken, that he might be about to plant a kiss on the mouth of someone other than Judith—like Jeremy Haverford!—passed through his mind. But then his lips met warm, sweet, eager lips, and his arms went around the familiar graceful curves and he felt the soft thrust of her breasts pressed against his chest, and he knew that it was Judith he was holding, Judith he was kissing.

For long moments they embraced, Judith's lips opening so that John's tongue could slide between them and explore her mouth. He drank deeply of her sweet sensuousness, knowing that he could never get enough of the taste, the feel, the smell of her. He lifted one hand and plunged his fingers into her thick blond hair, cupping the back of her head as his tongue delved even deeper into the hot, wet cavern of her mouth. Her hands clutched at his back, the fingers working back and forth in passion. John felt himself responding to her, and the way her soft belly was pressed against him, he knew she had to feel it, too. He almost groaned with the need for release.

Judith broke the kiss and stepped back away from him, panting softly like an animal. The sound enflamed John that much more. He knew she wanted him as much as he wanted her.

"I thought . . . I thought we came down here to watch the fireworks," she said breathlessly.

"You know why we came down here," he said, "and it had nothing to do with any holiday."

"We can make our own holiday," she murmured.

John liked the sound of that, but before he snatched her into his arms again, he said, "You didn't see Jeremy Haverford when you were coming downstairs, did you?"

"Jeremy?" She sounded genuinely surprised. "No, I didn't. Why on earth do you care about Jeremy?"

"I don't. It's just that I ran into him while I was trying to get out here, and I had to throw him off the scent."

Judith laughed. "Well, I certainly hope you were successful. I'd hate to think that a pompous bore like Jeremy was lurking around somewhere, spying on us."

"Yes, indeed." John reached out unerringly in the darkness, found her hand, drew her to him again. "I wouldn't want him to see us doing this."

He kissed her again, and Judith responded as eagerly as before, almost wantonly. John wanted to make love to her more than he had ever wanted anything in his life, or at least it seemed so at the moment. The Battle of Antietam, where he had been badly wounded and nearly killed, had receded in his memory with the passage of years. His desire for Judith seemed as strong now as his need for survival had seemed then.

Yet he knew he had to be careful. Judith was no farm girl he could take into a barn and have his way with. Her father was a very rich, very powerful man. Edward Faulkner could make a great deal of trouble for a young medical student if that were his wish.

Just as he could make the way much easier for that same medical student, John thought, if the young man in question were smart . . .

"Why don't we find a bench . . . and sit down?" John suggested when this kiss was over, trying to catch his own breath.

"I think that's . . . an excellent idea."

Arm in arm, they strolled through the garden, John

hesitating just slightly so that Judith could lead the way. She had grown up here; even in the pitch blackness she could find her way around this garden. But the night was not quite as dark as he had thought, John was beginning to realize. There was the glare from the fireworks, of course, although it came and went, and the stars also cast quite a bit of light. In addition, the moon was beginning to rise in the east. By the time they reached one of the backless stone benches that were scattered through the garden and sat down, John's eyes had adjusted to the point where he could make out Judith sitting beside him in her light blue gown.

He put his arm around her shoulders and drew her against him. "I've never seen you look lovelier than tonight," he murmured.

"Yes, but you're accustomed to being around sick people all the time in the hospitals and that medical school of yours," Judith said. "Am I really beautiful, or just . . . healthy?"

"Oh, you're quite healthy, I'm sure," John said as he bent over her. He found her mouth again with his, and this time he was daring enough to let his hand steal up to caress her breast through the fabric of her gown. This wasn't the first time he had been so intimate with her, and she didn't pull away. In fact, she put both of her hands over his and pressed it even harder against the mound of flesh. John began to knead her breast, bringing a whimper of passion from her.

God, he wanted to lay her down on this bench, raise her gown and petticoats, and take her right here and now!

A peculiar thumping sound made them both sit up sharply and move apart until there was a more proper distance between them on the bench. A shadowy figure came along the path toward them, then suddenly stopped short. A man's voice said, "Oh, I'm sorry. I hope I haven't interrupted anything."

"Of course not, Nathan," Judith said quickly. "John and I were just . . . just watching the rockets." Her voice took on a sheepish tone. "I have to confess, we wanted to get away from Congressman Reed for a while."

Her brother laughed. "The congressman's like all the others in his line of work," Nathan Faulkner said. "He can't pass up the opportunity to make a speech, even if it's an unofficial one. Do you mind if I join you?"

"Of course not," Judith said again. She slid over on the bench, moving closer to John.

"Sit down, Nathan," John invited. "Get off that leg for a while."

"Thanks." Nathan sat down on the end of the bench and gratefully stretched out his right leg in front of him. The leg ended in a short, thick peg which took the place of his right foot. That foot had been mangled beyond repair during the war, and it had been amputated in the field hospital where John worked as an aide to Dr. Matthias Borden. It had been Borden who performed the actual surgery, but John had tied off most of the bleeders and assisted in sewing up the wound, as he normally did. That had been enough to convince Edward and Dorothy Faulkner that John had saved their son's life. Judith believed the same thing, and John had never gone to the bother of correcting them. Besides, there might be some truth to it. Nathan probably would have bled to death if those veins and arteries had not been tied off, and it had been John who had slipped the ligatures around them and drawn them tight.

Now Nathan said in a musing tone, "You know, John, sometimes I could swear that the bottom of my foot is itching. That's not possible, is it? I mean, the foot's not even there anymore."

"If you feel it, then it's possible," John said. "I've heard of such things, and I don't believe they're uncommon. If someone went around and asked all the soldiers who came back from the war without arms or legs if they sometimes feel like the missing limbs are still there, I'll wager you'd find that most of them have had that feeling."

A shudder went through Judith, and John could feel it where her shoulder was pressed against his. "This conversation is entirely too gruesome for my tastes. Why can't you boys ever talk about anything pleasant?"

Nathan laughed. "We do sometimes, don't we, John? Why, just the other day when we were down at Red Mike's—"

"Red Mike's?" Judith broke in to repeat. "That horrible grog shop by the docks? What in heaven's name were the two of you doing there?"

"Having some grog, of course," Nathan said. "What else would we be doing there, eh, Johnny?"

John didn't like being called by the nickname, and he liked even less that Judith now knew about him carousing in the wharfside dives with her brother. He tried to repair the damage by saying quickly, "It wasn't anything like what you're thinking, Judith. Nathan and I were out walking—the exercise is quite good for his leg, you know—and since it was hot we thought we would stop for something cool to drink. We happened to be close to the docks, so we stopped at Red Mike's for . . . for . . ."

"Lemonade," Nathan said dryly, not sounding as if he meant it for a moment.

"I don't think you should go over to that part of town, either of you," Judith said. "It's dangerous over there. You could both be hurt."

"Don't worry about us, Judith," Nathan said, his voice light. "We know what we're doing."

They certainly did, John thought. Nathan was drinking in an attempt to blunt the pain he still felt and to forget the injury he had suffered. John went along to try to keep Nathan from getting into too much trouble. He intended to be part of this family someday, if everything went as he planned, and every kindness he did for Nathan put him that much closer to his ultimate goal.

"Now, as I was saying about our conversation in Red Mike's . . . ," Nathan went on, but his sister stopped him.

"I don't want to hear about it," Judith said. "I'll take your word for it, Nathan."

"All right, if that's the way you want it." Nathan looked up as a particularly bright rocket streaked across the sky over the river. "Ah, that was a good one, wasn't it?"

"Beautiful," John said, but he was thinking more of Judith than the rocket. His heart was still pounding from the excitement of kissing her, and part of him wished fervently that Nathan had not come along when he did. However, it was probably better that they had been interrupted, John thought pragmatically. There was no need to rush things. He had been enrolled in the medical school at Harvard for only a year;

he had two more years of instruction to complete before he would take the oral examination that would determine his fitness to be considered a doctor. John had no doubts even now that he would pass with flying colors when the time came; despite his lack of any real interest in the subjects of his courses, mastery of them came easily to him. No, there was no need to hurry where his romance with Judith was concerned. Getting carried away now might only complicate things needlessly.

And they had all the time in the world.

John whistled to himself as he walked toward the Charles River Bridge a couple of hours later. Although he hadn't had a chance to kiss Judith again before bidding her and her family good night, the evening had gone quite well in John's judgment. The way things were proceeding, he thought, he and Judith would be engaged by the time he finished his second year of medical school, and the wedding could take place following the awarding of his degree a year later. Then, as the son-in-law of Edward Faulkner, he would have his choice of opportunities. He could go into partnership with one of the well-established physicians in Boston, or join the medical staff of one of the major hospitals, or even start his own practice. If he did that, he was confident that he would soon have plenty of patients from the city's upper crust. After all, who wouldn't want to take their medical problems to a handsome young doctor with a beautiful wife and a wealthy, influential father-in-law?

A smile creased John's face and his step was jaunty as those thoughts ran through his head. He was so distracted by them, in fact, that he almost failed to notice the man who suddenly stepped out of the shadows in front of him, blocking his way.

John stopped short, his muscles tensing. This was a fairly respectable part of town, but thieves could turn up almost anywhere these days. If this man were after John's wallet, he might wind up getting more than he bargained for. John wasn't going to let anyone take anything of his without a fight.

But the next instant, a familiar voice spoke, and John relaxed a little. Jeremy Haverford said, "You sound positively cheerful, Black, skylarking along like that. Do it some more."

"What are you doing here, Haverford?" John asked curtly. Then before the other man could answer, he went on, "Never mind. I don't want to know. Just get out of my way."

"I think not. Not until I've had a word with you."

"You've already had a word with me, and I've nothing more to say to you. Good night."

John tried to move around him, but Jeremy moved smoothly to the side, still blocking John's path. John flushed angrily. He was damned if he was going to step off into the gutter just to avoid this annoying bastard. He growled, "I'm warning you, Jeremy. Get out of my way."

"I want to talk to you about Judith," insisted Jeremy. "It's important."

That gave John pause. He still didn't think Jeremy could have anything to say that would be important to him, but it might be easier just to humor him. John said, "What about Judith?"

"I saw the two of you in the garden tonight."

John tensed again. "I don't know what you mean," he said automatically.

"Of course you do. You slipped out of the house while everyone else was watching the fireworks, then she joined you a few minutes later. You kissed her, just outside the rear door of the house. The two of you walked to one of the benches and sat down, and then you kissed again." Jeremy chuckled. "I daresay you would have done even more if that brother of hers hadn't come clumping along when he did."

John felt his hands clenching into fists. He felt a little sick at his stomach from both anger and fear. Obviously, Jeremy had been spying on them, and that infuriated him. But armed with the knowledge he possessed, Jeremy could also do some damage to the plans John had worked out.

"I saw through your pitiful charade as soon as I encountered you downstairs," Jeremy went on. "I allowed you to think I went back up to the balcony, but actually I slipped into one of the rooms at the head of the stairs and waited for Judith to come along. After that it was child's play to follow her. She was thinking about you, not about the fact that someone might be watching. Especially not a . . . what was it she called me? A pompous bore like me?" There was bitterness in his voice as he spoke.

"You had no right to skulk around like that," John snapped.

"I had every right!" Jeremy shot right back with surprising strength in his voice. "I've been courting Judith, too, you know. I have a right to know how my competition is doing, don't I?"

"Competition," John repeated scornfully. "You know the only reason Judith puts up with you is because she doesn't want to anger her father."

"Is that so? Well, how angry do you think Edward

Faulkner would be if he knew that an upstate bumpkin like you was practically rutting with his daughter in his own backyard?"

John trembled with the urge to lash out at Jeremy. He said, "If you told Faulkner that, Judith would never have anything to do with you again."

"Quite possibly you're right. But beyond a shadow of a doubt, *you* would never be welcome in the Faulkner household again."

Galling though it was, John knew that what Jeremy said was true. The bastard could ruin him with Edward Faulkner, ruin all the plans he had made. John forced himself to swallow the hatred rising in his throat like bile and asked, "What is it you want from me, Jeremy?"

"I want you to withdraw gracefully before Judith's good name—and what little reputation *you* have—are ruined."

John couldn't stop the laugh that welled out of him. "Withdraw gracefully? Give up and let you have Judith?"

"I don't see that you have much choice. I can cripple you, financially and professionally, just as surely as that gimp brother of Judith's is crippled."

Despite the thick shadows in the street, a red haze seemed to slip down over John's vision. The only other time he could recall feeling like this was just before he had gone into battle against the Rebels at Antietam. He had fought then for his life. He had killed for survival.

He could do the same thing now.

He held back the shout that tried to burst from his mouth. This had to be done quietly, so as not to attract attention. Without warning, he threw a punch, smashing his right fist into the middle of Jeremy Haverford's face. John felt the man's nose pulp under the blow, and something hot and wet spurted across John's knuckles.

He didn't give Jeremy time to recover, stepping in and slamming a blow to Jeremy's midsection that knocked the breath out of him. As Jeremy bent over, gasping for the air with which to cry out for help, John swung his right in a sweeping punch that landed solidly on the other man's jaw. Jeremy's head was jerked around by the impact, and he slumped to the sidewalk.

John pounced on him, rolling him over, clubbing him back and forth with clenched fists. More blood splattered. Jeremy tried feebly to push him away, but John was in the grip of a rage much too strong to be turned aside. As he knelt on Jeremy's chest, his fingers went around Jeremy's neck and locked there in an iron grip. John squeezed harder and harder as Jeremy's thrashing beneath him became weaker.

Suddenly, a huge shudder ran through John's body. He was no brawler. He hadn't thrown a punch in anger since the early days of the war. And he certainly wasn't a killer. For God's sake, he realized, he was becoming a doctor to save lives, not take them!

He peeled his fingers away from Jeremy's throat and staggered to his feet, putting out a hand and resting it against the wall of the building beside him for support as a wave of dizziness went through him. He couldn't believe what he had almost done. As he heard Jeremy drawing huge, rasping breaths back into air-starved lungs, John was truly glad that he hadn't killed the other young man.

However, he still had a problem, and he knew it.

John's fate was in Jeremy's hands more than ever

now. But John had an advantage, and he had to press it. He went to a knee beside Jeremy, reached out and caught hold of the lapels of Jeremy's coat. He jerked Jeremy upright and put his face close to him.

"Listen to me," John said slowly and distinctly, in a voice as cold as the winter wind off Boston Harbor. "If you ever tell anyone about what Judith and I were doing in the garden tonight, or about what happened just now, I'll have nothing to lose by killing you, Haverford. Do you understand that?"

Jeremy made a wet, bubbling sound through smashed, bleeding lips.

"Damn you, do you understand?" John hissed, shaking him. Jeremy finally managed to nod his head, or perhaps it was just lolling on his shoulders as John shook him. John didn't know or care. He went on, "You can ruin me, but you can't stop me. I'll come for you. I'll come for you, and this is just a sample of what I'll do to you, Haverford. Is it worth it? Is ruining my life worth yours?"

This time, he was sure that Jeremy was shaking his head back and forth in a negative.

"Remember this night, and never cross me again. In fact, it might be best if you left Boston for a while. Take a tour of Europe, or whatever it is you rich boys do with your time. But don't let me see you again, especially around Judith."

With that, he gave Jeremy a hard shove that sent the young man sprawling on the sidewalk again. Jeremy's head smacked against the paving stones. John stood up, straightened his clothes, and started toward the bridge again. He would have to stay out of the light as much as possible, he thought, because Jeremy's blood was no doubt splattered all over his clothes. He would burn them when he got back to his apartment in Cambridge.

He didn't look back.

But he did stumble into an alley a couple of blocks farther on and heave up everything that was in his stomach—the fine dinner he'd had at the Faulkner mansion, the wine, the brandy—it all came spewing out of him until he was retching dryly and agonizingly. As difficult as it was to believe, he had almost killed a man, almost taken a human life. He prayed that Jeremy Haverford was smart enough to do as he had been told.

For Jeremy's sake, for Judith's . . . and for his own.

THREE

Handley's Mill

Andy Scott did not lose the sight in either eye, although his vision was considerably blurred after the accident, especially in the left one. Thomas prescribed a pair of spectacles, but there was no one in Handley's Mill who could make them. Andy's mother took him to Pittsfield, where Dr. Vincent Rawlings helped the boy pick out some spectacles at the local apothecary shop. The lenses improved Andy's sight somewhat, although it was Rawlings's opinion, and Thomas's, too, that the lad would never again see as well as he had before his mishap.

"There's no question in my mind, however," Rawlings said as he sat in the parlor of the Black home later that summer, "that Andy would have been totally blinded if not for your prompt action, Thomas."

Thomas snorted. "It was Sara who suggested the treatment, Vincent, and you know it. She deserves the credit for saving the lad's sight." He and Rawlings were alone in the parlor; otherwise he might not have spoken so plainly. He didn't want to put any more ideas in Sara's head than were already there.

"You would have bathed the boy's eyes," Rawlings pointed out. "You said so yourself."

"Perhaps. Who knows what I would have done? It never came to that because as soon as Sara spoke up I knew somehow that she had hit on the proper treatment. She has quite an . . . instinct for that, I suppose you could say."

"A doctor's instinct," Rawlings said quietly.

Thomas took a deep breath and pushed himself up out of his chair. He began to stalk back and forth, his movements sharp and almost angry. He clasped his hands behind his back and said, "I know what you're getting at, Vincent, and I resent it. It's impossible!"

"Other women have become doctors."

"Yes, but at what cost? You know as well as I do how female doctors are regarded by most people. They're ostracized and vilified at nearly every turn. Why, it's only in recent years that male doctors have gained a modicum of respect! Too many people still regard us as leech-waving butchers!"

By the time he was finished, Thomas had unclasped his hands and was waving his arms in the air agitatedly. He stopped suddenly, brought one hand to his chest, and pressed hard against it.

Instantly, Rawlings sat forward in his chair. "Pain in your chest again, Thomas?" he asked.

"It's nothing," Thomas snapped. "Nothing to be concerned about. I just need to stop getting so upset about things."

"Such as Sara's medical career?"

"Sara doesn't *have* a medical career!"

Rawlings sat back and sighed. "Whatever you say, Thomas. You *are* her father."

"You're damned right I'm her father." Thomas

strode over to the mantelpiece above the fireplace on one side of the parlor. He rested a hand on it and looked intently at a daguerreotype sitting there. The photograph showed Clarissa with John and Sara and had been taken when the children were both small. Clarissa was sitting on a chair with John standing beside her and Sara poised on her lap. All of them looked very solemn, but that didn't prevent Clarissa from being breathtakingly beautiful, Thomas thought.

"It's not just that I don't want to expose her to the hardships of being a doctor," he went on quietly without looking around at Rawlings. "I'm just not certain that a woman . . . any woman . . . has the mental fortitude to stand the strain of a medical career."

"You're thinking of what happened to Clarissa in Washington," Rawlings said.

Thomas nodded slowly. "The things she saw there in the hospital . . . all those horrible, gruesome injuries . . . they were too much for her, Vincent. They were too much for her to bear, so her mind simply . . . stopped working."

Rawlings stood up, came over to Thomas, rested a hand on his old friend's shoulder. "You can't be certain the same thing would happen to Sara. She's stronger to begin with than Clarissa ever was, and I mean no offense by that."

Thomas shook his head to indicate that none was taken.

"At any rate, you can't compare what Clarissa experienced in that military hospital to what Sara would face in a normal medical practice," Rawlings went on. "There was a war going on, for heaven's sake! You saw all manner of terrible cases that a doctor doesn't have to deal with in peacetime."

"That's true," Thomas admitted. "But a doctor sees more than his share of death, you know that, Vincent. A doctor sees entire families carried off by fever. He sees the cold, lifeless forms of drowned children pulled out of rivers and ponds. He sees people who have been run over by wagons and stabbed by jealous lovers. He sees practically every kind of injustice and inhumanity inflicted on one man by another or by nature. You *know* that, Vincent. And I won't expose Sara to it. I simply won't."

"Even if it's her choice?"

"Even if it's her choice."

Rawlings sighed. "Well, then, my friend, I wish you luck in convincing Sara of that. Because I fear you're going to need it."

Thomas kept staring at the photograph of his wife and children. He was afraid that Vincent Rawlings was right.

Sara carried the last of the dishes from supper into the kitchen. Dr. Rawlings had stayed for the meal, but Sara had not been able to ask him the question that had been nagging at her all day. She couldn't bring up the subject with her father and mother sitting right there. Thomas would have gotten upset, and even though Clarissa would have had no idea what was really going on, the simple fact that she was still Sara's mother had an inhibiting effect.

But before the evening was over, Sara told herself, she would find out what she wanted to know—one way or another.

After the meal, Clarissa went upstairs, and Thomas and Rawlings went back to the parlor, where they had already spent most of the afternoon. This time they would break out the brandy and cigars, though, Sara knew. Their medical discussions would have been fascinating to her, she was sure, if only she had been allowed to join them. But that was out of the question as far as Thomas was concerned. He wanted to keep her as far away from anything concerning medicine as possible.

She was going to spend the rest of her life keeping house and taking care of her mother, Sara thought as she washed the dishes. She was already an old maid, by her own choice. She hadn't been overwhelmed by suitors since the end of the war, true, but there had been a few young men who had come calling on her. All of them were mild and inoffensive and might as well have been totally bloodless, as far as she was concerned. After being with a man like Carver Gresham . . .

A warm flush came over her, and it had nothing to do with the hot water in which she was cleaning the dishes. She told herself not to think about Carver. Memories of his death were enough to make her melancholy for days, and she couldn't afford to slip into such a mood now. She had too many important things on her mind for that.

Such as listening for Dr. Rawlings so that she might be able to get a private word with him before he left.

When the dishes were done, Sara went upstairs to check on her mother. Clarissa was sitting up in bed, brushing out her long silver hair and humming softly to herself. Sara didn't recognize the tune. It was probably something from her mother's girlhood, she thought. Sara couldn't be sure where Clarissa's mind was these days, but she suspected that most of the time it was back there in that long-ago time, reliving precious memories.

Perhaps Clarissa was really the lucky one in the family, Sara thought as she straightened her mother's nightclothes and took the brush from her. She sat on the bed beside Clarissa and began running the brush through the silver strands. Clarissa smiled at her and stopped humming.

"Would you like to sing?"

The question took Sara by surprise. "I don't know the song," she said after a moment.

"Oh, it's easy. I'll teach it to you."

Clarissa began to sing in a clear voice that shook just a little. The words were something about the love of Barb'ry Ellen. Sara had trouble making them out because suddenly her eyes were filled with tears and the pounding of her own heart filled her head. She recalled the song now from her own childhood, when the sound of her mother's voice had been enough to make her feel safe and secure and loved. But those feelings were gone, and as Clarissa sang, it was nothing but a reminder of how fragile and fleeting happiness could be, how uncertain and treacherous the world really was. Her mother had vanished somehow, Sara thought as she swallowed a sob, and nothing was left behind but this empty shell, and it wasn't fair.

Sara fumbled the brush back into Clarissa's hands and stood up abruptly. Clarissa fell silent, the song dying away to nothingness. In a choked voice, Sara said, "I'm sorry, Mother. I have to go." Without waiting for a reply, she hurriedly left the room, never looking back.

Outside in the hall, Sara leaned against the wall and took several deep breaths, drawing the air into her lungs raggedly. She shook her head and shuddered, then lifted her arm and used the back of her hand to wipe away the tears on her cheeks. She hated it when she allowed herself to get this emotional. Her mother's case was very interesting medically, she told herself. She needed to keep things on that basis.

As she stood there, she heard male voices downstairs in the foyer. Her father was bidding Dr. Rawlings good night. Sara stiffened for a moment, then turned and hurried toward the rear stairs, her slipper-clad feet making little noise on the floor. At the bottom of the narrow staircase was the back door of the house. She opened it, slid out into the night, and closed it quietly behind her.

Rawlings's buggy was parked at the front of the house, the horse tied to the hitching post beside the gate in the picket fence. The doctor was untying the bag of grain from the horse's nose when Sara stepped out of the shadows cast by the trees in the front yard.

"You're leaving, Dr. Rawlings?" Her voice made it a question.

"What? Oh . . ." He heaved a sigh. "You startled me, Sara. Yes, I'd better be getting back to Pittsfield. It's already later than I intended."

In fact, it was almost completely dark, with only a faint rose tinge to the western sky, from the departed sun. The evening was quite warm, but a light, refreshing breeze rustled the leaves of the trees. Sara said, "Did you talk to my father?"

"I talked to Thomas a great deal. You know that, Sara, you were there at supper—"

"That's not what I mean, Doctor, and you know it," she said bluntly. "Did you plead my case, as you promised you would?"

Rawlings sighed again. "I did. I brought up the matter when your father and I were talking this afternoon. He was quick to admit that young Andy Scott has you to thank for his eyesight, diminished though it might be."

That made Sara feel a little better, but it didn't ease her main worry. "What about the idea of my attending medical school?"

"He's still as opposed to it as ever, I'm afraid."

Frustration welled up inside Sara. She wanted to curse, to flail her arms, to stamp around the yard. But none of that would do any good, and she knew it. She said, "For years now, I've been trying to bring him around to my way of thinking. But it's like trying to budge a stone. I thought he might have learned . . . after what happened in the war . . ."

"You mean when you ran off to Washington to work as a nurse in the military hospitals without getting your family's consent or even telling them where you were going?"

Sara looked down at the ground, shame washing over her. "I . . . I know I shouldn't have done that. It . . . it led to a great many terrible things. If I hadn't . . . then perhaps my mother wouldn't be . . . wouldn't . . ."

Rawlings stepped closer to her in the gathering darkness and placed his hands on her shoulders. "Stop that," he said firmly. "What happened to Clarissa was not your fault. She had suffered some . . . mental deterioration . . . even before she and Thomas went to Washington. Your father told me she mistook Miles Austin for Dr. Benjamin Everett, when Everett had been dead for years. And that was far from the only such incident."

Sara nodded slowly. Rawlings was right, she supposed. The time Clarissa had spent amid the horrors of the military hospital might have hastened her breakdown, but it had not been completely responsible for it. The ultimate reasons, as always in cases like this, were likely to remain a mystery.

"I was just hoping," she said miserably, "that my father might have changed his mind."

"I did my best," Rawlings said. "I tried to plant the idea that he could use an associate in his practice and that you would be perfect for the position. I told him what he's already known in his heart for a long time but refused to acknowledge: that you have a doctor's instincts, Sara. You'd make a fine physician."

She looked up at him as he stood close to her, his hands still on her shoulders. "Do you really think so?" she whispered.

"I know it." He swallowed hard. "Just as I know that there would never be a more beautiful doctor than yourself, my dear."

The words took her by surprise, but not as much as what he did next.

He kissed her.

She was a bit taller than he, so he didn't have to bend over her. All he had to do was lean forward and press his lips to hers. His hands tightened on her shoulders. Sara's eyes widened in shock. But she didn't pull away from him. She was too stunned for that.

Her surprise didn't last long. She jerked her mouth away from his and exclaimed, "Dr. Rawlings! I . . . I—"

"Oh, Lord, I'm sorry, Sara!" he said wretchedly. "I don't know what came over me—" Suddenly, his voice strengthened. "Yes. Yes, I do know. Your loveli-

ness overwhelmed me. I've watched you growing up.
I've seen you turn into such a beautiful, intelligent
young woman—"

"Young enough to be your daughter!"

"Yes, perhaps, but you're *not* my daughter. You're a
woman and I'm a man, and right now that's all we are.
I can't stand it anymore, can't bear the strain of not
telling you how I feel!"

Sara's head was whirling dizzyingly. She had never
expected behavior like this from Dr. Rawlings, would
never have believed that he could say and do such
things.

And yet, she remembered that moment on Independence Day when Rawlings had taken her arm and his
hand had brushed against the side of her breast. So that
"accidental" touch had been deliberate after all!

He confirmed that the next moment by moving his
right hand from her shoulder and sliding it down her
body to cup her left breast. His fingers molded the soft
mound of flesh through her blouse and the camisole
beneath it. Sara gasped.

"I've been burning with desire for you for so long,
Sara!" Rawlings said, practically panting. "These visits to your house are agony for me. I'm tormented by
the sight of you and the knowledge that I can't have
you . . . can I?"

A fine thing to ask while he was standing there pawing her! she thought. She tried to back away from him,
but the grip of his other hand was still too tight on her
shoulder. She said, "Doctor, I think you should leave
now."

"Vincent—call me Vincent."

She didn't want to, but maybe it would help her get
through to him if she did, she reasoned. She forced the

name out. "Vincent, that's enough. You're frightening me."

"There's no need to be frightened. I adore you, Sara. I'd never hurt you."

"You're hurting me now!" she said, her voice beginning to tremble a little from a mixture of anger, pain, and fear.

"Step up with me into the buggy," urged Rawlings. "Sit with me awhile. Be nice to me, Sara, please. Make an old man happy. Can't you do that?"

She gasped again at his boldness as he took his hand off her breast and reached down to press it against her groin through her skirt. He rubbed his fingers against her and continued to murmur, "Please, please. I'll give you anything you want, anything in my power." His words had the wheedling sound of a child begging for a forbidden treat.

"No!" The word burst out of Sara, but she managed to hiss it rather than shouting it as she wanted to. She still could hardly believe that Rawlings was doing this, but she was utterly mortified all the same. She went on, "If you don't stop, I . . . I'll call my father." It was an empty threat—she was much too embarrassed to let her father know what was happening—but Rawlings didn't have to know that.

What she really wanted to do was clench her hand into a fist and smack it into the face of the lustful old doctor.

Rawlings took his probing hand away from her body. He was quivering with emotion. "Are . . . are you sure?"

"I'm certain," Sara made herself say, hoping that she sounded stronger and calmer than she really felt. "Please leave me alone, Doctor."

He lifted his other hand from her shoulder and stepped back. "Oh, dear," he said. "Oh, my God. I've gone and made an old fool out of myself, haven't I?"

"I think you should go on back to Pittsfield," she told him, ignoring his question.

"I'm so sorry . . . I don't know what came over me." His head tilted suddenly toward her. "You . . . you won't tell Thomas about this, will you?"

Sara took a deep breath. "Do you promise that it will never happen again?"

"Good Lord, yes! I swear it, Sara. I . . . I must have gone mad there for a moment."

"All right," she agreed grudgingly. "I won't say anything to my father, or to anyone else. But if you ever do anything like that again, Dr. Rawlings, I . . . I shall have you arrested and put in jail!"

He began to climb into his buggy, shaking his head and saying, "You don't have to worry. You don't have to worry. I'll not bother you again. You have my word on that."

"See that you don't," Sara said. She crossed her arms tightly over her chest and glared at him.

"Sara . . ." He said her name very tentatively.

"What is it?"

"Can you . . . untie the reins?"

She swallowed her exasperation, jerked the horse's reins loose from the hitching post, and tossed them to Rawlings, who caught them clumsily in the shadows. He backed the horse and buggy away from the fence, then turned the animal and flicked the reins against its back. Sara stood and watched stonily as the buggy rolled away down the street.

When he was gone and she was convinced he wasn't coming back, her resolve evaporated. Shivering despite the warmth of the night, she hugged herself and turned toward the house, her mind still struggling to comprehend what had just happened. She could barely accept that the incident had occurred, let alone make any sense of it. She had never thought of herself as being particularly attractive, but Vincent Rawlings had acted as if she were some sort of . . . of trollop!

He was an old man, she told herself as she went slowly up the walk toward the house, and old men were prone to vivid memories of the days when they had been young. That was it, she decided. Rawlings had merely given in to a desire to relive his youth by kissing a younger woman and playing a little slap and tickle with her. It was probably all rather innocent, and if she had gone along with him, no doubt he would have panicked, made some excuses, and departed hastily rather than admit that he was actually no longer the passionate old goat he was pretending to be. Yes, that was it, of course.

Sara paused on the porch, took several deep breaths, and collected herself. She certainly didn't want to go inside until she was sure her father wouldn't be able to tell that anything was wrong.

After a moment, she opened the door and stepped into the foyer. As she was closing the door behind her, her father called out from the parlor, "Hello? Who's there? Did someone just come in?"

That was right, Sara recalled. She had slipped out the back and he didn't know she had been outside. She said, "It's just me, Father."

Thomas Black appeared in the doorway to the parlor, his collar and tie loosened, a copy of the Handley's Mill *Gazette* in his hand. With a frown on his face, he asked, "What were you doing wandering around out there in the dark?"

"Oh, it's not completely dark yet . . . or at least it wasn't when I stepped out. I was just getting a breath of air. It . . . it's a lovely evening."

"If you say so. Have you looked in on your mother?"

"Yes, she went to bed early. She's probably sleeping by now."

"Doesn't sound like a bad idea," Thomas muttered. He started to turn away, satisfied with Sara's explanation.

She stopped him by saying, "Father?"

He looked at her, apparently a bit impatient to return to his newspaper. "What is it?"

Might as well take the bull by the horns, Sara thought, since she obviously couldn't count on Vincent Rawlings for any help. She said, "I've been thinking again about medical school."

The newspaper crumpled in Thomas's hand as his fingers balled into a knobby fist. "We've had this discussion before, Sara," he said tightly.

"Yes, but it's never been resolved satisfactorily."

"I'm perfectly satisfied with my decision," Thomas said. "I see nothing wrong with you becoming a nurse, since you have a considerable amount of practical experience in that area. I might even hire you myself. But medical school is out of the question for you."

Her lips compressed into a thin line. She loved him, but he could be so damned condescending! Might even hire her himself . . . How dare he talk down to her like that!

But she kept her tone as reasonable and calm as possible, betraying little of the emotions seething inside her, as she said, "You seem to have forgotten that I've already been a doctor. For two-and-a-half years, I was the only medical officer that Confederate patrol had. And they were very glad I was on hand when they were injured or wounded."

Thomas grunted. "I'm sure they were. But I wish you wouldn't remind me of that time. It . . . it's very unpleasant for a father to think about his daughter being held captive by the enemy . . ."

What he meant, she thought, was that he didn't want to think about the fact that she and Carver Gresham had been lovers. They had never talked about it, but she knew it was in his mind. Would it make him feel better, she wondered for a second, if she lied and told him that every man in the patrol had raped her, had thrown her down on the ground and ripped her clothes off and had his way with her!

She caught hold of her raging thoughts. None of this really had anything to do with the real problem. She said coldly, "I'll ask you one last time—"

"And I'll answer as I always have," he interrupted before she could finish. "I'll not send you to medical school."

"Then there's nothing more to say, is there?"

"It would seem not." Thomas smoothed the wrinkled newspaper and nodded curtly to her. "Good night, Sara."

"Good night, Father." She turned and started up the stairs. She felt tears in her eyes again, but she blinked them away. She wouldn't let herself cry about this. She simply would not.

But once she was upstairs in her darkened bedroom, sprawled across the bed with her clothes still on, the tears came and she couldn't hold them back. The strain

of the evening's events was just too much. She shook
and shuddered and clenched her fists in the bedclothes
for long moments.

Until the tears brought with them a memory, and an
idea. The memory was a recent one, and it made her
lift her head and wipe her eyes as she drew a deep
breath.

I'll give you anything you want, Vincent Rawlings
had said. And he had meant it. Despite his apologies,
Sara was sure that he was completely infatuated with
her.

Anything she wanted . . . The idea was too strong to
go away. What she wasn't sure of was whether or not
she had what was necessary to take advantage of it.

But the words still rang in her head. *Anything you
want . . .*

Anything.

FOUR

By the time autumn arrived, the resolve in Sara's mind had firmed to the point that she knew there would be no turning back. As if she needed anything else to help her make her decision, she received a letter from her brother John, who was an infrequent correspondent. When he did write letters, though, he tended to fill up several pages with his tight scrawl, as if to make up for the months at a time when he hadn't written. His letter to Sara was full of the details of his life at Harvard. She knew he wasn't gloating, but it was all she could do not to rip the paper into pieces as she read about what he was doing in medical school. She would have done almost anything to have the same opportunities to learn that he was enjoying.

And *anything* was pretty much what she was prepared to do, she thought.

However, "enjoying" was not really the word to describe John's educational experience, she mused as she folded the letter and put it back in its envelope. He complained about the workload of his classes and the long hours spent learning from actual experience, accompanying the doctors who were his professors on their rounds in Boston's hospitals. Again, it sounded to Sara like a tremendous opportunity.

An opportunity that was going to be denied her, if her father had anything to say about it. Fortunately, her future no longer depended solely on Thomas Black.

John's letter sounded much more animated when he was talking about the Faulkner family, especially Judith. Sara had never met Judith, or any of the Faulkners, but she had heard John talk about the young woman enough to know that he was fascinated with her. His letter hinted that there was an actual romance between them, and Sara was glad to hear that. She and John had not been particularly close since they were children, not even after he had found her on the final day of the war and brought her home to Handley's Mill, but she still wished him well.

After putting the letter away, Sara went downstairs to begin preparing dinner. She wanted everything to be perfect, because they were having a special guest tonight: Dr. Vincent Rawlings.

Rawlings hadn't been back to the Black house since the incident beside his buggy. Sara assumed he was too embarrassed to show his face there again, perhaps even fearful that she had told her father what had happened, despite her promise not to. Or maybe he was just afraid to be around her, afraid that he wouldn't be able to control his feelings if he saw her. Not that she regarded herself as any sort of irresistible temptress, she thought as she began bustling around the kitchen. But evidently Rawlings did.

And that might just be sufficient for her purposes.

"Hello, Thomas," Vincent Rawlings said as he came into the foyer of the Black house that evening. He held his hat in his left hand and extended his right for Thomas to shake. His gaze darted past his host's shoulder and fastened on Sara, who stood behind her father, wearing a light green blouse and a brown skirt. She smiled at Rawlings, hoping to ease the flash of apprehension she saw in his eyes.

"How are you, Vincent?" Thomas asked as he pumped Rawlings's hand. "It's been quite a while since you've been here. Why have you become such a stranger?"

Rawlings laughed uneasily. "You know how it is, Thomas. The press of work. I'm not the only doctor in Pittsfield anymore, of course, but I still have an abundance of patients."

"Yes, I know the feeling," Thomas agreed. "Well, I'm glad you decided to honor us with a visit tonight. Come on in."

Actually, Sara had dropped enough hints that her father had had little choice but to send a note to Rawlings inviting him to dinner. She had been afraid that Rawlings would decline the invitation, but to her relief, he had accepted. Of course, if he had turned down the offer, she would have simply gotten her father to issue it again later. Once she made up her mind, she wasn't easily turned aside. Persistent, she called it, and persistence was a virtue; Thomas Black considered the quality downright stubbornness and had told her so more than once.

Sara stepped around her father and took Rawlings's hat and coat. "Let me take care of those for you," she murmured, and she made sure her fingers brushed across the back of his hand when she took the hat from him. While she was hanging the hat and coat on the rack just inside the front door, Thomas led Rawlings toward the parlor. Sara watched them and saw Rawlings glance back at her over his shoulder.

She smiled.

She had never been hunting, since the idea didn't appeal to her, but she had heard men from the village talk about the look in a deer's eyes when it was caught in the light from a bull's-eye lantern.

The look in Vincent Rawlings's eyes was probably similar to that of a deer, Sara thought. Surprised, confused, perhaps even a little afraid . . .

Thomas took him on into the parlor, saying, "Dinner will be ready in a few minutes, Sara tells me. Until then, have a seat, Vincent, and tell me what sort of cases you've been seeing lately."

"Oh, the usual ailments for this time of year, I suppose," Rawlings answered as he settled himself into a wing chair across from the divan where Thomas sat down. "The standard culprit is the grippe. Quite a few of my patients have come down with it."

"And you're treating it with . . . ?"

"Hot mustard plasters, primarily. They seem to be quite effective."

Thomas nodded solemnly. "I concur."

Rawlings looked around the room and asked, "Where is Clarissa this evening?"

"She won't be joining us," Thomas replied with a little frown. "She's not feeling well."

"I'm sorry to hear it. Nothing serious, I hope."

Thomas waved a hand. "Just the complaints of age, common to us all."

"Too common," Rawlings said with a knowing nod. "We're fighting a losing battle, Thomas, you know that."

"Of course we are. The victories are small ones, and

often fleeting." Thomas smiled. "But worth the struggle, my friend, well worth the struggle."

"Certainly," Rawlings agreed, returning the smile.

Sara stepped into the room a moment later and announced that dinner was ready. The men followed her into the dining room, where Rawlings overcame his nervousness long enough to hurry forward and hold her chair for her as she sat down. She looked up at him and said, "Thank you, Vincent."

If her father found anything unusual about her referring to their guest by his first name, he gave no sign of it. Sara warned herself not to overplay her hand. Slow and steady, she thought. That was what it would take. But not *too* slow.

"Well, Sara, it looks as if you've gone to a great deal of trouble," Rawlings commented as he went around the table and took his place opposite her. He had little choice in where he sat, since other than Thomas's position at the head of the table, his seat was the only other place that was set for dinner. Rawlings nodded at the thick slices of ham, the potatoes, the sweet corn, the greens, and the platter of cornbread so warm from the oven that steam still rose from it. "Everything looks and smells delicious."

"Thank you, Doctor," she replied, deliberately using his title instead of his name this time. She wanted to keep him slightly off-balance, unsure what to expect from her. She was allowing her instincts to guide her, since she had practically no experience at the elaborate dance of words that went on between a man and a woman who were interested in each other. In some ways, she reflected fleetingly, her life was sadly lacking in experience.

"Yes, indeed, quite impressive," Thomas said. "Your mother would be proud of you, Sara."

For a moment, Sara felt a flash of resentment. Her father was referring to her mother as if she were dead, instead of merely resting upstairs. But Sara knew Thomas hadn't meant it that way, so she made herself smile and nod to him. "Thank you, Father. I'm glad you're pleased."

Thomas lowered his head and began intoning a blessing. Sara tried to force herself to pay attention to what he was saying, but she could not. Her mind was too full of the plan she had formed over the past weeks. It was a simple plan, to be sure, but not so simple in its execution, she was discovering. As calm as she was on the outside, inside she was as nervous as she had ever been, even on that day when she had stood before Miss Dorothea Dix, trying to convince the old woman that she was qualified for a job as a nurse in one of the military hospitals in Washington, D.C. There were so many things that could go wrong: she could lose her resolve—unlikely but not impossible—or Rawlings could fail to respond as she thought he would. Her father might discover what she was up to before it was too late to do anything about it, and she didn't want to face his wrath if that happened.

Brooding about what might go wrong was just more likely to make it happen that way, she told herself. As with everything else in life, confidence was the key.

With that thought echoing in her mind, she was able to make it through the meal without missing a beat. Rawlings visibly relaxed during dinner, although he was still a bit wary every time he addressed her. By the time they were finished eating, Sara was sure everything would go just as she had planned. She stood up and said, "I'll just clear away these dishes. Why don't you gentlemen go into the parlor? You'll find the cigars and the brandy already laid out." She had excused herself briefly a few minutes earlier to tend to that task.

"You're going to spoil us, girl," Thomas said in a good-natured growl.

"Indeed," Rawlings added.

Sara smiled and didn't point out to either of them that it had been quite a few years since anyone would have considered her a girl. No doubt nearly everyone in Handley's Mill thought of her as an old maid by now.

"An evening like this is a rare treat for a bachelor such as myself," Rawlings went on. "I've begun to regret that I never married and had a family."

"It's never too late," Sara said.

Rawlings heaved a sigh. "For some things, it is, my dear. For some things, it unfortunately is."

Sara didn't argue with him. Her father took Rawlings back to the parlor while Sara cleared away the remains of the meal.

When she was done with that, she went quickly up the rear stairs and down the hall to her mother's room. She wanted to make sure that Clarissa was all right before she did anything else. A quick glance into the room, which was lit by a small candle on the bedside table, showed Sara that her mother was sleeping soundly. Sara smiled a little and backed out of the room, closing the door softly behind her.

Then, drawing a deep breath, she started downstairs again.

". . . article in the *New England Journal* concerning the use of aniline dyes in histopathological research,"

Thomas was saying as Sara came into the parlor a few moments later.

"Yes, Dr. Woodward is quite the erudite scholar," Rawlings agreed, "but I must admit, all this talk of research and studies makes me a bit nervous. You know how the public feels, even now, about vivisection and autopsies."

"But how else are we going to *learn*?" Thomas shot back vehemently. "If I thought it was going to help save a life if my body was cut up and studied after my death, I'd agree to the prospect without hesitation."

"On the other hand, how *could* you agree? You'd be dead. Sara and John are the ones who would have to agree to the procedure, and they might not want their father's body subjected to what some people regard as unholy desecration."

"Well, Sara's right here," Thomas said, gesturing at her as she crossed the room and lowered herself into a rocking chair with a padded seat and back. "What do you think, Sara? Would you give permission for an autopsy to be conducted on my body if you thought it would further the cause of medicine?"

"Of course I would, Father," she said.

Thomas looked at Rawlings and said, "You see?" Then he added, "However, knowing Sara as I do, I daresay she might want to perform the autopsy herself!"

"If it would further the cause of medical science," she said sweetly.

Thomas threw his head back and laughed, and Rawlings smiled broadly. "An excellent answer, darling," Thomas said. He turned his attention back to Rawlings and continued, "Vincent, perhaps we'd better talk about something else—"

"Nonsense," Sara cut in. "I'd rather listen to the two of you discuss medicine than anything else."

"You're sure?" asked Rawlings.

"I'm certain, Vincent," she said. She stood up and went over to his chair. "Let me refill that brandy for you."

She took his empty snifter without waiting for an answer and went over to the sideboard to pour more brandy into it. While she was doing that, Thomas said, "I hear that Woodward is also making some significant advances in photomicrography. Imagine that, Vincent! One day we may be able to actually produce photographs of what's going on at a cellular level."

"That will be fascinating, I'm sure," Rawlings said. He murmured, "Thank you, my dear," as Sara handed his brandy snifter back to him.

For the next hour, Sara sat and listened raptly as her father and Rawlings discussed the current state of medical knowledge and research. They might be small-town doctors, but they faithfully read the *New England Journal of Medicine and Surgery* and the *American Journal of the Medical Sciences*. They were in contact with other doctors, and they did their best to keep up with all the latest developments. Unknown to her father, Sara also read his journals, and she could have joined in the conversation intelligently if she had chosen to. She remained silent for the most part, however, speaking only when Rawlings asked her directly for her opinion, which he did several times. Her father, she noticed, asked no such questions of her.

Finally, Rawlings put out his cigar, which he had barely smoked but rather had allowed to smolder in the ashtray at his elbow for most of the conversation. He drank the last of the brandy in his glass and placed it next to the ashtray on the small table. "I suppose I should be going," he said. "I must say, this has been the most pleasant evening I've spent in quite some time. Thank you, Thomas."

"Most of the credit should go to Sara," Thomas said, nodding at his daughter.

"And so it should," Rawlings agreed. He came to his feet and stepped over to the chair where Sara sat. As he reached out, she lifted her hand, thinking that he intended to shake it, but instead he clasped it and bent over to press his lips against the back of it. He murmured, "Thank you, my dear."

"You're very welcome, Doctor," she said, smiling at him. As he unobtrusively caressed her hand, unable to withstand that temptation, she tried not to think about the fact that his fingers were wrinkled and gnarled.

Thomas snorted. "Gone a bit continental on us, haven't you, Vincent? I mean, kissing the back of a woman's hand!"

"Leave him alone, Father," Sara said quickly, then beamed up at Rawlings. "I think it's positively charming, Vincent."

With another snort, Thomas shook his head. He stood up and headed for the sideboard. "I could use some more brandy."

With her hand still clasped in Rawlings's fingers, Sara rose and said to him, "I'll see you out, Doctor."

"Oh, that's not necessary," Rawlings began. "I know my way—"

"I insist."

"Well . . . in that case . . . I'd be delighted." Rawlings turned his head. "Good night, Thomas."

"Good night, Vincent. Have a safe journey back to Pittsfield."

"I'm certain that I shall."

Sara linked her arm with Rawlings's and walked beside him from the parlor into the foyer, where she handed him his hat and coat. He shrugged into the coat, then, holding his hat in his hands, looked intently at her and said, "Well, good night, Sara. Thank you again for a lovely evening."

"It was very nice. I wish it didn't have to end quite so soon . . ." She played her next card. "I believe I'll step outside for some air."

"The night may have gotten rather chilly," Rawlings said with a slight frown. "It is autumn, you know. Won't be long until winter is here."

"That's all right. I have a shawl right here."

Indeed, it was hanging on the rack where she had placed it earlier in the day, before his arrival. She took it down now and allowed him to help her drape it around her shoulders. She thought his hands rested on her shoulders a little longer than they really needed to, but tonight she didn't mind. In fact, she was grateful for the gesture. It meant she was coming closer to achieving her ends.

"Shouldn't you tell your father . . . ," Rawlings said, gesturing vaguely back toward the parlor.

"I don't think that's necessary," Sara said. "After all, I *am* a grown woman." *Keep that uppermost in his mind,* she thought.

Together they stepped out onto the porch, and Sara quietly pulled the door closed behind them. With Rawlings beside her but not touching her at the moment, she strolled down the walk toward the gate in the fence around the yard.

Rawlings was right; the air had indeed grown cooler since the sun had gone down. There was a definite chill to the breeze that tugged at Sara's hair and flipped the ends of her shawl. Within a month or two, the first snowfall would arrive.

But until then, the air was crisp and clean and Sara enjoyed breathing deeply of it. She smiled over at Rawlings in the moonlight and said, "It's a lovely evening, isn't it?"

"It certainly is," he said, "but not half as lovely as you, my dear."

His words and the way he rested his hand lightly on her arm, just above the elbow, took her back to that other night, the night he had revealed his true feelings for her. He had to be thinking about it, too. Although he had been quite cautious during the evening, she could tell that his feelings hadn't really changed during the intervening weeks. He still wanted her.

Her heart began to thud with anticipation.

They arrived at the gate, and Rawlings reached down to grasp it and swing it open. He looked over curiously at Sara. "Are you coming out . . . or going back to the house?" His voice was taut with some anticipation of his own.

Sara answered him lightly. "Oh, I'll step out . . . for a moment."

Rawlings held the gate wide open, and she stepped through with a swish of her long skirt. He followed her and let the gate shut quietly behind them. They stood beside his buggy, and once again Sara took a deep breath. He would think she was simply enjoying the night air, but actually she was trying to calm the turmoil raging inside her.

It was time, she told herself. If she was going to go ahead with this, she could delay no longer.

"Vincent . . . ," she said tentatively.

His answer came back quickly. "What is it, Sara?"

"I've been thinking about . . . about that other night. When I came out here to talk to you."

"I know which night you're talking about." His voice had a hollow sound to it. "The night I made a fool of myself."

"No," she said quickly, "I was the fool."

"What . . . what do you mean?"

"You thought highly enough of me to be honest with me, and I reacted like a silly young girl."

"Oh, no, you had every right to feel as you did—"

"Perhaps, but that doesn't really change anything. You chose to honor me with your affection, and I turned you away. The most intelligent, compassionate, attractive man I know, and I was too blind to see that at the time."

He was breathing harder now, leaning closer to her. "Sara, what are you saying?" he asked hoarsely.

"I'm saying that . . . if you still want me, Vincent . . . I'm ready now to be yours."

And just to make sure he understood, she rested her hands against his chest, leaned forward, and pressed her lips to his.

The kiss took him by surprise, but he recovered quickly. His arms went around her, drawing her tightly against him. Sara cast her mind back in time, remembering the passion she had shared with Carver Gresham. That helped a little. Besides, Rawlings wasn't totally repulsive. He was much older than her, true, but there was still strength in his arms, and his mouth tasted of brandy. She opened her lips and darted her tongue through, spearing his mouth. He stiffened, evidently shocked by her brazenness, but then he crushed her to him even harder. He panted into her mouth, consumed by excitement.

She felt his hardness pressing against her belly. Just how daring could she be? she wondered. She didn't want to scare him off. Better to make him wait a bit, she decided.

She pulled back, leaving him breathless. He released his hold on her reluctantly and lifted a shaking hand to his face. "My God," he said. "My God, I never expected . . ."

"The best things in life often take us by surprise," Sara said. She smiled, held her arms out, and turned in little half circles as she walked around the buggy, enjoying the night breeze and the silvery moonlight. While she certainly felt no real attraction to Vincent Rawlings, kissing him hadn't been too bad. She was more confident than ever that she could carry this off.

He came after her, saying, "Sara, you're the most beautiful thing I've ever seen in my life. If . . . if you're only teasing me, leading on an old man, I think I shall die right here and now."

"You're not old, Vincent," she told him easily. "When you were holding me, it was with the arms of a young man."

"Oh, my dear, if only you could know what it means to me to hear you say that!"

She stopped, turned back to him, and held out her arms. "That's enough talking for now," she said with a smile.

The invitation was more than plain enough for Rawlings. He sprang forward, caught her in his embrace again, and kissed her lustily. His right hand slid down her back to the soft swell of her rump, his fingers pressing into the flesh and holding her tautly against him. He took his lips away from hers and whispered, "I want you."

"And I want you, Vincent," she whispered back. "But not here. Not now."

"Of course not. Your father . . ." He looked toward the house. "Perhaps you could arrange to visit me in Pittsfield. A shopping trip . . . you could stop by my house . . . no one would have to know."

Sara frowned. This wasn't going exactly the way she had planned. Best to steer it back onto course now, she decided.

"I'll not be your mistress, Vincent," she said, allowing a hint of coolness to creep into her voice. "I may be an old maid, but I'm still a respectable woman."

"Of course you are! I didn't mean to imply—"

She cut in on his desperate response. "I want you very much, but it has to be open and honorable. That's the only way I could be with you properly." She let her belly push lightly against his groin for emphasis.

Rawlings moaned quietly. He leaned forward and kissed her again. "I told you, on that other evening, that you could have anything you wanted, Sara. I meant that. Your love is worth the world to me. Will you . . . will you marry me?"

She lifted her hand to her mouth and widened her eyes in seeming surprise. "I . . . I don't know," she said, suddenly hesitant—or at least appearing so. "My father might not give his blessing . . ."

"Don't worry about Thomas. He'll come around. You'll see. And at any rate, you are a grown woman. You said so yourself."

"That's true. But I won't trade the tyranny of a father for that of a husband. I'm sorry, Vincent, but if

I'm to marry you, I must be sure that I will have some say in my own life."

"Of course you will!" he exclaimed. "I would never dream of dictating to you. I . . . I have too much respect for you to ever do that!"

"Then you wouldn't object if I went to medical school?" She hoped her voice didn't betray her true feelings as she asked the question. Everything that had happened tonight had pointed to this moment, and everything rode on the answer.

"Certainly not," Rawlings said. "I think it's a wonderful idea! I've said all along, you have the instincts of a doctor. You'll make a fine physician."

Sara's pulse thundered in her head. Relief made her knees weak. She had only Rawlings's word, but she believed she could trust him. He was so consumed with desire for her that he would not dare go back on his promise.

She brushed her lips lightly over his. "Thank you, Vincent," she breathed. "Of course I'll marry you."

"Oh, my dear, you've made me the happiest man in the world!"

Then he was hugging her again and kissing her wildly and letting his hands roam over her body. Sara gave herself over to the moment, thinking that she might as well take what pleasure she could from this bargain. She intended to give good value.

But in the back of her mind was only one thought, and it was the most important of all.

She was going to medical school.

FIVE

"Absolutely not," Thomas Black said. "I forbid it."

Sara laughed. "I'm well past the age where I have to have your permission to marry, Father."

"I don't care. You're still my daughter, and I forbid you to marry that . . . that old man!"

"He's no older than you," Sara pointed out. "In fact, I think he's a bit younger, isn't he?"

"Not young enough!" Thomas clasped his hands behind his back and stalked back and forth as if he intended to wear a hole in the rug on the parlor floor. "Where did this insane idea come from, anyway?"

"It's not insane, and Vincent and I have been attracted to each other for quite some time now. He's very intelligent, as you well know, and he's also quite distinguished. Not to mention his kindness. I'm sure he'll treat me very well."

Thomas shook his head. "I don't understand how you can do this to me, Sara. All I've ever wanted is your happiness."

She stood up abruptly from the chair where she was sitting. "My happiness?" she repeated. "You've never been concerned with my happiness!"

"That's a bloody lie!"

She caught her breath. Getting into a shouting match with her father wasn't going to accomplish anything. If everything was going to proceed as planned, she had to stay calm and rational. She waited a moment, letting her pounding pulse slow a bit, then said, "I'm sorry, Father. I didn't mean to upset you. You have to believe that."

"Well, you did upset me," snapped Thomas. He continued pacing. "Coming in here and announcing out of the blue that you're going to marry Vincent Rawlings!" He stopped and looked at Clarissa, who was sitting placidly in a chair by the window, looking out into the side yard with a smile. "Why, if your mother was still . . . still . . ."

"Still sane?" Sara knew she shouldn't say it, but the words came out anyway.

Thomas stopped short in his pacing and glared at her. "I'll thank you not to take that tone," he said coldly. "You know what I meant. If things were different with your mother, she'd be just as upset by all this as I am."

"What about her family?" Sara asked. "Were they pleased when she decided to marry a penniless medical student instead of one of her wealthy suitors?"

"That was different," Thomas said. "Clarissa and I were about the same age. And besides, your Grandfather Palmer did rather like me."

"And you like Vincent. At least, I've always thought that you did."

Thomas drew a deep breath, sighed, and said, "Blast it." Sara knew she had scored with her last comment. Her father and Rawlings had been close friends for years. Thomas was going to have trouble bringing himself to dislike Rawlings too much, no matter what happened.

"You'll see, Father. Everything will work out just fine." She paused, then sat down again and laid her final card on the table. "Besides, Vincent has agreed to send me to medical school after we're married."

Thomas swung around sharply to face her, his eyes widening in horror. "My God," he said in hushed tones. "So that's what this is all about."

Sara fought the urge to squirm a bit in her chair. She hadn't expected her father to see through her ruse quite so quickly. Perhaps she had made a mistake somewhere.

"You would really marry Vincent Rawlings just so you can go to medical school?" Thomas asked, still sounding as if it were too much for him even to comprehend. "Becoming a doctor means that much to you?"

"Vincent and I love each other," Sara said stiffly. "That's why we're going to get married."

Thomas's eyes narrowed suspiciously. "And if I was to offer to send you to school, Sara? Would that . . . change things between you and Vincent?"

She tried not to let him see the excitement that coursed through her. Everything she had done had led up to this moment. She had to handle it correctly, or the entire plan could still fall apart.

"Of course not," she said, trying to sound as if he had offended her dignity. "What sort of woman do you think I am?"

"I'm beginning to wonder about that," Thomas said wearily.

Sara kept a tight rein on her emotions. She said, "Of course, if you were to offer to send me to school, I'm sure Vincent would understand why I would want to postpone the wedding . . ."

And once the wedding had been postponed, once she was actually a doctor at last, the plans for the marriage could eventually be called off completely. Vincent was a reasonable man. He would not give her any trouble, she was sure of that.

Besides, at his age, there was a good chance he might not even be alive by the time she finished medical school.

"Are you totally without a conscience?" Thomas asked curtly. "Or are you just so determined to get what you want . . . so damned stubborn . . . that you can't help hurting other people in your quest to achieve your goals?"

Sara lifted her chin. "It's not my desire to hurt anyone."

"And you don't think Vincent will be hurt when you call off the wedding? You're right, Sara, he is intelligent. He's going to realize that you were just using him to force me into doing what you want."

"Think whatever you like," she told him. "Obviously, I can't convince you of the truth."

"Oh, I know the truth, all right. I'm well aware of it now."

Sara didn't like the sound of that. Perhaps her plan hadn't been as devious as she had thought, because her father had figured it out immediately. She had never intended to actually marry Vincent Rawlings, of course. Her acceptance of his proposal was a means to an end, nothing more. And as long as it worked, she could live with her father's disapproval. He had certainly sounded just now as if he intended to send her to medical school, and that was all that mattered.

Suddenly, Thomas swung around and walked over to the chair where Clarissa was sitting. He stood behind the chair and gently put his hands on her shoulders. "Clarissa, dear, I have some news," he said.

An icy-cold finger seemed to touch Sara's backbone and go gliding along it.

Clarissa twisted her head to look up at Thomas. She was still smiling, but her eyes were as vacant as ever.

That didn't stop him from going on, "Our little girl is getting married, darling."

Sara stood up sharply. "Leave her alone, Father," she said, her voice trembling a little. "You know she doesn't understand."

He turned his head to look at her. "I'm afraid it's you who doesn't understand, Sara. I made my decision long ago, and I see no reason to change it now. I'll not send you to medical school."

"But . . . but what about Vincent?" She knew she was sputtering, but she couldn't help it.

"I'm sure the two of you will be very happy in your marriage."

Sara wanted to cry out. This was wrong, all wrong. She had been so certain that her father would not allow her to go through with the wedding. He had to know that she didn't really want to marry Vincent Rawlings.

"You gave your word, Sara," Thomas said quietly but firmly. "I expect you to honor it, if you still want to consider yourself my daughter."

"You . . . you'd disown me if I don't marry Vincent?" She couldn't believe the turn this conversation had taken. "But you were so opposed to the idea—"

"I still am," he said, a touch of heaviness coming into his voice. "But you're so determined that I'll not stand in your way." He patted Clarissa's shoulder.

"Your mother and I wish you and your new husband every happiness, Sara."

With that, he turned and stalked out of the room, no longer able to look at her as he cleared his throat loudly.

Sara stood there, stunned and blinking. She looked at Clarissa and said in a half whisper, "Oh, Mother, what am I going to do?"

But Clarissa just sat there and smiled, and said nothing.

The wedding date was set for early in January 1868. That would give the newlywed couple time to move to Boston and settle into their new home before the spring term began. Vincent was going to keep his house in Pittsfield, of course, although he would suspend his medical practice there for the three years it would take Sara to complete her studies. He had put away enough money over the years that he could easily afford to do such a thing. Nothing but the best for his bride, he said frequently, and the medical college there certainly fit that description. Once Sara had been awarded her degree, they could return to Pittsfield and practice there together. Vincent had everything worked out.

Sara wanted to scream.

She jumped as a knock came on the door of her room. She was standing in front of her dressing table, looking at herself in the mirror. Staring in disbelief was more like it, she thought. She had never really expected to see herself in a long, white wedding gown. She took a deep breath, tried to control her raging emotions, and turned toward the door. "Who is it?"

"John," came the reply.

Sara frowned a little, not sure why John would be coming to her room. He had come home for the wedding, of course, taking a few days off from his studies, and had surprised the rest of the family by bringing Judith Faulkner with him. Judith was staying in the guest room. She had only smiled prettily when Thomas greeted her and asked her if there might be another wedding in the future for the Black family. Sara found herself hoping that would be the case; she liked Judith, and John obviously adored the pretty young blonde.

None of that was on Sara's mind, however, as she went over to the door and opened it to admit her brother. Her brain was too full of her own impending nuptials. She still wasn't quite sure how everything had come to this.

John grinned at her as he stepped into the room. "I'm not sure I'm supposed to see the bride in her wedding dress before the ceremony," he said as he bent over to brush a kiss across her cheek.

"That's the groom, not the best man," she snapped. "It doesn't matter what *you* see."

"Well, I'd better close the door just in case. Wouldn't want Dr. Rawlings to wander by and catch a glimpse of something he's not supposed to, although I think he's going to stay downstairs. Probably won't stray far from the brandy, if you take my meaning."

"I do," Sara said, "and I don't like it. A man has a right to have a drink or two on his wedding day, I suppose."

"I can't argue with that."

"And you should call him Vincent. He's going to be your brother-in-law, after all."

John shook his head and said dubiously, "I'm not sure I can do that. I was raised to respect my elders."

Sara's jaw tightened and her breath hissed between her teeth as she glared at her brother. She shook her head and turned away from him. "Why did you come up here?" she asked. "Just to taunt me?"

"No, that's not my intention," John replied, sounding serious now. "I just wanted to ask you a question, Sara."

He paused, and she said, "Well, go ahead."

"All right. Why are you really marrying Vincent Rawlings?"

For a long moment, she didn't say anything. She tried to meet John's eyes but had to look away. Finally, she said, "Why does anyone get married?"

"There are a lot of reasons. Business, convenience, ambition, love . . . lust." He shook his head. "I can't see any of those applying in this case. Unless, perhaps, it's ambition . . ."

"I think you should go back downstairs now," Sara said, still not looking at him.

He put his hand on her shoulder and turned her to face him. She stared defiantly into his eyes as he said, "I won't pretend there's a great deal of closeness between us, Sara. We both know it isn't there and hasn't been for years. Life took us down different paths."

"We're both going to be doctors," she said quietly.

"And that's what this is all about, isn't it? Dr. Rawlings has said he'll send you to medical school. I've heard him talking about your plans. He's very excited about them, Sara. He thinks he's doing a wonderful thing by marrying you and helping you fulfill your ambition." He chuckled humorlessly. "There's that word again. But what about you, Sara? Is that all there is to it?"

"What business is it of yours?" she asked coldly.

"You *are* still my sister. I'd like to see you happy."

"I'll be happy . . . when I'm a doctor."

He let go of her shoulder and stepped back. "You'd marry Rawlings . . . you'd give yourself to him . . . just for that?"

"Yes!" Sara hissed savagely. "Yes, damn you! That's exactly what I'm going to do."

"Well, then, dear sister . . ." John sighed wearily. "That makes you no better than a whore."

Her arm flashed up and her hand cut through the air toward his face, but he was quicker. He caught her wrist before she could slap him. She trembled with anger and shame as he held her. "Get out," she said. "Goddamn you, get out!"

"Am I the best man in this wedding, or the pimp?" He laughed, a hollow sound. "Do you know the worst thing about this, Sara, the very worst?"

She said nothing, not trusting herself to speak. There were tears in her eyes, and her chest felt hot and tight.

John leaned closer to her and said, "The worst thing is that I can see now just how much alike you and I really are. I always thought you were better than that."

With that, he dropped her wrist and stepped back, then paused with his hand on the doorknob. With a jaunty grin, he looked over his shoulder at her and said, "I'll see you downstairs. Don't be late."

Then he was gone, and all Sara could do was plunge her face into her hands and try not to give in to the wracking sobs that shook her body.

Because she knew that everything he had said was true.

She barely remembered the carriage ride to the Congregationalist Church or the wedding itself. She was vaguely aware that a few flurries of snow were drifting down from a leaden gray sky, matching her mood. The ceremony was a blur to her. Afterward it was a jumble of memories: strains of music from the church organ echoing hollowly from the high ceiling of the sanctuary; the faces of the congregation turned toward her as she walked down the aisle on the arm of her father; the look in Thomas's eyes, grim but resolute, as he bent over and kissed her before relinquishing her arm at the altar; the mocking smile on John's face; the anticipation in Vincent's gaze as he looked at her; the drone of the minister's voice; then more music and Vincent was lifting her veil and leaning toward her and his lips touched hers and the music grew louder and louder as he took her arm and they walked together away from the altar, the place where they had been joined together and let no man put asunder . . .

She leaned forward and rested her forehead against the window. The glass was cold, and it felt good against her flushed skin. When she opened her eyes, she could faintly make out the snowflakes swirling down from the night sky outside. The snowfall was heavier now. By morning, there would be a foot or more of the white, fluffy stuff on the ground.

She was inside the master bedroom on the second floor of Vincent Rawlings's house in Pittsfield. The supper after the wedding, where the well-wishers had gathered to celebrate the happiness of the new couple, had flown by without leaving much of an impression on her brain, much like the ceremony itself. When the feast was over, she and Vincent had been bundled under a lap robe in a carriage while the driver brought them from the church in Handley's Mill to Vincent's home in Pittsfield. She remembered the clip-clop of the horses' hooves on the snowy road, and she almost recalled how the driver had carried in her bag once they reached this place. Then the man had been gone, and she was alone with Vincent . . . with her husband.

Her breath fogged the window, and she lifted a hand to idly trace patterns in the moisture with a fingertip. She wondered if this vagueness were like what went on in her mother's mind, this feeling of almost remembering things, of trying to reach out and touch reality but having it always slip away from her grasp. Was *she* going to descend into madness, too?

Sara's spine stiffened. She would not allow that to happen. Perhaps she had made a bad bargain, but she would live up to her part of it, and in the long run, everything might be worthwhile. After all, this marriage was going to enable her to do the thing she had always wanted.

She was going to be a doctor.

Vincent had brought her upstairs to this room and handed her a package, murmuring that it was a special present for her and that he would see her later. She had unwrapped the package, and now she was wearing what she had found inside: a gown of green silk, so thin it was almost transparent, adorned with white lace. It was beautiful, of course, and she knew it must have been quite expensive. But she wasn't sure whether it was actually a present for her—or for Vincent.

The sound of the door opening made her turn sharply from the window. Vincent stood there in a dark blue dressing gown belted at the waist, a tray in his hands. On the tray were a pair of snifters and a carafe of brandy. He looked somewhat alarmed and nervous as he said, "Oh, dear, I didn't mean to startle you, Sara."

"That . . . that's quite all right, Vincent," she forced herself to say. She even managed to summon up a faint smile. "Please, come in."

"I thought you might like something to drink," he said as he placed the tray on the small table beside the large four-poster bed.

"That was very thoughtful of you."

He straightened and turned to look at her, and after a moment he breathed, "My God, Sara, you're the most beautiful woman I've ever seen."

She felt herself blushing under his scrutiny. The room was lit rather dimly by a lamp on a table on the other side of the bed and the embers of a fire in the fireplace, but she knew that he could plainly see the contours of her smallish breasts through the fabric of the gown, as well as the coral circles of her nipples and the smooth whiteness of her belly and the thick triangle of reddish-brown hair at the juncture of her thighs. No one had looked at her like that since . . . since Carver Gresham.

There had been no discussion of purity before the wedding. Vincent was a physician; soon he would know beyond a shadow of a doubt that she was not a virgin. But he had known from the first that she had been with that Confederate patrol for more than two years. He probably assumed she had been forced to submit to at least some of her Rebel captors. He couldn't know, of course, that none of them had ever touched her except Carver, and that had been her own choice, something that she wanted every bit as much as the young Rebel captain. Obviously, none of that mattered to Vincent. She was here with him now, his wife, and that was all he cared about.

She swallowed hard. "You . . . you said we were going to have something to drink."

"Oh." Vincent gave a little shake of his head. "Oh, yes, of course. Pardon me. I was just so caught up in your loveliness that I completely forgot." He went to the table and poured brandy from the carafe into each of the snifters. Then he picked up one of the crystal vessels, turning it and warming it in his hands before he gave it to her. He did the same with his own glass. After a moment, he lifted the snifter and clinked it against hers. "To us."

"To us," she echoed, trying not to allow her voice to sound too hollow.

She brought the glass to her lips, sipped the brandy, then drank deeply of it. She felt its warmth spreading through her and was grateful for it. After a breath, she tossed down the rest of the liquor.

Vincent didn't seem to notice how quickly she had polished off the drink. He sipped his brandy for a moment, then set the snifter aside on the table. "I almost can't believe this is happening," he murmured as he stepped closer to her.

Neither could Sara, but her disbelief had a totally different source. If only her father had reacted as she had thought he would to the news of her engagement . . . !

But it was too late to do anything about that now, much too late. She had to make the best of the situation. Perhaps it wouldn't be too bad, she told herself. She knew that Vincent would be gentle, and considerate of her feelings.

He reached for the ribbon that was tied at the neck of her gown.

"Vincent, can't we—" She tried to back away, but there was nowhere to go.

"I have to see you," he said, his voice low and intense. "I've waited so long."

The ribbon came loose as he tugged at it, and the gown began to open down the front. He spread it apart even more, revealing her breasts. His head bent toward her, and she gasped as his lips fastened over her left nipple, already erect from the chill in the room. His arm went around her waist, holding her tightly as he suckled her breast for a moment, then moved to the right one. His other hand continued to spread the gown open, and she felt his fingers move through the thicket of fine-spun hair. She breathed, "Oh, God," as his hand cupped her mound and his middle finger found her core, but she didn't know if it was a prayer or a curse.

All she knew was that every instinct in her body was screaming for her to run, to get out of this place and away from this man as quickly as she could.

But he was her husband. She no longer had any choice in the matter. And besides, she told herself, he had something she wanted every bit as badly as he wanted her.

"Could you . . . blow the lamp out?" she whispered.

"In a moment." Vincent straightened and finished pushing the gown off her shoulders. It slithered around her hips and legs and crumpled in a heap around her feet, leaving her nude before him. His gaze played over her and he smiled, his eyes shining with lust. He reached for the belt of his robe and pulled it loose, shrugging out of the garment. He wore nothing beneath it.

His body was old, just as she had expected, his legs thin, his chest a bit hollow, his arms spindly. But obviously she had inspired other parts of his anatomy to recapture their lost youth. She found her eyes drawn to his shaft, surprised at its burgeoning length.

"Please, Vincent," she said shakily, "the lamp."

"Of course, my dear." He went around the bed, leaned over, and blew out the flame. Then he reclined on the bed and held his arms out to her. They could still see each other, faintly, in the glow from the embers in the fireplace.

She went to him. There was nothing else she could do. He took her hand, placed it on his organ, and parted her legs, not roughly but insistently. A second later, despite the fact that she wasn't really ready, he was inside her, thrusting uncomfortably. His breath came harshly between his lips as he loomed over her. Sara tried to respond. Make the best of it, she told herself grimly. Make the best of it.

She cried out.

"Oh, yes, my dear," Vincent gasped. "Oh, yes!"

But it was not passion that brought the cry from her, or the tears that began to roll down her face. Vincent could think whatever he wanted to, could take pride in his prowess if that was what he desired, but Sara knew, deep down, that her response came from despair, utter despair.

Because she knew now, medical school or no medical school, that today she had made the worst mistake of her life.

BOOK TWO

It is not ours to separate
The tangled skein of will and fate.
—JOHN GREENLEAF WHITTIER

The future is no more uncertain than the present.
—WALT WHITMAN

SIX

Boston, 1869

"Judith, John, come up here!" Edward Faulkner
called, waving to catch their attention as he summoned
them from the back of the ballroom. Behind Faulkner,
the orchestra began to play "The Wedding March."
The approximately one hundred and fifty people in the
room broke into applause.

John tried not to smile too broadly as he took Judith's arm and led her toward the front of the room. It
wouldn't be very dignified if he were grinning like a
jackanapes as he escorted his bride-to-be.

But he couldn't help being excited. Judith's father
was about to announce their engagement. In two
weeks, he would be Dr. John Black, and a month after
that, Judith would be his bride.

After that . . . who could say? The only thing John
knew was that the future held nothing but good things
for him.

The crowd in the ballroom parted to let them
through. Several of the women hugged Judith, while
most of the men who could reach John slapped him on
the back and called their congratulations to him. Edward Faulkner had not made the official announce-

ment yet, but everyone in the room knew the reason this ball was being held.

John's eyes suddenly spotted Nathan leaning against the wall, well clear of the dance floor, of course. Nathan smiled mockingly and lifted his hands, clapping them together lightly, noiselessly. His way of saying congratulations, John knew. Nathan never took anything too seriously.

John couldn't help but grin at his friend and future brother-in-law. He lifted his free hand in a little wave, then turned his attention back to guiding Judith through the press of well-wishers. Finally, they reached the front of the room, and Judith's father put his hands on her shoulders and leaned over to kiss her cheek. He turned to John and put out his hand.

"I know you'll take good care of my girl, John," Faulkner said as they shook hands. His words were pitched quietly, so that only John and Judith could hear him over the music.

John nodded. "I certainly intend to do my best, sir."

"See that you do," Faulkner said, then turned to the crowd and lifted his hands for silence. The orchestra leader was watching him and made a sharp motion with the baton. The music died away as a hush also fell over the crowd.

"My friends," Faulkner went on, his voice booming now, "it gives me great pleasure tonight to announce that my lovely daughter Judith will soon become the bride of Mr. John Black!"

A wave of cheers and applause went up. Faulkner waited for it to recede, then continued, "I suppose I should say Dr. John Black, because by the time the wedding takes place six weeks from now, my future son-in-law will be one of Boston's newest and most promising medical practitioners!"

John nodded and smiled at the fresh spate of clapping, then someone called, "Speech! Speech from the groom-to-be!"

He glanced over at the wall and saw Nathan lowering cupped hands from his grinning mouth. *I should have known,* John thought. The idea of saying even a few words in front of these people, who were the very cream of Boston society, made him nervous, but he knew he would have to get over that. After all, it wouldn't be long before some of these very people were patients of his. He would be seeing them not as wealthy industrialists, merchants, and politicians, but rather as people suffering from all sorts of indelicate, downright embarrassing ailments. That thought calmed his nerves somehow, and as Judith gave his hand a squeeze of encouragement, he was able to step forward and speak.

"I doubt that any man could feel luckier than I do tonight," he said. "I'm surrounded by my friends, and at my side is the loveliest woman in the world, the woman who has done me the honor of consenting to be my wife. I . . . I feel truly humble. I want to thank all of you for helping to make this evening truly special, although the biggest thanks of all goes to my bride-to-be . . . Judith Faulkner!"

With that, John turned and took her into his arms and kissed her, softly and sweetly, as the ballroom erupted with noise and the musicians began playing again.

Life truly—truly!—could not get any better than this, he thought.

The rest of the ball passed in a dizzying whirl for

John. He danced with Judith and her mother, as well as with quite a few of the ladies in attendance at the party. More than one society matron wished him well in his marriage, then sighed regretfully and expressed the hope that *their* daughters could find such a handsome husband with the same type of prospects that he had. The praise made John beam with pride.

Judith must have overheard some of the comments, because as he danced with her again near the end of the evening, she said quietly to him, "Many more nights like this one, and that head of yours won't fit into any of your hats, John Black!"

He laughed. "Is the swelling that obvious?"

"To me it is."

He pressed his groin lightly against the softness of her belly, covering the brazenness of the gesture with the movements of the dance. "What about this one?"

She blushed, but a laugh bubbled out of her mouth. "Oh, yes, very obvious."

They had never made love, and John was fairly certain Judith would come to the marriage bed a virgin, but he knew she wanted him as much as he desired her. Their long, passionate kisses and fevered gropings whenever they were alone had told him that much. But she had always pulled back, unwilling to take the last step, frustrating them both.

Of course, John wasn't marrying her just to get her into bed. Anytime he left Judith with lust gnawing at his vitals, it wasn't a problem to find a willing wench at one of the many taverns Boston sported. He could slake his physical needs with hardly any effort. Marrying Judith would fill a much deeper need. With her as his wife, his ties to the Faulkner family would assure him of success in his profession.

And she *was* beautiful. Anytime he held her in his arms like this, he found himself anticipating their wedding night very much.

Guests began drifting away from the party a little after ten o'clock, and by midnight all of them were gone. John bid Judith good night with a discreet, almost chaste kiss under the proud but watchful eyes of her parents, then put on his top hat and overcoat and strolled out into the cool night. He could have caught onc of the carriages for hire that were still waiting outside the mansion, but he felt so good, not tired at all, that he decided to walk back over to Cambridge instead. Maybe that would make him weary enough so that he could sleep; otherwise, he might be awake until dawn.

"John! Wait up a moment!"

John stopped and turned, recognizing the voice and also the clumping sound that Nathan's peg made as the young man hurried after him. Nathan came up and clapped him on the shoulder. "Hell of a party, wasn't it?"

"It was very enjoyable," John said.

"Yes, I could tell by the way you were swinging my sister around the dance floor—along with every other attractive woman in the room."

John felt a little uncomfortable. Nathan couldn't dance, of course, not with that peg on the stump of his right leg. But usually, Nathan didn't seem to let such things bother him, so John didn't see why he should, either.

Nathan was wearing an overcoat but no hat. "Where were you going now?" he asked.

"Why, home, I thought."

"It's much too early for that," Nathan said with an

emphatic shake of his head. "I thought we might do a little private celebrating of our own at, say, Red Mike's."

It was John's turn to shake his head. "No, thanks. If we go into that hellhole dressed like this, some thief is liable to mark us and jump us in an alley when we leave."

"So you're getting cautious already," Nathan said with mock disapproval. "I'm not so sure my sister has been a good influence on you after all, laddy."

John chuckled. The idea of going out for a few drinks with Nathan appealed to him, but he wanted to pick a place that was a bit more respectable than Red Mike's. On second thought, they could probably find a place that was a *lot* more respectable.

"How about Abernathy's?" he suggested.

"An excellent idea. Come along. We'll take one of those carriages."

"Don't you want to get your hat?" John asked.

"What for? It's a lovely evening."

True, the night air was cool but not cold by any stretch of the imagination, John thought. He nodded, and he and Nathan walked over to one of the carriages parked on the narrow, cobblestoned street. "Abernathy's Tavern," John called up to the driver as they climbed inside.

"Aye, sir," the man replied, and when they were settled inside and had the door closed, he popped his whip and got the team of horses moving.

Abernathy's was a crowded, noisy, neighborhood tavern not far from Boston Common. As John and Nathan strolled in, one of the barmaids greeted them with a friendly smile. "Good evening, gentlemen," she said. "Would you like a booth, or are you going to sit at the bar?"

"A booth, I think," John told her. That would be easier for Nathan than trying to perch on one of the stools along the bar.

The young woman led them across the room to an empty booth that was paneled in dark wood. The table was rough-hewn and heavy, as were the benches on either side of it. As they took their seats, John cast his memory back to previous visits and plucked the name of the barmaid out of his brain. "Thank you, Elaine," he said.

"Why, you're welcome, Mr. Black," she replied, proving that she recognized him, too. "What can I get for you and Mr. Faulkner?"

"Whiskey," Nathan answered without hesitation. "And bring the bottle."

John frowned a little. It sounded like Nathan had some serious drinking in mind, and John wasn't sure he was up to that. He said, "I'll just have a beer."

"A beer?" repeated Nathan. "How can you do any real celebrating with a *beer*?"

"Let me worry about that," John suggested.

Elaine leaned closer to him, her hip brushing his shoulder lightly. "What are you celebrating, Mr. Black," she asked, "and can I help?" The smile was still on her face, but it had become rather seductive now. John tried to remember if he had ever bedded this particular barmaid.

Nathan answered Elaine's question. "John's engagement was announced tonight. He's marrying my sister Judith. It'll be in all the papers tomorrow, in the society sections."

"Oh," Elaine said, and the pressure of her hip

against John's shoulder went away. "I don't suppose you need my help then, do you, sir?"

"*I* might," Nathan said with a laugh before John could reply. "Come here." He reached up and across the table, caught hold of the sleeve of Elaine's low-cut dress, and pulled her toward him. With a little shriek, she fell into his lap and he put his arms around her.

A tall, burly man appeared beside the booth in what seemed like the blink of an eye. "Here now," he said in a hard voice. "What's goin' on here?"

Elaine was giggling as Nathan nuzzled her neck under the thick brunette hair. "It's all right, Rory," she told the bouncer. "These gentlemen are just celebrating a wedding engagement." She put her hands on Nathan's chest and pushed herself away gently. "Behave yourself, Mr. Faulkner. Do you want me to bring those drinks or not?"

"Oh, bring them, by all means!" Nathan said. "I didn't mean to delay you."

Still laughing, Elaine stood up and said, "I'll be right back." She put a hand on the bouncer's arm. "Come on, Rory."

John looked across the table at Nathan and shook his head. "I think you're already feeling a little too good. Are you sure you need more whiskey?"

"What do you mean, more whiskey?" Nathan asked with a frown. "You know there was nothing at the ball tonight except some punch."

John reached across the table and tapped a finger against Nathan's side, feeling the hard object tucked away in an inside pocket of his coat. "I also know about that flask you carry. I think you must have slipped out of the ballroom a time or two for a little nip."

"And what if I did?" Nathan asked, his voice suddenly taking on a slight tone of belligerence. "There's no harm in that, is there? A man's got to do something while everyone else is dancing."

John heard the bitter edge in the words. This was a side of Nathan that was usually kept hidden, but John had seen it come out from time to time, usually with little or no warning. He didn't want Nathan to descend into maudlin self-pity, so he said, "No, there's nothing wrong with that. You go ahead and enjoy yourself."

"I intend to," Nathan said, his grin reappearing as abruptly as it had vanished. "I may even enjoy that little barmaid. What's her name? Elaine?"

John nodded, hoping what was left of this night wouldn't deteriorate into some sort of drunken orgy. He just wasn't in the mood for that. His mind was too much on the future.

He looked around the room. A thick haze of tobacco smoke hung in the air, blending with the smells of spilled liquor, fried food, and human bodies that were not washed quite as often as they should be, to create an unmistakable, universal tavern odor. Abernathy's was a far cry from a dive like Red Mike's, but it was also pretty remote from the rarified atmosphere of the Faulkner mansion.

"Say, you know what would have been funny?" Nathan asked, and without waiting for an answer, he supplied it himself. "If Jeremy Haverford had showed up at the ball tonight."

"Jeremy?" John repeated in surprise. "I haven't seen him in over a year."

"Neither has anyone else around here. I've heard that he went off for a tour of the Continent. His father could certainly afford to send him." Nathan shook his head. "There was a time when Jeremy was convinced *he* was going to marry Judith. He's going to be upset when he finally gets back and discovers that you've beaten his time."

John shrugged, trying to appear casual. "That's his problem, not mine."

He didn't feel casual, though. It had been months since he had even thought about Jeremy Haverford, but Nathan's mention of him made all the memories come flooding back into John's mind.

For several weeks after the incident with Jeremy, John's hands had been swollen and sore. He had been lucky he hadn't broken several bones in each of them, he knew. In one way, attacking Jeremy had been an incredibly stupid thing to do. A physician needed strong, deft, supple fingers. John had taken a chance on ruining his.

And yet, in the long run the result had been exactly what John wanted. Jeremy faded out of the picture and had not returned. He hadn't been serious competition for Judith's affections, of course, but he could have caused a great deal of trouble for John with Edward Faulkner. John got along well with the banker, but like most financiers, Faulkner was on the stuffy side. If he had known about what was going on between John and Judith in the garden that night, he might have been angry enough to banish John from the Faulkner mansion. Something that extreme would have put a serious crimp in John's plans.

There was nothing to worry about now. Obviously, Jeremy had been so frightened that he might not ever show his face in Boston again. That was the way John wanted it, and he would have been just as happy if Nathan had not even mentioned the name.

Elaine returned with their drinks before any more discussion of Jeremy Haverford could take place. John was thankful for that. Nathan picked up the bottle of Irish whiskey that Elaine placed on the table, and he didn't spill a drop as he splashed some of the liquor into the empty glass the barmaid had also brought. John picked up his mug of beer, which was overflowing slightly from the tall head on the brew. Nathan lifted his glass and held it out toward John.

"To the future," he said.

"I'll gladly drink to that."

Nathan tossed back the whiskey while John took a healthy swallow of the beer. It was cold and good. He was willing to nurse this mug along for a while, but Nathan was already refilling the glass with whiskey. He lifted it to his lips and drank it almost as fast as the first shot.

John frowned a little. He knew Nathan drank regularly, but the pace at which the young man was putting away the liquor tonight was even faster than usual. "Something bothering you, Nathan?" he asked.

"What makes you say that?"

"Just curious," John said with a shrug. "After all, you're going to be my brother-in-law, so naturally I'm concerned about you. And I've always felt a certain responsibility—"

"Because you saved my life after that Rebel shell blew my foot off?" Nathan cut in, his face turning dark. "Is that it, John? Like the old Chinese proverb about being responsible for someone if you save their life?"

John had never heard that saying, but it made sense to him. He wished Nathan's moods weren't so volatile tonight, but it was too late to do anything about that.

He said, "That was an awful time, and I didn't mean to bring it up. It's just that if you have any problems, Nathan, I want to help. You're my friend."

"Your crippled friend," Nathan said as he filled the glass with whiskey again. "And as for my problems, there's no way in hell you can help me, John, unless you can tell me how to grow a new foot." He threw back the drink, set the empty glass down on the table with a thump. "Maybe the only way you ever could have helped me would've been to let me die on that operating table in the field hospital. Let me bleed to death. That would have saved me a lot of pain."

John looked down at the table and grimaced. These fits of despair from Nathan were few and far between, but when they did come they were sometimes quite intense. This was shaping up to be one of the bad ones. Perhaps there was something John could do to stop it before it got started properly.

"Look," he said as he looked up, "I know that leg must pain you quite a bit at times, but you have a great deal to be thankful for."

"Oh? And what, *Doctor* Black, would that be?" The scorn in Nathan's voice as he spoke the title was almost more than John could take.

John kept a tight grip on his temper. "You have parents and a sister who love you," he said. "You have friends, and your work—"

"My work!" Nathan interrupted. "Shuffling papers around on a desk in my father's office. That's all I'm fit for anymore." He leaned forward. "Did I ever tell you what I wanted to do before . . . before the war? When I was just a boy?"

"No . . . no, I don't believe you ever did."

"I wanted to go west." There was a hushed quality

in Nathan's voice, as if he were in awe of what he was talking about. "I wanted to go to California and hunt for gold."

"No one's hunting for gold out there now, from what I've heard, except the big mining companies. The Gold Rush is over, Nathan."

"Maybe it is, but there are other adventures to be had. I could have ridden for the Pony Express or helped build the Union Pacific railroad. Did you know that right now cowboys from Texas are driving herds of longhorn cattle up the trails to the railheads in Kansas? Doesn't that sound exciting?"

"Riding through a lot of dust and heat to follow a bunch of stinking cows?" John stared at Nathan in disbelief. "It sounds awful to me, my friend, absolutely awful."

"Yes, but you have no sense of adventure! You just want to marry my sister and raise a family and make a lot of money doctoring a bunch of pampered society bluebloods!"

John looked at him squarely and said, "You're damned right that's what I want to do. I'd be a fool not to." He wondered how the conversation had veered off into these uncharted areas.

Nathan stared at him for a moment, then sighed and shook his head. "You're just like everyone else," he muttered. "Can't see past the end of your nose. But I can. I can see all the things I've missed, all the things I'll never have."

"I can see that as long as you're in this mood, you don't need to do any more of this so-called celebrating." John finished the beer in his mug. "Come on. Let's take you home."

"Not yet." Nathan said stubbornly. "Not yet." He

seemed to be looking around for something. He lifted his arm and called, "Elaine!"

The barmaid came over as Nathan clumsily stood up. John frowned again, wondering what Nathan was up to. Elaine was carrying an empty tray at her side. She asked, "What can I do for you, Mr. Faulkner?"

Nathan took the tray from her and placed it on the table in the booth. "You don't need that anymore," he said.

"Oh, yes, sir, I do. I have to work, you know—"

"Forget about all these bastards. You're going to dance with me."

Elaine was beginning to look confused and worried. "I . . . I don't think I can do that, Mr. Faulkner."

"Why not?" Nathan snapped.

John started to come to his feet. "Nathan . . . ," he said warningly.

"Why not?" Nathan repeated roughly to Elaine. "Because I'm a cripple? Because of this goddamned peg?"

"N-No, of course not. I just have to work—"

Nathan caught hold of her shoulders and jerked her closer to him. The sudden movement and his rising voice drew attention to him as he went on, "Too good to dance with a cripple, but how about going to bed with one? Surely not. You'll do it with anybody who's got enough coins in his pocket, even a grotesquerie like me!"

"That's a lie!" Elaine shot back at him angrily, her pity for him finally evaporating in the face of his continued abuse. "I'm a respectable girl. I'm not a trollop!"

"All of you are," Nathan insisted. "And you're the

only kind that'll have anything to do with the likes of me, the kind I have to pay—"

"That's enough, Nathan," John said as he put a hand on Nathan's shoulder and tried to tug him away from Elaine. "Let go of her. Come on."

"No!" Nathan cried. The whole room was quiet by now. "I want an adventure."

The big bouncer called Rory suddenly appeared on the other side of him. "I'll give you an adventure, you bloody gimp!" the man growled as he balled one hand into a knobby fist and reached for Nathan with the other one.

Nathan released Elaine and twisted toward Rory with surprising speed. His right hand flashed underneath his coat and came out again. Light from the tavern's lanterns glinted on the blade of a knife. "Attack a helpless cripple, will you!" he shouted as he slashed at Rory with the weapon.

Rory jumped back to avoid the blade, a bellow of rage coming from his throat as he did so. John stood a couple of feet behind Nathan, his eyes wide with shock, barely able to believe what was going on right in front of him. From the corner of his eye, he saw the bartender starting around the corner of the bar, a bungstarter gripped in the man's hand. At several nearby tables, some of the husky patrons of Abernathy's were getting hurriedly to their feet, and John sensed that they were going to come to the aid of big Rory. This unexpected confrontation was on the verge of becoming very ugly, very fast.

And Judith would never forgive him, he knew, if he allowed her brother to be badly hurt.

Without wasting any more time thinking, John lunged forward and reached past Nathan with his left hand. He grasped Nathan's right wrist and jerked him around toward him. Slightly off-balance as he was—not to mention drunk—Nathan was unable to stop himself from turning. At the same time, John brought his right fist up sharply, and the blow caught Nathan on the jaw, snapping his head to the side. John let go of Nathan's wrist and he collapsed to the sawdust-littered floor, the knife clattering away as it slipped out of his fingers. Nathan lay there breathing heavily, stunned.

"Thanks, mister," Rory said with grudging gratitude. "But I could'a handled the son of a bitch."

"I'm sure you could have," John said as he fumbled in his pocket and brought out several bills. He pressed them into Elaine's hand, saying, "For the drinks . . . and for the trouble we caused."

"Thanks, Mr. Black," she said. "And I . . . I'm sorry about your friend."

"So am I," John muttered as he looked down at Nathan, who was moving around groggily on the floor, trying to push himself upright again.

Rory stepped up, caught hold of Nathan's collar and belt, and jerked him up. As he frog-marched Nathan to the door, he said, "Get on home and quite causin' trouble for honest folks, ye fancy-dan bastard!"

John hurried after them and got there in time to see Rory shove Nathan through the tavern door that someone had opened for him. There was no way Nathan could catch himself, so he sprawled heavily in the street.

As John went past Rory, the bouncer said, "Don't bring him back here, mister."

"Don't worry, I won't," John assured him. The door closed behind him as he went over to kneel beside Nathan.

"Sneaking son of a bitch," Nathan was saying as he came up into a sitting position. "Hit me from behind."

"Nathan, I'm sorry—"

"Did you see who did it, John? Did you see who jumped me?"

John's breath caught in his throat. So Nathan didn't even remember who had clouted him. Well, so much the better, John thought. He bent and put his hands under Nathan's right arm. "No, I'm afraid I didn't," he said as he started to lift. "Come on, let's get you home—"

Nathan let out a cry of pain and sat down hard. John wasn't able to hold him up. He said, "What is it? What's wrong, Nathan?"

"Something here . . ." Nathan put a hand to his mid-section, sliding it underneath his coat and vest. "I don't think I can stand . . . Well, what do you know?"

He had taken his hand out from under his coat, and in the glow from a nearby street lamp, both of the young men could see that Nathan's fingers were smeared with something black and sticky.

"I seem to be . . . bleeding rather heavily . . . Dr. Black," Nathan said, his voice thick. John stood over him and stared as Nathan swayed back and forth once and then pitched over on his side, out cold.

SEVEN

Sara leaned back in the uncomfortable chair and lifted a hand to rub her weary eyes. She had spent the past two hours studying the thick, leather-bound volumes spread out on the table in front of her. The small, dense print was beginning to be indecipherable in the light from the lamp at the other end of the table, and the illustrations had long since lost any real meaning to her. The hour was growing late, probably after midnight, and she knew it was time to stop studying.

And yet she hated to waste the time on something like sleep. She had begun her studies at the medical college of Harvard University a year earlier with an advantage none of the other students had: she was married to a doctor, and they had brought his entire medical library with them when they came down here to Cambridge. She was determined to exploit that advantage as much as she possibly could, because she also had a disadvantage none of the other students shared.

She was a woman.

As the only woman taking courses in the medical college—although she was officially enrolled at the

Salem Street School in Boston, since Harvard did not accept female students—she was an oddity. No one took her seriously at first, not her fellow students and not even her professors. But they soon learned that she was quite serious about earning a medical degree, and even though her professors seemed reluctant to grade her work as fairly as they did that of the male students, her efforts were so exemplary that they soon had no choice but to recognize her intelligence and dedication. At present, none of the students in Sara's class ranked ahead of her—and she intended to see to it that things stayed that way.

She closed her eyes and rolled her head around on her shoulders, trying to ease the stiffness in her neck. She had spent the entire evening on the circulatory system, and she thought she could trace it now to the tiniest capillary, as well as recognizing the symptoms of virtually every disease and condition that could affect it. But she wanted to make sure she had everything down perfectly before tomorrow's lecture.

Besides, there were other reasons for continuing to study.

As if reading her mind—an annoying trait he had—Vincent appeared in the doorway of the kitchen and said, "Sara, dear, it's very late. Aren't you coming to bed?"

He was wearing his robe and had a pipe in his hand. There was a slight whine in his voice as he spoke, the wheedling sound of a small child begging for a treat but trying not to appear too obvious about it. Sara glanced up at him, then immediately turned her attention back to the medical books.

"I'm still studying, Vincent," she said, putting a note

of distraction in her voice. "I'll be along presently. You go ahead."

"It's awfully late—"

"I know, but it's important that I have all of this material straight in my mind before tomorrow's lecture."

"Surely it can't be that vital—"

"Yes. It is."

Vincent sighed. "Very well." He came over to her, moving slowly, and bent to kiss the top of her head. As he straightened, he said, "You know, my dear, you're pushing yourself too hard. You ought to take more time to enjoy the, ah, finer things of life."

She knew what he meant. She ought to be in his bed whenever he wanted her so that he could push himself into her and slake his lust. A shiver went through her as he dropped his hands onto her shoulders and began to massage them gently.

Sara breathed deeply and didn't look around at him as she said, "There'll be plenty to time to enjoy life— after I've been awarded my medical degree and established my practice."

"Of course. And we both know that will happen. But there's no need to devote every waking minute until then to your studies. Everyone has to rest and enjoy life sometimes."

He didn't understand. He would never understand. Sara knew that. It wasn't just that he was old and rather unskilled as a lover. He could have been young and handsome, a veritable Adonis, and it wouldn't have mattered. Her work would still come first.

"Go on to bed, Vincent," she said coldly. "I'll be up later."

His hands fell away from her shoulders, and even without turning around, she knew they were hanging dispiritedly at his sides. "Yes, dear," he said, his voice small with defeat.

She listened to his footsteps retreating across the kitchen and then ascending the staircase to their bedroom. When she was certain he was gone, she turned her attention back to her studies.

Her concentration had been broken, though, and now her mind was wandering. Despite her resolve, she found her thoughts turning back to the day she and Vincent had arrived here in Cambridge.

The house was a small, neat, two-story cottage within easy walking distance of the university. Vincent had taken care of renting it and furnishing it, and as a result, it lacked much of a feminine touch. Sara had done what she could to remedy that—some curtains here, a rug there, lace doilies on the tables—but if the truth were told, she had never been very interested in frills and fripperies herself. As long as the house was livable, it would serve just fine as a way station on her journey to her ultimate goal.

Someday, of course, when her practice was well established and successful, there would be enough time and money for nice things, and Sara was sure she would enjoy having them around . . . when the time came. But until then, as she had told Vincent, everything else would just have to wait.

He was easier to put off now than he had been at first. While they were living in his house in Pittsfield right after the wedding, getting ready for the move to Cambridge, he had been insatiable. Every night he had pawed her breasts and pushed her nightgown up and insinuated himself between her spread thighs. She was always dry, and it was nothing to her except an irritating annoyance as he thrust back and forth and wheezed for a minute or two before spilling his climax in a couple of feeble spurts. Then he rolled off and began to snore almost immediately, leaving Sara wide awake to stare at the ceiling and wonder just what in God's name had ever possessed her to marry this man.

But logically, she knew quite well why she had done it. Vincent Rawlings represented her best chance—perhaps her only real chance—to get what she wanted out of life. She was willing to put up with a few uncomfortable moments every now and then in return for that. And if that made her nothing better than a whore, as her brother John had said, then so be it.

Once they were actually living here in Cambridge, after Vincent had shut down his practice in Pittsfield and closed up his house there, things had improved somewhat for Sara. She had her classes to occupy her mind, although it was disturbing sometimes the way her fellow students and her professors looked at her, as if she were a rather interesting specimen of some type but nothing remotely human. She had learned quickly to pay no attention to that reaction, and they had begun to take her seriously, perhaps even give her a little grudging respect, after she had demonstrated her intelligence over and over. Things were going to work out at school, she sensed.

And at home, she had taken a firmer hand with Vincent, refusing to drop everything and make love whenever the urge struck him, which was still too often to suit her. She no longer worried about rejecting him; he always came panting back later. As long as she submitted to him a couple of times a week, she had no worry that he would start to think twice about the bargain *he* had made.

Of course, he wouldn't see it that way, she mused.

He probably still thought, even after all this time, that she had married him for love . . .

The sound of a knock on the back door broke into her reverie and made her look up sharply.

Who in the world . . . ? Sara thought as the knock was repeated and she got to her feet. She and Vincent had no real friends here in Cambridge, only acquaintances, who would not be coming to call in the middle of the night like this. The knocks had been soft, but there was an urgency about them nonetheless.

Sara went to the door and leaned against it. "Who is it?" she called quietly.

"John," the reply came back through the door. "Your brother."

He hadn't needed to add that last part, Sara thought a bit indignantly as she reached for the doorknob. As if she wouldn't recognize her own brother's voice!

Yet, he *was* one of the last people she would have expected to find on her rear doorstep in the wee hours of the morning. He and Judith Faulkner had come to the house for dinner once since she and Vincent had moved down here, but the evening had been rather awkward and uncomfortable and had not been repeated. She and Vincent had been to the Faulkner mansion once, as well, but that had not gone much better. Her path rarely crossed that of John at the university, since despite being two years younger than her, he was also two years ahead of her in his studies.

She swung the door open and gasped as the light from the kitchen lamp spilled out over the two men standing there. John had his arm around the second man, holding him up. The front of this man's white shirt was sodden with blood, and he appeared to be only half-conscious at best. It took Sara a moment to recognize him, due both to her shock and the fact that his features were so pale and haggard. But then she realized he was Nathan Faulkner, Judith's older brother.

"Oh, my God, John! What happened?"

"Help me get him inside," John said with a grunt of effort as he started to drag Nathan over the threshold of the door. "He's been cut badly."

Sara got on Nathan's other side and put her arm around him as well, not worrying about the possibility that she might get blood on her clothes. In the face of a bad injury, such considerations always vanished where she was concerned. "Take him through to the parlor," she said. "We'll put him on the sofa there."

"That would be better," John said, nodding toward the table where Vincent's medical books were spread out. "We're liable to get blood all over your sofa if we put him there."

That was typical thinking on John's part, Sara told herself. He was more worried about getting bloodstains on a piece of furniture than helping a wounded man. But he was probably right in his way, she admitted. The table would be a better place to examine Nathan and find out just how badly he was hurt.

"All right, let's bring him over here," she said as she led them toward the table. She reached out with her free hand and shoved the books off, letting them fall helter-skelter to the floor. She kicked them aside as she helped John lower Nathan onto the tabletop. It was a good thing she had put away the linen tablecloth earlier in the evening before spreading out the books and beginning to study, she thought.

Nathan was breathing rapidly and harshly, and when Sara felt the pulse in his neck, she found that it was also fast and somewhat irregular. John said needlessly, "He's lost a lot of blood."

"I can see that," Sara snapped. "How was he injured?"

"He . . . fell . . . while he was holding a knife. As far as I can tell, the blade must have sliced across his midsection then. But I'm not sure how deep it went. I just tried to stop the bleeding as best I could and then brought him here."

"Why here, for God's sake?" asked Sara as she began pulling Nathan's clothes aside so she could get to the wound. "Why didn't you take him to a hospital?"

"There were . . . circumstances you wouldn't understand."

She felt a flash of anger, then suppressed it. She could deal with John later. Right now, she had to see what she could do for Nathan. However, she couldn't resist saying, "There had to be medical attention you could have gotten closer than Cambridge. And failing that, you're about to graduate. I'm just a first-year student."

"Just see what you can do for him, all right?" John asked impatiently.

Sara gave him a curt nod. She had Nathan's coat, vest, and blood-soaked shirt laid open now. There was a compress of cloth over the wound itself, tied tightly in place with a belt looped around Nathan's middle. She glanced at John and saw that he wasn't wearing a belt. That answered one question.

She asked another. "Where did you get the cloth for the compress?"

"Tore it off the tail of my shirt. It was fairly clean, but hardly sterile."

Sara nodded. While the compress had soaked up quite a bit of blood, it was not as sodden as Nathan's shirt, indicating that the wound had bled quickly and heavily but that John's actions had slowed the bleeding considerably. If not for that, Nathan might well be dead by now, so she grudgingly gave her brother credit for that.

"Let's get this off and clean up the wound," she said as she loosened the belt. John lifted Nathan slightly so that Sara could pull the belt completely off and remove the compress. Nathan was muttering something, but he seemed to be out of his head and not really feeling the pain of the wound. Sara asked, "Did you give him some sort of anesthetic?"

John gave a short, humorless bark of laughter. "Nathan took care of that himself before the injury. He must have been drunk as a lord, although I didn't fully realize it at the time. And the loss of blood put him out even more."

"Probably a good thing," Sara commented, as much to herself as to John. She had the wound exposed now. It was an ugly one, some six inches long, slanting across his stomach from a point just above his waistline on the right to one just below on the left. The edges of the gash appeared to be fairly clean.

"There are still some embers in the stove," she told John. "Stir them up and get a good hot fire going. There's water in that basin over there, pots in that cabinet."

"Right," he said, knowing without being told what she wanted him to do.

While he got a pot of water boiling, Sara fetched some clean cloths from a closet in the hall between the kitchen and the parlor. She went into the small room

Vincent had set aside as a study for himself, as well, and brought his black medical bag back to the kitchen with her. The wound would have to be thoroughly disinfected and stitched up, and luckily she had everything here she needed to do that.

The water was boiling by the time she got back. She dropped the cloths into the pot and put the black bag next to Nathan's head on the table. John was standing beside his friend, his face grim. "I'm sorry, Nathan," he murmured. "You don't know how sorry I am."

Sara looked sharply at her brother and gestured at the wound. "Did you have anything to do with this?"

"What? No . . . no, of course not. I told you, he fell."

Sara wasn't sure whether or not to believe him, but she couldn't think of any reason why John would stab Nathan, either. They were good friends, and Sara strongly suspected that they would be related soon. Unless she was badly mistaken, John was going to wind up married to Judith Faulkner.

"Get one of those cloths from the pot, and let's get some of this blood washed off," she said. John did as she told him, using a long fork from one of the drawers in the kitchen cabinets to fish out the cloth from the boiling water. He brought it over to Sara, who carefully swabbed the dried blood away from the wound, which was barely seeping crimson now. John had to bring two more cloths from the pot before the gash and the area around it were clean.

The next thing to do was see just how deep the wound was. Sara took a pair of forceps from Vincent's bag, wiped them down with carbolic acid, then inserted them into the center of the wound and carefully spread the edges of the cut apart. She frowned as layer after layer of skin and tissue separated smoothly. Nathan let out a groan.

"It's deeper than I thought it would be," Sara said without looking up from what she was doing.

"Did it penetrate the peritoneum?" John asked.

"I can't tell yet. Get me another pair of forceps from Vincent's bag and spread this part of the wound."

John took the instrument from the bag, disinfected it with the carbolic acid, and then did as Sara had told him. Sara slid the pair of forceps in her hand toward the other end of the wound, so that they had nearly the entire length of the gash spread open.

A moment later she gave a small sigh of relief. "The peritoneum is intact, which means that none of the intestines were nicked by the blade. We're lucky. I wasn't looking forward to trying to sew up an intestine. That would have required an even bigger incision to give us room to work."

"But you'd have done it, wouldn't you?"

"Of course, if it was necessary."

"You never hesitate, do you, Sara?"

She glanced up at her brother. "Hesitation doesn't accomplish anything."

"Neither does bulling ahead stubbornly."

"I thought you brought Nathan to me because he was hurt, not because you wanted to debate medical philosophy," she said. "Let's get this wound disinfected and then stitch it up. He ought to be all right. I saw saber wounds during the war that were similar to this, only much worse, and they healed just fine with the proper care."

John nodded and let Sara take the forceps from him. She had a pair in each hand now, and she was able to keep the wound open while John cleaned it out with a piece of cotton soaked in carbolic. Once that was done, Sara removed the forceps and let the lips of the injury come together naturally. She looked across the table at John and said, "Close him up, Doctor."

He glanced up sharply. "I'm not a doctor yet. Not for another month. I thought that maybe you . . ."

"Me? You're two years closer to being a doctor than I am!"

"But you've had experience with this sort of injury. You said so yourself. Those saber wounds during the war."

"All right," Sara said with a sigh. If she waited for John to do something on his own, they might be there all night. "I'll need some sutures. There should be some already threaded in the bag."

Proceeding smoothly and efficiently, Sara took the sutures John handed her and stitched together each layer of tissue, working her way back up to the skin, which she also sewed closed. As she pushed the needle through Nathan's flesh and then drew the suture after it, she said, "I happen to know that you closed up quite a few patients when you were working for Dr. Borden in those field hospitals. You could have done this, John."

"Not tonight," he said. He held up his right hand so that she could see it. A steady tremble went through it. "Too much has happened. And besides, it's different when you're working on someone close to you. Nathan's going to be my brother-in-law."

Sara glanced up. "Is that official?"

"It is now. Judith's father announced the engagement tonight at a party."

Looking back down at what she was doing, Sara drew a suture tight and said, "I suppose congratulations are in order." *Even if Vincent and I weren't invited,* she thought. Not that they would have been likely to attend anyway. "I hope your marriage is more . . . rewarding than mine."

"Oh? Trouble in the Rawlings household, is there?"

Sara felt another surge of anger at the mocking tone in John's voice. She told herself it was just a matter of habit where he was concerned, though. He was much too shaken to mean anything really malicious, especially considering the great favor she had done for him tonight. She said tightly, "Vincent and I have our problems. I suppose all married people do."

"I suppose. But I expect my marriage to Judith to be very rewarding indeed."

As well it probably would be, Sara thought. Edward Faulkner's wealthy friends and business associates— and there were a great many of them—would line up to take their aches and pains to Faulkner's new son-in-law. Sara was confident of that, and she was equally confident that was exactly what John had in mind.

Obviously she wasn't the only one in the Black family who looked on the idea of marriage as expedient.

"There," she said when she was finished and the stitched-up wound had a fresh, clean bandage tied on it. "We can take him up to the spare room now and put him to bed."

John shook his head. "No. I'm going to take Nathan home."

"You can't do that! He'll need care. He ought to be in a hospital, but if you won't do that—"

"I'll take care of him."

"If you move him, those stitches are liable to give way," Sara warned.

"I'll be very careful. I have the carriage that brought

us here waiting out on the street. I told the driver we might be inside for a while. He thinks Nathan is just drunk."

Sara shook her head in amazement. "I'm not sure why you're doing all of this, John, but as usual, you seem to have everything figured out."

"Thanks," he said offhandedly, not realizing that she hadn't really meant the comment as a compliment. "And thank you for everything you've done, Sara. When I saw the light in the window and decided to come around back here, I . . . I hoped it would be you who came to the door." He looked around, suddenly frowning. "Where *is* your husband, anyway?"

"Upstairs sleeping," she replied, "and I'm glad we didn't wake him. I didn't fancy the idea of having to explain why there was a bloody, unconscious man on the kitchen table."

John chuckled. "If you'll give me a hand, I'll get him back to the carriage and we'll be out of your way."

"Good." Sara looked around at the books scattered on the floor, the bloody cloths dropped in heaps beside them, and the medical instruments lying next to Nathan on the table. He was unconscious but breathing deeply and steadily now. "Then I can clean this mess up. I'm not certain I want Vincent even knowing that anything happened down here."

"I couldn't agree more. This will be our secret, eh?"

Sara nodded but didn't say anything. She helped John lift Nathan onto his feet. He roused a bit, but he was still more asleep than awake. Sara could smell the reek of whiskey still on him, underlying the acrid scent of the carbolic acid. She had been prepared to use the ether inhaler on him if he had come back to his senses while she was working on his wound, but that hadn't been necessary. As John had said, Nathan had anesthetized himself—and done a good job of it.

With one of them on each side of him, they took him out through the rear door.

Thirty minutes later, Sara was finished with the task of cleaning up the kitchen. The bloodstained cloths were in with the rest of the laundry, where Vincent would never see them. His instruments were packed away in his bag again, and the bag was back in the study where he kept it. There were still some spots of blood on the table, but Sara had cleaned them as best she could and then replaced the linen tablecloth, spreading it over the stains to conceal them. She picked up the medical books, closed them, and stacked them neatly on the table. As she looked around the room, she nodded in satisfaction.

No one could tell now that only a short time earlier, she had sewn up a knife wound in a man's belly right here in this kitchen.

She was more weary than ever, but her eyes were wide open and a peculiar excitement lurked inside her. She knew she couldn't go to sleep, not right now. Even though she would be exhausted tomorrow during the lectures, she was too tense to just let go of everything and fall into slumber.

An idea slipped into her head, taking her totally by surprise. She smiled in amazement that such a thing could be possible.

Yet, there was no denying what she was feeling. There was a warmth inside her, an insistent prodding that would not be ignored. She gave in to it, blew out the lamp in the kitchen, and went upstairs.

She dropped her skirt and blouse and underclothes to the floor as she entered the bedroom she shared with

Vincent. The room was dark, with just enough moonlight filtering in through the gauzy curtains to let her see the shape of him lying in bed underneath the covers. She kicked off her slippers and padded, nude and barefoot, across the room.

He stirred a little when she slipped under the covers with him, and then he rolled toward her as she snuggled against him and put her arm around him, reaching under his nightshirt to caress him. "Wha—what . . . *Sara?*" he asked in astonishment. "Is that you? What are you—oh, my God! Sara!"

She opened herself to him, and for the first time in her marriage, when she cried out a few minutes later, it was in passion, not despair.

EIGHT

Luckily, tonight wasn't the first night Nathan had needed to sneak back into the Faulkner mansion without rousing anyone, and he was lucid enough by the time the carriage reached Beacon Hill to tell John how to slip through the garden, into the back door, and up the rear stairs. John recalled the night he and Judith had ventured into the garden for the first time; he was glad he had Nathan to serve as their guide, because he still didn't know his way around the maze-like place.

Like the other members of the family, Nathan had a suite of his own on the second floor, with a small sitting room that had to be passed through to reach the actual bedchamber. There was a divan in the sitting room, and as John helped Nathan get into a nightshirt, he said, "I'm going to sleep out there on that divan tonight, just in case you need anything."

"That's nice of you, but how will you explain your presence in the morning?" asked Nathan.

"I'll just tell your family that I was a bit under the weather and didn't feel like going all the way back over to Cambridge."

"They'll think you were drunk," Nathan warned

him. "At least Father will. Mother and Judith might accept that story on face value."

John shrugged. "It can't be helped. Besides, I doubt if your father will hold it against me that I was out celebrating on the night my engagement to his daughter was announced."

"Maybe not," Nathan said as he lowered himself gingerly to the edge of his bed. He placed a hand on his stomach. "Lord, as if I wasn't in enough pain already from this pounding head, I feel like a fish that's been gutted!"

"That's nearly what happened when you fell holding that knife. You were very lucky you weren't hurt worse, Nathan. And as for your head, you have only yourself to blame for that—and it's going to be a lot worse in the morning."

Nathan grimaced, then lay back on the pillow and placed his arm across his eyes. "I know," he said with a resigned sigh. "The things I do to forget . . . You know, I still don't remember exactly what happened there in Abernathy's."

"There was a scuffle with one of the men who works there. You pulled a knife on him, and someone in the crowd knocked you down," John lied. "That had to have been when you were hurt, because you dropped the knife when you hit the floor. I'm afraid I didn't think to retrieve it, either. You were already being tossed out of the place, and I wanted to make sure you were all right."

Nathan flapped his free hand. "Don't worry about the knife. I can easily afford another one. But I'm shocked at myself for doing such a thing. I must have really been in my cups."

"Buckets is more like it," John said.

Nathan managed to smile. "And you said you took me to your sister's house . . . ?"

"I thought you might want me to be discreet about this, and I knew Sara would have what I needed to tend to your wound. We were able to disinfect it and sew it up, and now no one is the wiser. Your father doesn't have to find out about that brawl in the tavern."

"I appreciate that, John," Nathan said sincerely. "I really do."

John nodded. If Nathan wanted to think that John had kept the affair quiet for his benefit, then so be it. In point of fact, of course, John had been more concerned that Edward Faulkner not find out his future son-in-law had been out carousing in a lower-class tavern and had gotten mixed up in a fight in which Faulkner's only son had been seriously wounded. That would have looked quite bad for him, John thought. It might have even been enough to make Judith angry with him.

Nathan was half-asleep again. "Do you think . . . we can keep this mess . . . a secret from the family?"

"If we're careful," John replied. "I'll help in any way I can. You just take it easy for a few days and let the wound heal. I'll be around, and we can steal a few moments each day to check on the dressing and change it if need be. I believe it'll be fine."

"I hope so." Nathan took the arm away from his eyes, reached up and caught hold of John's hand. "You're a good friend, John. A better friend than I deserve."

"I doubt that," John told him honestly. "You rest now, Nathan. I'll be right outside in the sitting room if you need me."

"Good night," Nathan whispered.

"Good night." John blew out the lamp and slipped out of the room.

He sank down wearily on the divan in the sitting room. It had been a much longer, more difficult night than he had anticipated when it began. It seemed like a week since he had been dancing with Judith, swirling her lightly around the floor while the musicians played, instead of a matter of mere hours. He moved a throw pillow into position for his head, swung his legs up onto the divan, and stretched out as best he could. This wasn't going to be the most comfortable place he had ever slept.

But it would do, and he drifted off thinking about Judith and the way things would be after the two of them were married at last.

To no one's surprise, the wedding of Miss Judith Faulkner and Dr. John Black was the social event of the season in Boston. The church was packed, with all of the city's leading families in attendance. Nathan, fully recovered from his wound, with no one the wiser, served as John's best man. Thomas and Clarissa journeyed down from Handley's Mill for the ceremony, and although his mother had little or no idea what was really going on, as usual, John thought she enjoyed herself. Sara and Vincent were there, too, of course, prompting John to worry that Sara might say something about the injury Nathan had suffered. She remembered, however, that it was supposed to be a secret, and nothing was mentioned about it, although John thought he saw a brief look of shared knowledge pass between his sister and his new brother-in-law during the reception following the ceremony.

Those were all of his relatives, so his side was heavily outnumbered by Judith's. The Faulkners had a large family, with plenty of aunts, uncles, and cousins, not to mention all the friends and acquaintances and business associates. The crowd was large enough to remind John of his commencement ceremony at Harvard a couple of weeks earlier. His medical degree had been conferred upon him in front of many of these same people, with no mention of the fact that he had ranked well down in his class. That no longer mattered. He was a doctor, and that was all that counted.

John passed through the marriage ceremony itself in something of a daze, and he wondered if that was the way everyone felt when they got married. It seemed likely to him. The step was such a large one, so overwhelming in its implications, that the human mind was naturally stunned. Or at least the male mind was, he reflected afterward. Judith had seemed quite alert, as if she were trying to soak up every detail of the day and imprint it on her memory so that it would never be forgotten.

As far as John was concerned, he was ready to get on with it. The wedding night, the months-long trip to Europe which his wife's parents were giving them as a wedding present, then the return to Boston and the opening of his medical practice—he looked forward to all of those things with ever-mounting anticipation.

But first there was the reception to get through. He found himself standing next to Judith and shaking the hands of hundreds of well-wishers as they passed by. When that ordeal was over, there was food and drink and dancing, and the party went on merrily for a long time. At one point during the evening, John was standing in a corner of the huge ballroom in the Faulkner mansion, by himself for a change. Judith was dancing with her father at the moment.

"Very impressive," a woman's voice murmured beside him.

He looked over at her and saw an attractive woman in her thirties. Ash-blond hair was piled on her head in an elaborate arrangement of ringlets and curls, and the gown of sky-blue silk she wore was cut low enough to show the rounded swells of her upper breasts. There was a small scattering of freckles across those breasts, he couldn't help but notice.

"Thank you," he said. "I assume you're referring to this reception . . . ?"

"And the wedding itself. Of course, one would expect as much when Edward Faulkner's only daughter gets married."

"I suppose so . . ." John hesitated.

The woman gave a throaty laugh. "You don't know me, do you?"

"I'm sorry. I've met so many people today."

"I'm Roberta Ingersoll. My husband is Michael Ingersoll."

John nodded, recognizing the name. Michael Ingersoll owned a highly profitable shipping line and did business through Edward Faulkner's bank. A good man to know, John reflected . . . and it never hurt to make the acquaintance of such a man's wife, either.

"I'm pleased to meet you—again—Mrs. Ingersoll, and I promise I'll remember you this time. I trust you're enjoying yourself?"

"I'm having a fine time, I suppose. Or I would be, if it wasn't for this pain . . ."

John frowned slightly. "Pain?" he repeated.

"Yes, in my back. It's not that bad, you understand,

but it's very annoying. I must have someone look at it one of these days."

"Well, it's certainly better to have any sort of pain tended to before it has a chance to become even worse—"

She cut into what he was saying to ask, "Exactly when will you and your lovely bride be back from the Continent, Dr. Black?"

"That's . . . difficult to say," John replied slowly. "In eight to ten weeks, I imagine." This woman couldn't be hinting at what he suspected, could she? Surely it was just wishful thinking on his part.

"Would it cause a problem if I waited until then to see a doctor about this pain in my back?" Roberta Ingersoll asked.

There was no doubt about it, John thought. He had read her correctly. "As long as the pain isn't too great, I suppose it could wait that long," he said with a smile.

"Shall I make an appointment now?"

"I'm afraid that won't be possible. I don't have an office yet, or a nurse." He paused, then added, "I can make a note to myself, though, concerning my first patient."

"Your first patient? I like the sound of that, Doctor. It makes me feel rather like a virgin again." The hooded smile she gave him made his fingers tighten on the glass of wine he held in his hand.

Roberta went on, "I do hope you and dear Judith enjoy your grand tour. I'll be in touch when you return."

"Thank you. I'll be looking forward to it."

"And so will I." She smiled again, then moved off into the crowd.

John took a deep breath, checked his forehead to see

if there were any beads of sweat there, then drank the rest of his wine in a single swallow. Obviously, there might be some fringe benefits to his medical practice that he hadn't even considered.

Judith came up to him a bit later, looking radiant in her magnificent white wedding gown with its long, lace-covered train. The gown, though high-necked, was cinched tight at the waist, and the silk molded itself to Judith's breasts. John thought she was stunningly beautiful.

She said sharply, "What were you doing talking to Roberta Ingersoll?"

The question took him by surprise. From the look in Judith's eyes, he thought perhaps it would be wise not to tell her exactly what the Ingersoll woman had said to him. "She was asking about our trip to Europe," he said, telling himself that was not exactly a lie; Roberta *had* mentioned the tour he and Judith were going to be taking. "I gathered she wished she could go to the Continent."

"She's been there before," Judith said peevishly. Then her tone softened as she went on, "I didn't mean to sound so suspicious, John. It's just that Roberta has a reputation as a, well, a rather predatory woman, if you know what I mean."

"Her conversation with me was entirely proper." That was a lie, of course, but a necessary one.

"I'm sure it was." Judith laughed suddenly. "I'm being ridiculous, aren't I? This is my wedding day. If a woman can't trust her husband on her wedding day, when can she trust him?"

John made himself laugh, too, and hoped it didn't sound hollow. "I'll take it as a compliment," he said easily, then put his arm around Judith and leaned over to kiss her lightly on the forehead. "Now, Mrs. Black, may I have this dance?"

"You certainly may, Dr. Black."

And as they swung back out onto the floor, John thought to himself that married life might well turn out to be even more interesting than he had expected.

Sara was thoroughly exhausted by the time she and Vincent got home from her brother's wedding and the reception that had followed it. They had taken her parents to the railroad station after the reception and seen them off on the train that would take them to Pittsfield, where Thomas's buggy would be waiting for the drive back to Handley's Mill. Sara had felt decidedly uncomfortable amid all the luxurious finery of the church and the ballroom. She was glad to be back to the cottage she and Vincent shared. At the moment, she wanted nothing more than to get out of the tight, forest-green gown she had worn to the wedding.

"Quite an event," Vincent said as he hung up his hat and overcoat on the rack just inside the front door.

Sara was slipping her shoes off and not paying much attention to him. "What did you say?"

"I said it was quite an event, that wedding. Your brother was quite handsome, and his bride is very lovely."

"I suppose."

"It reminded me of our wedding, you know."

That gave Sara pause, since she and Vincent had gotten married in the Congregationalist Church in Handley's Mill. That was quite different from the massive Boston edifice in which today's ceremony had taken place.

"I'm afraid I don't understand that at all," she told Vincent honestly.

"Well, it's quite simple, really. In both cases, a very lucky man was marrying an extremely beautiful young woman." His smile threatened to become a leer. "Although I daresay, John can't possibly enjoy his wedding night as much as we enjoyed ours."

Sara turned away so that he wouldn't see her roll her eyes. "Don't be crude," she told him, adding to herself, *It's bad enough that you're already so dense you don't even know when a woman is enjoying herself!*

He came up behind her and reached around her to cup her breasts. "Would you like to relive our wedding night, Sara?" he asked as he caressed her.

She stiffened, forced herself not to whirl around and cry out at him to get his damned hands off of her. He was her husband, after all, with certain rights and privileges. And it was true that she had been truly aroused that night six weeks earlier when she had patched up the knife wound in Nathan Faulkner's belly. But since then she had gone back to feeling little or no desire for Vincent.

"I'm much too tired for that," she said as she reached up and took his hands away from her breasts. "Perhaps another night, Vincent . . . all right?"

He sighed heavily and stepped away from her. "Of course," he said without looking at her. "That's fine, just fine. Another night it is."

Damn him! She knew what he was trying to do. He wanted her to be wracked with guilt just because she didn't feel like falling into bed with him. Well, damn it, she wasn't going to do it! She refused to feel guilty for something that wasn't her fault.

Or was it? Despite her resolve, guilt *did* gnaw at the

edges of her mind as she went upstairs, undressed, and got into her nightclothes. Perhaps she wasn't living up to what the world saw as a wife's duties.

But there were other duties, the duties of a healer. *Those* were the ones that were really important. Those were the responsibilities to which she had dedicated her life.

With those thoughts in her head, she went to sleep and never even stirred when her husband joined her in the bed later on, sometime during the night.

Judith sang softly to herself as she leaned against John in the backseat of the carriage that was taking them from the Faulkner mansion to the hotel where they would spend their wedding night. She was still wearing her wedding gown, and John was sure she would have attracted a great deal of attention if they had entered the hotel through the lobby. He had already made arrangements with the management to come in through a rear door, however, from which they could reach the bridal suite on the third floor with a minimum of fuss.

John had drunk enough wine during the reception so that a pleasant glow suffused his mind. His right arm was around Judith's shoulders, and he moved his fingers in little caressing circles on her upper arm, enjoying the warmth of her flesh through the silk of the gown. She twisted her head toward him and lifted her face and he brought his mouth down on hers in a long, lingering kiss. When it was over, she sighed, snuggled tighter against him, and said, "Mrs. John Black."

"Indeed you are, my dear," he told her.

"Did it seem like this day would never come? We've been waiting so long."

"Yes, we have," he agreed. "But I had faith. I knew that sooner or later we would be together."

"And so we are. Now we don't have to wait any longer." She reached down and put her hand on his thigh. "I hope you won't think I'm being too forward when I say how much I want you, Dr. Black."

"And I hope you won't think I'm crude when I tell you that I intend to ravish you this entire night, Mrs. Black."

She laughed and moved her hand a little higher, then kissed him again. He could taste the wine she had drunk and knew that she was feeling some of the effects of it, too. That was all right, he thought. He knew that Judith possessed a healthy curiosity about the sensual things of life, but it wouldn't hurt if the wine lowered some of her natural inhibitions.

She was still caressing him, and he said, "Darling, I think that unless you really want to shock the driver of this carriage, we had best slow down a bit. We'll be at the hotel soon."

"It can't be soon enough to suit me," she said with another laugh.

But it didn't take long, and everything went according to plan as they climbed the rear stairs to the third floor, followed by a couple of porters bringing up their luggage. John and Judith stood aside while the servants took the bags into the suite, then he tipped them generously and sent them on their way. The two of them were alone in the hallway as he turned to her and scooped her up in his arms without warning. Judith gave a little cry and threw her arms around his neck.

"Tradition, I believe," John said. "Carrying one's bride across the threshold, I mean."

He stepped into the suite and kicked the door closed

behind them with his heel. The sitting room was as luxurious as he had known it would be, with thick carpet on the floor, overstuffed furniture, and beautifully patterned wallpaper. Several tables with elegantly slender legs sat along the walls, each of them decorated with a bowl of fresh flowers. A crystal chandelier hung from the ceiling, the small glass lamps inside it hissing slightly. Thick velvet drapes hung closed over the windows. It was a lovely room, made even lovelier by the presence of Judith, who turned in a small circle when John placed her on the floor. "I love it," she said, "and I love you!"

"Why don't we take a look at the bedchamber?" he asked, nodding toward a door on the other side of the room.

"Yes, let's!" Judith said.

Eagerly, she preceded him into the other room. The bedchamber was much the same as the sitting room, only larger and even more luxurious. The huge four-poster bed had an ornate lace canopy suspended over it. There were more flowers in here, and one of the tables also held a bottle of champagne and a pair of crystal glasses on a tray. Another door led to a dressing room. Judith went into the sitting room, picked up a small bag, and hurried toward the dressing room. "I'll be back shortly, John," she said. "Will you pour us some champagne?"

"Certainly, darling."

He busied himself with that while she went into the dressing room and shut the door. His mind was fevered with the thought of what she was doing in there, and his hand trembled slightly as he poured the champagne. Then he took off his cutaway coat, the black silk cummerbund, and his silk cravat. He unfastened the collar of his ruffled shirt.

The door to the dressing room opened behind him.

John turned slowly, prepared to be dazzled by the sight of Judith. But she was even more beautiful than he had expected, and his breath caught in his throat. She wore a gown so thin and light as to almost not be there. It was cut low, its neckline sweeping down almost to her nipples, which showed plainly through the gauzy fabric. The small brown buds crowning her breasts were pebbled with arousal. John could see her slightly rounded belly as well, and her smooth white thighs and the triangle of fine-spun hair that was a little darker blond than what was on her head.

He tore his gaze away from her body and lifted his eyes to her face. She was smiling, a faint curving of her full red lips that promised fulfillment of all the delights he could possibly imagine. Her hair was loose, falling around her shoulders, and he longed to tangle his fingers in it. He felt himself trembling and aching with desire.

"Well," she said, "what do you think?"

How could he answer her? What words could do justice to her beauty? He took a deep breath and said, "I think I'm the luckiest man on the face of the earth."

"Prove it," she whispered.

"The champagne—"

"It can wait."

He was no fool. He wasn't going to argue with her. Instead, he went to her, opened his arms, and she came into them with her face uplifted, her lips slightly open, her eyes heavy-lidded but still pulsing with hunger. He kissed her.

After that, he wasn't quite sure how his clothes

came to be scattered wildly around the room. All he knew was that he was naked, with Judith's hands clutching at his back as he lifted her again and placed her on the bed. He spread the gown open, baring what had previously been almost completely exposed. His lips fastened on first one nipple and then the other as she cried out softly. One of her hands stroked his face gently while the other traced its way down his body, exploring, moving in maddeningly smaller circles around what was at this moment the center of his being. Finally, her soft, cool fingers closed around him and he gasped.

Neither of them could wait any longer. Judith spread her thighs and John moved between them, reaching down to probe momentarily with his hand. She was slick with need. She still had hold of him, and she drew him to her. He shuddered a little as he entered the hot, wet, enfolding tightness. Judith's breathing quickened, became harsher as he began to move back and forth. Her arms went around him again, clasping him to her, and as she opened her lips to cry out once more, as he plunged past her maidenhead, he brought his mouth down on hers. He could tell from the way she stiffened momentarily that there was a flash of pain for her, but then it was over and her hips were moving sensuously to meet his every thrust. He drove deeper and deeper into her, and as he did his tongue dueled with hers and their arms tightened around each other until it seemed that they had truly merged into one being, as if he had somehow crawled into her skin and her into his. John had been with many women, but he had never experienced anything like this. Their climaxes erupted together, shaking them to their depths.

For a long moment after he was finished, John

couldn't move, couldn't do anything except lie there and gasp for air and listen to the hammering of his own heart as it blended with the beat of Judith's heart. Finally, worried that he was crushing her, he rolled to the side and fell onto his back, sinking down into the soft mattress. Beside him, Judith was as breathless as he was. A fine sheen of sweat covered both their bodies.

"Oh, my," Judith said after a few minutes. Her voice was weak and shaky.

John turned on his side toward her. "Are you all right?" he asked anxiously.

"Oh, yes . . . I'm fine, John, just fine." She looked at him and smiled. "I don't think I've ever been better."

"I'm glad to hear it. I'm told that some women . . . well, that the first night is rather a shock for them."

"The only thing I'm shocked about is that we didn't do this sooner!" She laughed as she cuddled against him. "Do you think I'm too brazen?"

"Just brazen enough," he told her as he ran a hand along her smooth flank and then cupped the rise of her left buttock. They lay there like that with their faces only inches apart, exchanging a series of soft, gentle kisses.

"John," Judith whispered after a few minutes, "I . . . I know you've been with other women."

"That's all in the past. It meant nothing." The answer came from him smoothly and quickly, well rehearsed.

"I know. And you won't need any other women in the future, will you?"

"Of course not," he said, but even as the words

came from his mouth, he saw in his mind's eye the lovely face of Roberta Ingersoll.

"Good. Because I don't know what I'd do if I ever found out you'd been unfaithful to me. I . . . I think I'd just die."

"You don't have to worry about that," he assured her.

She reached down to fondle him, and to his surprise he found himself hardening again in her hand. "I couldn't stand sharing you," she said, her long fingernails prodding his flesh in a mixture of pain and pleasure. "It would make me insane."

"I . . . I told you, that won't ever happen." Something was strange here, he thought. The look in Judith's eyes had changed from one of satiated lust to a much more alert expression. John was reminded suddenly of a hawk circling lazily over its prey but still ready to strike suddenly and violently.

She surprised him even more the next moment by moving over him while he still lay on his back. She swung her leg over him and lowered herself, tucking him into her with an ease he would have thought practiced if he had not been certain that she had no real experience in these matters prior to tonight. Obviously, she had an instinct for lovemaking. She let that instinct take over as her hips began to pump back and forth. She leaned over him so that her breasts swung enticingly in front of his face, and he couldn't stop himself from lifting his head to kiss them.

"Don't ever betray me," she said.

"I . . . I won't." His voice was little more than a gasp as he reacted both to what she was doing as well as to what she was saying. He was surprised that the conversation had taken this tack, but the rising tide of desire in him carried away his doubts. He was sure he would be faithful. It was more than clear that his new bride was a perfect match for him when it came to lovemaking.

But as he poured himself out into her again a few moments later, he wished he could get that image of Roberta Ingersoll out of his head!

NINE

"And the best course of action in a hemorrhagic emergency? Anyone? Mrs. Rawlings, how about you? Mrs. Rawlings?"

Sara looked up sharply, jolted out of her doze by the prodding question of Dr. Arthur Jimmerson. She heard a few faint chuckles from her fellow medical students in the lecture hall, but she ignored them, showing no sign she even heard the reaction, save for a slight reddening of her ears. She forced her mind to concentrate on what the doctor had been saying and silently cursed herself for the continued pattern of studying late at night. "A hemorrhagic emergency, Dr. Jimmerson?" she repeated.

"Do you need me to define that, Mrs. Rawlings?"

Sara flushed even more. "Of course not, Doctor. You're speaking of a situation in which the patient has lost a great deal of blood through some sort of injury and requires immediate treatment to save his life. Naturally, that blood has to be replaced, and the preferred method for that is an infusion of sterile saline solution, in whatever quantity is necessary to stabilize the patient. This, of course, follows whatever means are required to stop the bleeding in the first place."

"Of course," Jimmerson said dryly. "Why not use a transfusion of human blood?"

"Too risky," Sara said with a shake of her head. "There have only been a few such transfusions carried out, and in most cases the patient has died."

"But what about the cases in which the patient has lived? Those transfusions are credited with saving their lives."

"That may well be true, but the odds are against it. The risk is so great that no reputable physician will take the chance."

Jimmerson nodded slowly, his expression unreadable. He was a tall, stoop-shouldered man whose bald head had always reminded Sara rather unpleasantly of a vulture. He had a reputation for being a hard taskmaster in his courses, and Sara had already been on the receiving end of his sharp tongue a few times, even though this session of classes had begun less than a month earlier.

She could stand it, she told herself. She could tolerate whatever came her way, because less than a year from now, she would be a doctor. Her course of instruction would be completed. Any doubt that she might fail her final examinations never entered her head.

"So," Jimmerson said after a moment, "you do not hesitate to speak for all reputable physicians, Mrs. Rawlings. You must be very well informed."

"There could be exceptions," Sara said tightly. "I suppose an emergency might be so extreme that a transfusion would be warranted. But I never saw any—"

She stopped herself. She had been about to say that she had never seen such a situation during the war, but that was a part of her life she had kept to herself during her stay here at Harvard. She was willing to tell people that her father was a doctor and that she had assisted him in the past, as well as to admit that she was also married to a doctor, but the time she had spent with the Confederate patrol led by Carver Gresham was her business alone. Anyone who wondered how she had come by her proficiency in treating gunshot and knife wounds would just have to live with that curiosity.

Jimmerson arched his eyebrows. "You were saying, Mrs. Rawlings?"

"I just think it would be very risky to attempt a human blood transfusion, Dr. Jimmerson. I wouldn't do it unless I had absolutely no other choice."

"And that would be very wise of you," he said, taking her somewhat by surprise. Looking around at the rest of the students in the big lecture hall, Jimmerson raised his voice a little and went on, "Mrs. Rawlings is correct. The procedure known as a human blood transfusion is uncertain at best and should not be attempted except as a last resort. Why this is true, we do not know at the present time. However, research is being carried out in this country and in Europe that may someday give us the answer and present us with another usable tool for the treatment of humanity's ills. Until then, gentlemen—and lady—it would behoove all of you to remember that there are limits to medical knowledge and in all likelihood always will be. There are boundaries beyond which even the physician may not go." Jimmerson paused, then continued, "Now, as for emergencies that do not involve a hemorrhagic crisis . . ."

Sara listened with half an ear as Jimmerson's droning voice spread out over the room. She knew he would not ask her any more questions during this class. He never involved a student more than once per lecture. She was safe for the time being.

Of course, she still paid attention to what he was saying, at least enough so that she could scribble notes on the pad in front of her with the stub of pencil in her fingers. But this course involved primarily treatments and procedures for dealing with emergency situations, and she had already had plenty of experience with those when she was riding with the Rebels. You couldn't get a much bigger emergency than being shot up by a Yankee patrol. She had dealt with those situations, and she was confident that she could deal with anything she would run into in a regular medical practice.

The part of her mind that she allowed free rein wandered to the future. She had to decide what she would do once she had completed her education. When she first came to Harvard, she had assumed that when she was a doctor she would return to Handley's Mill and take some of the load off her father. Thomas Black wasn't getting any younger, and Sara knew that it was a strain on him, trying to keep up with his patients and take care of Clarissa as well. For the past five years, Thomas had been having pains in his chest from time to time, and Sara was convinced his heart was weakening. He might have many years of life left, if he was able to slow down and take some of the pressure off himself—but if he kept trying to do as much as he had always done, the outlook was decidedly more grim. Thomas might wind up like his old friend Dr. Miles Austin, who had been Sara's friend as well; he had been with her through some terrible times during the war. Austin had survived being wounded when the field hospital in which he and Sara were working was overrun by Confederate troops. That was the same day, in fact, that Sara had wound up a prisoner of Carver Gresham's patrol. After the war, Austin had carried on as spritely as ever . . . until the day a couple of years later he dropped dead with no warning. At least, there had been no warnings that anyone was aware of. Sara had wondered more than once if Austin had suffered symptoms similar to those of her father but kept them to himself, unwilling to have anyone worry about him or make a fuss over him.

But as much as the idea of going back to the small town where she had been raised appealed to Sara in one way, in another she had become very undecided. A good portion of her time here at Harvard had been spent visiting the wards of the major hospitals in Boston, accompanied by her instructors and the other students. There they were able to observe the workings of medicine first-hand. Sara remembered her father saying that he had learned more from the time he spent in observation at the hospitals than he did in all of his instructional courses. She understood that now. No lecture could take the place of watching surgery being performed or observing the doctors on their rounds through the wards. That was the real thing; everything else was theory and supposition.

Seeing the suffering of the patients in those hospitals had also convinced her that she might be able to do more good right here, rather than back in Handley's Mill. Boston was teeming with people, and they fell prey to every ailment and accident known to man. Practicing in one of the hospitals there would be a continuing education in itself. Later on in her career, there

would always be time to go back to Handley's Mill.
Right now she was leaning strongly toward staying in
Boston. There was only one problem, as far as she
could see.

What was she going to do about Vincent?

Although neither of them had ever really articulated
the situation, Sara knew he had financed her medical
education with the understanding that after she had
completed it, they would return to Pittsfield to live.
That was close enough to Handley's Mill so that she
could practice in the smaller town, if that was what she
wanted. Also, Sara was sure that Vincent would have
welcomed her in his own practice. Whatever would
make her happy was fine with him; he had made that
clear.

But did that desire to please her extend as far as
staying in Boston? Sara couldn't answer that question.
If she remained here, they would have to find a permanent place to live, and it was doubtful that Vincent
would ever be able to return to his own practice in
Pittsfield, not at his age. Nor was it likely that he
would be able to develop much of a practice in Boston.
Of course, that might be all right with him. He was financially well off, and he might enjoy a life of retire-
ment while his young, pretty wife established her own
practice.

There was no way of knowing without asking him,
Sara told herself. But she was going to have to do it
soon, so that she could plan for the future. She didn't
want to wait until after she had her medical degree,
then have Vincent disrupt everything she wanted to do.
There had to be some sort of agreement.

Of course, if he was totally opposed to what she
wanted, there was always the possibility of divorce. It

would be rather scandalous, but Sara could live with scandal if it enabled her to achieve her goals.

Maybe it wouldn't come to that. She hoped it would not. After living with Vincent for over two years, she had developed a sort of affection for him, she supposed, along with the gratitude she felt toward him. She didn't want to hurt him.

And she wouldn't, if she could avoid it. All he had to do was be reasonable.

"Stay here in Boston? But . . . but why? I always thought we would go back to Pittsfield. My friends are there, and my patients . . ."

Sara told herself sternly not to lose her temper with him. It would do no good right now to tell him that most of his former patients were probably seeing other doctors by this time and would continue to do so even if he returned to Pittsfield.

"I know that, Vincent," she said as she reached over and took hold of his hand. They were sitting side by side on the divan in the parlor of their rented house in Cambridge. Sara had prepared Vincent's favorite meal, a roast of beef cooked with potatoes and carrots, even though she knew her culinary skills would never come close to equaling her medical ones, then brought him here into the parlor after the meal was over. She had filled his pipe and poured him a glass of brandy, and he hadn't suspected a thing. He was too busy enjoying this rare occasion of her fussing over him. There was already a gleam in his eyes that told her he would be expecting something else later, too.

But first she had said there was something she wanted to discuss with him, and he had been more than willing to listen. She had laid it all out quickly, telling him of her desire to remain here and seek a position at one of the hospitals in Boston. Her final year at Harvard was more than half-over, and even though her mind had been made up for months, she had been postponing this conversation. She had been afraid that he would react . . . well, just as he was reacting. He looked intently at her, frowning in his confusion and hurt feelings.

"I wish you had said something about this earlier," he said peevishly. "I never dreamed that you would want to stay here, Sara. You're a small-town girl. A big city like Boston isn't the place for you."

"It's not like I never left Handley's Mill before we came here," she replied. "I lived for quite some time in Washington City during the war. Perhaps it wasn't as big as Boston, but it was every bit as crowded."

"Yes, yes, I know, but that's different. We all knew the war wouldn't last forever. You're talking as if you want to reside here permanently."

"I want to be where I can do the most good for people. Surely you can understand that, Vincent. You've been a doctor for many years. You know that the real reward of medicine is the good you can accomplish. Well, I want to accomplish some of that, too."

"Of course, of course," muttered Vincent. "But I still think you can do just as much in Pittsfield or Handley's Mill—"

She stood up abruptly, unable to control her impatience. "For God's sake, Vincent, practicing medicine in Pittsfield or Handley's Mill is nothing more than setting a few broken bones and passing out powders to help relieve the grippe or a stomachache! It's not real medicine!"

His neat salt-and-pepper beard trembled a little as

his jaw tightened. "I'm glad Thomas isn't here to hear you say that!" he snapped. "You know very well there's more than that to medicine, no matter where you're practicing. Why, your father was one of the first doctors in this part of the country to perform an appendectomy, right in Handley's Mill!"

"I know," Sara said with a sigh. "I was there with him, remember? But what else has he done there?"

Vincent stared angrily at her. "He's helped sick children to heal. He's been a source of comfort and assurance to the people he couldn't help in any other way. He's a good doctor, but more than that, Sara, he's a fine man!"

"Yes, yes," she said, nodding. "I know all that. And I'm not trying to disparage anything he's accomplished. My God, considering his background, he was lucky to ever amount to anything. But while practicing in Handley's Mill may have been enough to satisfy him, it's not going to satisfy me. I want more than that out of my career, Vincent."

"And if you want it, you shall have it," he said sarcastically, speaking under his breath but still loudly enough for her to hear.

She pushed her long red hair back and let her own temper slip a bit. "I resent that," she said.

"Resent it all you want. It's true. You've always known your own mind, Sara, and you've never let anything stand in the way of achieving your goals." He laughed bitterly. "You even married a dried-up old man like me just so you could go to medical school."

Her breath caught in her throat. She knew he was no fool, at least not completely; he had to have an inkling of why she had really married him. But she hadn't expected him to state it so bluntly. His words made her sound like some sort of . . . of adventuress!

She crossed her arms and said stiffly, "I'll not dignify that with a response."

"I'm afraid you just did." He waved a hand. "Never mind that. It's in the past, and we were both old enough to know what we were doing—especially me. What we have to decide now is the future." He looked shrewdly at her. "You're sure this is what you want, Sara?"

She sensed his resolve weakening. Quickly, she said, "Of course it is, Vincent. I've thought about this a great deal, and I'm convinced it's the right thing to do."

"You may not have as easy a time of it as you seem to think you will. The resistance you've encountered during your education has been formidable in itself. Things may be a great deal worse once you're actually in practice."

She shrugged and declared, "I'm not worried about that. I've won over my instructors and my fellow students—well, most of them, anyway—and I know that once people have seen what kind of medical skills I have, they'll forget all about the fact that I'm a woman."

Vincent laughed again, but this time the sound was not bitter. It was sad instead. "That's my Sara. So sure of herself. So sure of the world and her place in it."

"Why shouldn't I be?"

He stood up and put his hands on her shoulders, looking squarely into her eyes. "You should be," he said. "I've never doubted your skills. But they can only take you so far. You have to have the cooperation of the rest of the world . . . and I fear you may find it lacking."

"But only in Boston, not in Handley's Mill or Pittsfield."

"There you would have either your father or myself to ease the way for you, to help people become accustomed to you."

She turned away from him, jerking her shoulders out of his grip. "Damn it, Vincent! I don't *want* anyone easing the way for me! I want people to accept me for what I am—a good doctor! Not a good *woman* doctor, just a good doctor."

Vincent sighed heavily. "I'm afraid you may find that quite difficult. But . . . I know you'll never be happy unless you try."

She looked around at him and asked, "Are you saying that we can stay in Boston?"

"I don't suppose it would hurt anything to let you, shall we say, explore the opportunities here for a medical career."

She turned back to him and came into his arms. "Thank you, Vincent," she said. "I knew you'd understand."

"Only too well, my dear," he said. "Only too well."

She ignored that comment and leaned forward to kiss him lightly. She had been prepared to win him over with lovemaking if she had to, but thankfully he had accepted the logic of her argument instead. However, she had to admit that she was a little disappointed. To her surprise, she found herself somewhat aroused.

Maybe she hadn't had to use the bed to convince him; she could still show her gratitude there, couldn't she?

She kissed him again, harder this time, and her tongue slid out to caress his mouth. Vincent's arms went around her, pulling her tightly to him. After a moment, he took his lips away from hers and said, "Sara . . . you don't have to do this . . ."

"I know," she whispered. "I want to."

She really did, she thought. Suddenly, she wanted this very much.

And as Vincent had said . . . what she wanted, she usually got. Tonight was no different.

Sara's heart pounded heavily in her chest all the way through the commencement ceremony, which was held in one of the auditoriums at Harvard, which would award her degree even though she had never been officially enrolled there, through an arrangement with the Salem Street School for Physicians. The speakers were all long-winded and boring, of course, but she didn't care. She hung on every word, wanting never to forget anything about this day. It was the culmination of so many years of dreaming and hoping.

She sat with the other medical students, wearing a sober dark gray gown as befitted the solemnness of the occasion. A week earlier, she had taken her final qualifying examinations, which had been administered orally by a panel of doctors who were also instructors in the medical college. She had been a bundle of raw nerves during that questioning, but she hoped none of the professors could tell that. She had answered correctly all the questions they posed, and she knew they could not deny her certification unless they decided to do so on the basis that she was a woman.

And if they had done that, they would have found themselves in for all sorts of trouble, she had vowed to herself. They would have regretted the day they ever heard of Sara Black Rawlings.

But her worries had been for nothing, because when the results of the final examinations were posted a few days later, her name was there among those who were being awarded degrees in medical science. Not only there, but at the top of the list.

She led her entire class, just as she had set out to do.

There was still some resentment over that honor, too, among the other graduates. She was aware of the sidelong glances many of them sent her way, the little frowns, the looks of outright hostility. She no longer cared. Let them resent her. That was just one more indication of her superior skill as far as she was concerned.

She looked around and met Vincent's eyes as he sat in the audience, a broad smile on his bearded face. He seemed genuinely happy and proud of her, despite the fact that his plans to return to Pittsfield had been completely changed in order to please her. Next to Vincent sat her father, but Thomas was not smiling. His expression was quite solemn, and Sara could tell that he was worried.

He still didn't believe she could handle being a doctor, she thought bitterly. After all this time, all the evidence that she knew what she was doing, he still doubted her. He wouldn't be convinced until she was the leading physician in all of Boston.

And knowing Thomas Black as she did, she knew he might not be won over even then.

There was no point in worrying about that, no purpose to be served in dashing her head against a stone wall. She let her gaze move on to her brother, who along with his wife sat next to Thomas. John had grown a mustache and put on a little weight, making him look more like the distinguished, successful physician that he was. He had a growing practice among the city's elite, due no doubt to his connections through his wife's family. Sara tried not to let herself feel resentful over John's success. Beside him, Judith sat with a chubby-cheeked toddler on her lap. Harvey was a little over a year old and evidently quite a handful, to hear Judith talk about him. She was pregnant again, Sara knew, and in another five months, there would be a new infant for the small army of servants in John's house to tend to.

At least that was one thing she'd never had to worry about since her marriage to Vincent. He might still have the desires of a younger man, but not the potency. Also, Sara took precautions, just in case there might be a surprise or two still lurking in his loins. A child would have completely disrupted her plans. Perhaps someday, if she ever remarried, following Vincent's inevitable death, it might not be so bad to have children, but like everything else, that could wait until she had accomplished what she set out to do.

The only member of her family not in attendance at today's ceremony was her mother. Clarissa was too ill to make the trip from Handley's Mill to Boston; Thomas had left her in the care of the nurse who was employed permanently in the Black household now. He hadn't really wanted to make the journey himself, Sara knew, but he had felt compelled to do so. In spite of his opposition to what she wanted to do with her life, he still loved her. He always would.

The speeches were drawing to a close. Sara leaned forward in her seat, barely able to contain her eagerness. The president of the university stepped to the

podium a few minutes later. Sara knew what was about
to happen. In suitably stuffy tones, the man announced, "We will now award the degrees in medical
science, which carry with them certification to practice medicine in the State of Massachusetts, as well as
all other states in the Union. Please come forward
when your name is called." He looked up from the
podium. "Mrs. Sara Black Rawlings."

Sara stood and started forward. Her pulse ham-
mered loudly in her head and she seemed unable to
breath. She hoped her steps were not too shaky. When
she reached the podium, the president turned, shook
her hand, then gave her the certificate and diploma.
Both documents were covered with elaborate script
and embossed with the seals of the university and the
state, then rolled up into scrolls and tied with ribbons.
Sara's hands trembled as she took them.

"Congratulations, Dr. Rawlings," the president said.

Sara made her way back to her seat. The president
was calling out the names of the other students, but
Sara was only vaguely aware of them. Instead, she
kept hearing two words that played over and over
again in her mind.

Dr. Rawlings . . . Dr. Rawlings . . . Dr. Rawlings.

She saw Vincent beaming at her and felt a surge of
genuine affection. If not for him, she wouldn't be here
today. She wouldn't be Dr. Sara Rawlings.

Beside Vincent, her father was still trying to look
stern and even disapproving, but he was failing miserably, Sara saw to her surprise. His eyes glittered with
tears, and a smile tugged stubbornly at his mouth underneath the bushy mustache. John and Judith were
smiling, too, although Judith looked somewhat distracted by the squirming toddler in her lap. Sara was a

little surprised they had brought Harvey with them, instead of leaving him with one of his nannies.

Perhaps they hoped this was the beginning of a family tradition, she thought as she sat down and took a deep, ragged breath. One day in the future, she might be sitting here and watching while Dr. Harvey Black received *his* medical degree. All of John's children might become doctors.

That was too far away to think about, she decided. Today was hers, and hers alone. Her fingers tightened a little on the scrolls in her hands, but not too much, since she didn't want to crumple them. She had been waiting her entire life for this moment.

"Dr. Sara Rawlings," she whispered, her lips barely moving.

It was the sweetest sound in the world.

BOOK THREE

There is no good in arguing with the inevitable. The only argument available with an east wind is to put on your overcoat.

—JAMES RUSSELL LOWELL

The setting of a great hope is like the setting of the sun. The brightness of our life is gone.

—HENRY WADSWORTH LONGFELLOW

TEN

Boston, 1872

"Mrs. Ingersoll is here to see you, Dr. Black," the nurse said from the doorway of John's private office. He looked up in surprise from the desk where he was writing his notes for the day's cases, then took his heavy gold pocket watch from his vest and flipped it open.

"It's after office hours," he grunted. "Mrs. Ingersoll didn't have an appointment today, did she?"

"No, sir." The nurse was a plain-faced, middle-aged woman in a dark, heavily starched gown. She wore the standard white cap on her mousy brown hair. Judith had helped John settle on her from among all the applicants for the job, and although John knew his wife had her own reasons for that, he had to admit that Miss McLowry was very competent. The woman went on, "She says it's very important that she see you, Doctor."

John nodded slowly and put his pen back in the inkwell. "Very well. Send her in, Miss McLowry."

A moment later, Roberta Ingersoll swept into the office. As usual, she looked stunning, in a burgundy dress, with a hat of the same color perched on her upswept blond hair. She wore gloves and carried a small reticule. John stood up and reached across the desk to take the hands she extended toward him. She leaned forward for a kiss. John checked to make sure Miss McLowry had closed the office door completely before he brushed his lips across Roberta's cheek. It never hurt to be careful.

"Please sit down, Mrs. Ingersoll," he said, letting go of her hands to wave at the padded leather chair in front of the desk. "What brings you here this evening?"

He wanted to take her in his arms and give her a proper kiss, wanted to tell her how much he had missed her, how desperately he desired her. But there was no way of knowing when the nurse might be lurking around just outside the door. He didn't think Miss McLowry was a nosy busybody, but he couldn't be certain of that. It was possible that Judith might have even recruited the woman to act as a spy for her.

"I was having a bit of a pain this afternoon, Doctor," Roberta said. "Right here." She touched her chest between her breasts and then slowly, tantalizingly, ran a fingertip down over her stomach toward her groin. John's hands were clasped together in front of him on the desk, and his fingers tightened on themselves as he watched her.

He swallowed and asked, "Is it still hurting, Mrs. Ingersoll?"

"Not now," she said. "But I'm afraid it will start again later."

"Perhaps not, but just to make sure, I had better take a look . . ."

He stood up, walked silently to the door, and pressed his ear against it. He could hear some faint sounds coming from the other end of the hall, past the examining rooms that were now empty. Miss McLowry was probably straightening up the outer office in preparation for going home.

When he turned back to Roberta, a smile on his face, she was already on her feet waiting for him. She came into his arms and lifted her face for a real kiss. John brought his mouth down hungrily on hers. She writhed a little in his embrace, thrusting her pelvis toward him, rubbing her soft belly against the stiffening of his desire. John took his lips away from hers to say breathlessly, "We can't . . . not while the nurse is still here . . ."

"Then go out there and send her away," Roberta urged. "You can do that, can't you?"

"I . . . I suppose so." John nodded abruptly, and sounded more decisive as he went on, "Of course I can. I'll be right back."

He stepped away from Roberta, straightened the shoulders of his coat, and willed his erection to go away. It wouldn't do to stride into the outer office and send Miss McLowry home for the day with the front of his trousers tented out like that.

Luckily, by the time he reached the outer office his arousal had subsided, and he was able to speak fairly normally as he explained that he would no longer require the nurse's services today.

"But what about Mrs. Ingersoll?" Miss McLowry asked. "If she's ill, you might need my help, Doctor."

"Oh, it's not a medical matter that brought her here," John said with a casual wave of his hand. That much was true, but his next statement wasn't. "She's come to see me about the arrangements for that charity ball she and Mr. Ingersoll are giving next month. It's nothing you need to concern yourself with, Miss McLowry."

"Oh. Well, in that case . . ." She gave him a smile and reached for her coat. "I'll be getting on home then. I'll see you in the morning, Doctor. Good night."

"Good night, Miss McLowry." John went to the door and shut it behind her.

His practice was housed in a building that had once been a private residence, in an exclusive neighborhood not far from Beacon Hill and the Common. The current owner of the building had divided it into four separate apartments, two on each floor. John had half of the ground floor for his practice, while another doctor rented the other half. On the second floor were a bookkeeping firm and the offices of a freighting concern. All of the apartments were expensively furnished, and the address was still a good one. The location no doubt helped John's practice somewhat, although he was confident he would have been successful no matter where his office was. The main advantage this place had, however, was that it was slightly more than a mile from the house he and Judith shared.

Not that he disliked his wife; John still loved Judith very much. But she was extremely jealous and suspicious of him, and, John knew, not without reason. There were so many temptations . . .

Like Roberta Ingersoll.

John would never forget the day Roberta first came to his office. After he and Judith had returned from their trip to Europe and he had made arrangements to rent the apartment for his medical practice, John sent a discreet note to Roberta apprising her of that fact. He wasn't surprised when she immediately made an appointment to see him.

She was not his first patient, but he had been practicing for less than a week when she came for her appointment. John's first nurse, a young woman named Blaylock, had shown Roberta into one of the examination rooms and informed John she was there. John wanted to skip the patients who were in front of her and see Roberta immediately, but he resisted that impulse. It was important to keep up appearances, and besides, it was always possible he had misread the way Roberta had acted at the wedding reception. Not very likely, though, he thought, as he hurried through a sore throat and a couple of cases of gout.

Then it was time to see Roberta, and as he came into the examination room, he leaned on the door and closed it behind him. Roberta smiled at him from the chair where she was seated.

"Hello, Dr. Black," she had said. "How wonderful to see you again. And how was your trip to Europe?"

"Magnificent," John said, but he would have been hard put to decide if he was answering her question or describing the way she looked that day. She was wearing a dark brown dress and had removed her hat and taken down her hair. It fell around her shoulders in thick, ash-blond waves. Her blue eyes seemed to bore into him as he moved slowly across the room and propped a hip on the corner of the examining table. "How have you been feeling? Still have that pain in your back?"

"Yes, I do. Would you like to see where it hurts?"

John nodded, feeling a little shaky inside. It looked as if he hadn't misjudged her. She stood up and came over to him, then turned her back to him and reached behind her.

"Give me your hand," she said. "I'll show you."

His mouth dry, John put his hand in hers, and she guided it to the small of her back, just above the swell of her hips. Pressing his fingertips against her flesh, she said, "That's it, right there."

"Does it hurt when I rub it?" he asked, adding some pressure of his own.

"Oh, no! In fact, that feels very good, Doctor. Can you do it some more?"

John kept up the circular motion with his fingertips, gradually working them into a larger circle. He let his hand move downward so that he was rubbing the fleshy rise of her buttocks and the cleft between them.

"How about that?" he asked hoarsely a moment later.

Roberta was breathing faster, and her voice was hushed as she said, "Yes, Doctor, that's much better."

The hell with this, John decided. He had never liked playing games. He took his hand away from her and stepped over to the door, putting his key in the lock and turning it swiftly. It might be very embarrassing if anyone found him locked in an examination room with Roberta Ingersoll, but at the moment he didn't care. He was too overcome with his lust to worry about such things.

When he turned around from the door, she was ready for him, several buttons of her dress already undone. She came into his arms.

He took her, then and there, on the examining table, the two of them coming together in a welter of arms and legs and clothes hastily thrust aside. Neither of them undressed completely, and the lovemaking was fast and almost savage. The only sounds they made were little pants of breath and an occasional moan that they did their best to suppress. When it was over, John felt surprisingly sated. If she was able to do that to him under such hurried, awkward circumstances, he wondered what she would be capable of if they had more privacy and the leisure to thoroughly enjoy each other. It was an amazing prospect.

And when that reality finally occurred, it was even better than any of his fantasies had been, he thought now as he approached his private office again. He had been having an affair with Roberta for more than a year and a half, and she could still arouse him like no other woman he had ever known.

He was feeling that excitement as he stepped into the office. Roberta was sitting in the chair in front of the desk again, and she looked around with a smile as he came up behind her and rested his hands on her shoulders. He began to rub gently, knowing that she liked being caressed like that.

After a moment, though, she sighed and said, "John, I think you should stop doing that and sit down. There are things we need to talk about."

He frowned a little, not liking the sound of that. "You're sure?"

"I'm certain. Please, John."

He shrugged and went behind the desk. "What's wrong, Roberta? You were so playful earlier, I thought—"

"I know what you thought, and that's what I intended for us to do first. But these other things are weighing on my mind, and I've decided it would be better to talk about them first."

John spread his hands. "By all means, go ahead. What's bothering you?"

"It's Michael."

John stiffened and said hurriedly, "He doesn't know about us, does he?"

"Of course not." Roberta laughed hollowly and went on, "If he did, he might get his gun and shoot me first, then you."

"God, I don't like the sound of that!"

"I wouldn't worry about it. He'd probably be satisfied with divorcing me and ruining you with the scandal. Anyway, I told you that's not why I'm here."

"Then why, damn it?"

She looked squarely at him and said, "I'm worried about Michael's health. I'm afraid there's something wrong with him."

John stared at her, hardly able to believe what he had just heard. She was telling her lover how worried she was about her husband's health. There was something wrong with that picture, John thought wryly.

"Are you saying that you came to me for . . . medical advice?"

"And why not?" Roberta asked defiantly. "You *are* a good doctor, aren't you?"

"Of course I am, I just never thought—" He stopped with a shake of his head, then said, "Michael has his own physician, doesn't he?" It might be better to play along with this situation, he thought, bizarre though it was.

"Yes, he's been seeing Dr. Abraham Jenson for years."

John sniffed in contempt. "Jenson's a quack. He still uses leeches, for God's sake!"

"I know. I don't trust him, but Michael does. But I'm afraid that unless Michael sees a better doctor and finds out what's really bothering him, that he might . . . might . . ."

She's worried that he'll die, John realized. Her concern seemed genuine, and that was something of a revelation to him. He would have thought that she would look forward to the prospect of being a wealthy widow.

However, the Ingersolls had no children, no one to take over the business and run it after Michael was gone. Roberta was probably afraid of being left alone with that much responsibility. There was also the chance that the shipping line wouldn't be nearly as profitable if Michael weren't around to oversee its operation. Roberta wouldn't like that, either.

So he couldn't blame her for worrying, he decided. Quietly, he asked, "Would you like for me to take a look at Michael?"

She leaned forward eagerly in her chair. "Would you?"

John shrugged and said, "Of course, if he comes to see me of his own accord. I can't very well go to him and tell him that I've heard he's not well. He'd be bound to wonder how I found out about that."

"Not necessarily. He knows I come to see you when I'm sick. He heartily approves, in fact, since he does so much business with Edward Faulkner's bank."

"He wouldn't approve if he knew why you really come to see me," John pointed out.

"Well, no, he wouldn't. But he doesn't have to know, does he?"

"You're right. Very well, if you can get him here, I'll take a look at him and see if I can find out what's wrong."

Roberta stood up and came around the desk. "Thank you, John," she said. "Thank you so much! If you can help Michael, I'll be so grateful."

"How grateful?" he asked in a mock growl as he reached up, caught hold of her wrist, and pulled her down into his lap.

"So grateful you won't be able to walk straight for a week," she said with a laugh as she reached down to caress him and bent her head to kiss him.

That would be payment enough right there, John thought.

But he would be sure to soak Michael Ingersoll for a nice healthy fee, too . . . !

"So, Michael," John said a few days later, "I hear you're not feeling very well."

The man sitting in front of the desk scowled darkly. "What else has Roberta told you?" Michael Ingersoll demanded.

John spread his long, slender fingers and shrugged. "Why, nothing. What should she have told me?"

"She shouldn't have been blathering on to strangers about private matters at all," snapped Ingersoll.

"I'm her doctor and a family friend, Michael. One would hardly consider me a stranger."

"No offense, Black, but you're not *my* doctor. If I have a medical problem, I'll go see Dr. Jenson."

"Then why are you here today?" John asked, his voice still mild but now containing an undertone of impatience.

Ingersoll squirmed a bit against the leather cushions of the big chair. He was a short, muscular man of middle age, with thin iron-gray hair, a prominent jaw, and eyes that protruded slightly, just enough to remind John of a frog. Not a handsome man or even a particularly attractive one, but he had an undeniable air of power about him that would be intimidating to most men and appealing to many women.

"I'm here because Roberta is worried about me and insisted that I come to see you," he finally said. His attitude of defiance left him with a sigh. "I suppose she could tell that something has been bothering me."

"And what might that something be?" John prodded gently, not willing to let Ingersoll off the hook now that he had him wiggling.

"I have a . . . a rather annoying sore . . . ah, on a certain portion of my . . . anatomy. Damn it!"

John tried to conceal his reaction, but he couldn't stop one of his eyebrows from quirking upward in surprise. He looked down at his desk with a frown to hide the emotions he felt. He wanted to laugh, but at the same time, this could mean trouble. He said, "I see . . . or rather, perhaps I should see. I'll need to examine this sore place, Michael."

Ingersoll stood up sharply, his features set in a stoic mask. "No, that won't be necessary," he said. "Just forget I told you anything about it, Dr. Black. I'll be leaving now."

He turned toward the door, and John practically lunged around the desk to stop him. "Wait!" John said urgently. "If you're worried about my discretion, I assure you, you needn't be. I'm bound by my oath, you know. What's said—and examined—in this office goes no further."

"You're sure about that?" An even deeper flush was creeping over Ingersoll's normally ruddy features.

"Of course. You have my word."

The man's shoulders slumped a little. "Very well, then. I must admit, I've been worrying like blazes about this." He reached for the buttons of his trousers.

It took only a moment for John to confirm what he had immediately suspected. He looked up at Ingersoll and said, "You have a syphilitic chancre, Michael."

"Oh, Lord!" Ingersoll let out a groan as he practically fell back into his chair. "That's what I was afraid of. I'm a fool, a damned fool . . ."

John's heart was pounding heavier now, and his mouth was suddenly dry. He couldn't allow Ingersoll to see that, though. He took a deep breath and brought his hand to his mouth, stroking his mustache in what he hoped looked like concern. And he *was* concerned, of course, but not particularly for Michael Ingersoll.

If Roberta had been exposed to the disease, that meant he had been exposed, as well . . .

"Listen, Michael," John said as he sat down, "I don't mean to be indelicate about this, but there are certain questions I have to ask."

Ingersoll nodded miserably. "I know. You want to know where I got this . . . this hellish condition!"

"Well, yes," John said, although he didn't really give a damn about that. He would allow Ingersoll to proceed in his own manner, however.

"There's a young woman of my acquaintance who . . . who works in a tavern downtown."

A whore, John thought.

"I've been seeing her, paying her to keep company with me."

Paying her to take you to bed.

"That's the only way I . . . I could have been exposed to this horrible thing. I'm just so surprised. She seemed like such a nice young woman . . ."

A disease-ridden slut! John clasped his hands together on the desk to keep his fingers from trembling.

"Does Roberta know about this young woman, Michael?" he asked.

"Good God, no! What kind of idiot do you take me for?" Ingersoll frowned. "What business would it be of Roberta's?"

"She *is* your wife," John pointed out in amazement. "If you have a disease that could be communicated to her—"

Ingersoll stopped him with a wave of a hand. "Don't worry about *that*," he said curtly. "Roberta and I haven't had . . . marital relations . . . for quite some time. It was a long time before I met the other young lady, in fact. That's why . . . No, never mind. That's neither here nor there." Ingersoll squared his shoulders and looked directly at John. "Is there anything that can be done about this, Doctor?"

For a few seconds, John was so overcome with relief that he couldn't answer Ingersoll's question. Although it came as somewhat of a shock to him that Roberta had not made love with her husband for a long time, he was overwhelmingly grateful for that turn of events. He blinked a couple of times and said, "What? Oh, yes, of course. Yes, there is a treatment for this condition, Michael. It's rather painful and it's not always effective, but it's the only course of action open to us."

Ingersoll nodded, his face glum. "Whatever it is, go ahead, Doctor. It can't be anything worse than what I deserve."

Now that the man's icy, controlled exterior had cracked, his guilt and despair were welling out. John had never seen Ingersoll looking so down in the mouth. He said heartily, "Cheer up, old man. At least we caught this matter fairly early, when there's still a chance for a cure." He stood up and went over to one of the glass-fronted cabinets that lined the walls of the office. He took out a small round tin about half an inch thick and a brown glass bottle with a cork stopper in its neck. He held up the tin and went on, "The ointment in here is a compound of mercury. Apply it to the chancre twice a day. And I want you to take a dose of calomel twice a day, too, to purge your system. There's a good chance that will take care of the problem." He hesitated, then added, "Especially if you stay away from other young women of that sort in the future."

"You don't have to worry about that, Doctor," Ingersoll said fervently.

"And of course, relations with your wife will no longer be possible." *Might as well not take any chances,* John thought. And as long as Roberta was doing without at home, she would be sure to continue coming to see him . . .

"Of course," Ingersoll agreed. "Anyway, Roberta has made it plain that she no longer has any interest in such things."

If only you knew, you poor bastard. If only you knew . . .

John handed the tin of ointment and the bottle of calomel to Ingersoll and said sincerely, "I've very glad that you came to see me today, Michael. Since I've become Roberta's physician, I like to have an idea how the entire family is doing."

"I'm not sure I'd call us a family," Ingersoll said without looking up. "There's a question I'd like to ask you, Doctor."

John stiffened a little, wondering what the man had in mind. He said, "Go ahead."

Ingersoll lifted his head and met John's eyes. "How is Roberta?"

John's breath caught in his throat. Was Ingersoll asking how Roberta was as a lover? Or as a patient? There was only one way to proceed, of course.

"I'm afraid that a person's health is a confidential matter between patient and doctor," he began, but Ingersoll waved off that answer.

"I'm her husband," he snapped. "I have a right to know. She comes to see you so often . . ."

Was he suspicious, or simply concerned? John hesitated, then said, "I can tell you this much, Michael. Your wife has no life-threatening condition or serious illness, as far as I know. Her health is not quite as strong as some—"

"She's always been a bit frail," Ingersoll put in with a nod.

He might not think that if he had seen the way she threw herself into her lovemaking or felt the strength in those arms and legs when they wrapped around a man . . .

John gave a little shake of his head and thrust that image out of his mind. He said, "I assure you, Michael, you needn't worry about Roberta. You know how some women are. They like to be pampered a bit, made to feel as if they're at death's door when they're really not."

Ingersoll nodded knowingly. "Yes, of course. I understand now. Thank you, Doctor." He sighed and stood up. "How much do I owe you?"

"Ten dollars for the office visit and the medicine," John said without hesitation. The price was high, but Ingersoll could easily afford it.

The man took a gold piece from his pocket and

handed it across the desk. Then he looked at the tin in his hand and said, "Twice a day, eh? And I suppose it's rather painful?"

"So I've been told. But well worth the discomfort. A condition like this cannot be allowed to continue unchecked. The disease can become quite serious, leading to insanity or even death."

Ingersoll nodded slowly. "Quite a price to pay for a bit of fluff," he said bitterly.

Yes, it was, John thought. Especially when Ingersoll had a woman like Roberta at home. Obviously, the man had no earthly idea how to handle her.

But John did. And he was looking forward to the next opportunity he would have to do exactly that.

ELEVEN

Angrily, Sara slammed the door behind her. She stalked into the parlor and glared at her husband, who sat there reading a newspaper. After a moment's silence, he slowly lowered the newspaper and raised his bushy white eyebrows. "Trouble, my dear?" he asked in a mild voice.

"*Oh!*" She whirled away from him and began pacing across the room. "Trouble, he asks. As if you don't know very well what's wrong, Vincent!"

Vincent Rawlings closed the newspaper and placed it in his lap. "I assure you, Sara, I don't."

"Dr. Hasbrook has decided that my services are no longer required on the staff of Boston Memorial Hospital!"

"I see," Vincent said quietly. "Does this come as a great surprise to you, Sara? You knew that Hasbrook didn't really want you practicing there in the first place. He made that very clear when you first approached him."

"Yes, but he said he would give me an opportunity to prove myself because he knew you and Father and Miles Austin and Benjamin Everett."

"Quite generous of him, I'd say."

Sara glowered at him. "Well, I wouldn't. He's done nothing these past three months except hover around and watch over my shoulder, just waiting for me to make a mistake! He's been looking for any excuse to get rid of me, and when he couldn't find one, he made one up!"

"That doesn't sound like Hasbrook," Vincent said with a slight frown. "I've always found him to be fair."

"To you, perhaps, or to any other male doctor. But not to a woman who dares trespass in the sacred halls of medicine!"

Vincent placed the folded newspaper on the small table beside his chair and stood up. He went to Sara, put his hands on her shoulders, and said, "You're overwrought, my dear. Why don't you try to calm down and tell me what happened."

"Calm down? I'm perfectly calm!" Sara pulled away from Vincent's hands, stalked back and forth across the room again, then stopped and drew a deep breath. "I suppose you're right," she said. "I *am* upset. But I have every right to be."

"I'm not saying you don't."

She nodded and sank down into a chair. "All right, I'll tell you. But you have to promise not to take Hasbrook's side."

"I can't make any promises without hearing what happened."

"I made a diagnosis, and Dr. Hasbrook disagreed with it. When I tried to point out that I was correct, he became angry and told me that the hospital could dispense with my services. He dismissed me from the staff, Vincent!"

"I understand that, my dear."

He understood a great deal, in fact. When Sara said that she had tried to point out to Dr. Hasbrook that her diagnosis was correct, he knew that that had probably involved an argument and a good deal of shouting, quite likely in front of the patient involved. Tact and discretion had never been Sara's strong suit, at least not where her medical judgment was concerned, and her strong-willed nature had grown even more pronounced during the year and a half since her graduation from medical school. She had clashed with her superiors at every hospital where she had worked; her position at Boston Memorial was the fifth one she had held in that time.

From the beginning, he had urged her to go into private practice, reasoning that she would encounter less resistance in that field. Any patients who came to her would have to be at least somewhat disposed to the idea of allowing a female physician to treat them. But perhaps sensing that patients would be few and far between, at least at first, Sara had decided instead to seek a staff position at one of Boston's prestigious hospitals. Besides, she said, she would see a wider variety of complaints working in a hospital, and that was where she could do the most good. Her academic record, plus the fact that many of the doctors who ran the hospitals knew Vincent Rawlings and Thomas Black, made it possible for her to get what she wanted.

And then, of course, she had immediately alienated everyone with whom she worked.

"You don't understand at all, Vincent," she was saying now. "Hasbrook insisted that *his* diagnosis was correct, and he's treating the patient in a manner that's absolutely wrong!"

"What were the patient's symptoms?" Vincent asked, his own medical curiosity aroused.

"A young girl, five years old, was brought into the hospital with a bad cough and a high fever. I used a stethoscope to listen to her lungs, and I'm convinced she's suffering from pneumonia." Sara looked down at the floor. "I've heard my father talk about the illness that took his parents when he was a boy, and I think that was pneumonia, too. I've made a study of the disease for that very reason."

"What did Dr. Hasbrook say?"

Sara made a slight noise of derision. "He examined the girl and claimed she had nothing more than a normal case of catarrh. He overruled my diagnosis and prescribed a purgative for her."

Vincent frowned and said, "But if the girl actually has pneumonia, a purgative will just weaken her and place her in that much more danger."

"Exactly! That's what I told Hasbrook. I told him he was risking that child's life by being too mule-headed to listen to reason—"

"Ah," Vincent said. "And Dr. Hasbrook responded by dismissing you from the hospital staff."

Sara grimaced. "I suppose I could have been more tactful in my disagreement with him. But it made me so infuriated when he prescribed the wrong treatment for that little girl. I couldn't stand it, Vincent. I simply couldn't stand it."

He went over to her and patted her on the shoulder, knowing that he was risking an annoyed reaction from her if she thought he was being condescending. All of the anger and resentment seemed to have gone out of her as she talked about the ill little girl, though, and she slumped against the back of the chair in despair.

"You did what you thought was best, Sara," he told her. "No one can fault you for that. What happened to the child?"

"She was given a purgative, as Hasbrook ordered, then sent home with her parents."

"Well, all you can do now is hope for the best. Perhaps, if she really did have catarrh, the treatment will help her."

"You doubt my diagnosis, too." The words were more of a statement than a question.

"I didn't say that," Vincent replied firmly. "Would you like for me to go down to the hospital and have a word with Dr. Hasbrook?"

She looked up sharply at him, some of the fire returning to her eyes. "Intercede on my behalf, you mean? Go down there and defend your poor helpless wife?"

Vincent had to laugh at that, and again he hoped she wouldn't take offense. "My dear, no one could ever make the mistake of thinking you defenseless. No, I simply wanted to speak with Hasbrook and see if the two of you could come to an understanding. You're welcome to come along, but only if you let me do the talking at first. Sometimes a cooler head is all that's needed to settle a problem."

She glared at him for a moment, and he thought that she wasn't going to go along with his suggestion. But then she sighed and nodded. "All right, Vincent," she said. "But you'll see that my diagnosis was correct."

"I never doubted it, darling. I never doubted it at all."

Sara was still seething inside when she and Vincent arrived at the hospital a half hour later, this time with

Vincent at the reins of the team pulling their buggy. Normally Sara handled the horses herself, but she was willing to relinquish the task to her husband. It made Vincent feel better, she knew, and she suspected that he was about to run up against a brick wall in the person of Dr. William Hasbrook. He was going to be disappointed when he found himself unable to change Hasbrook's mind about dismissing Sara.

She was convinced that was what the outcome was going to be. Hasbrook had disliked her from the day she first joined the staff at Boston Memorial. This disagreement over a diagnosis—which would have been a minor thing had not the life of a child been depending on it—was simply an excuse to get rid of her. Hasbrook didn't like her because she was a woman with the temerity to become a physician, but he disliked her even more because she was right so often and he was barely competent. He might have been a good doctor once; it was unlikely he would have risen to the position of chief of staff if he had not been. But the times and the medical advances that had come with them had definitely passed him by.

Vincent brought the buggy to a stop in the curving drive that ran up to the entrance of the hospital, which was an impressive four-story brick edifice not far from the Charles River Bridge. He climbed down, then turned to assist Sara, who didn't need any help but allowed him to take her hand anyway. Vincent tied the reins to the rack that was there for that purpose, then took Sara's hand again and led her toward the entrance.

They found Dr. Hasbrook in a ward on the second floor. He looked up in surprise as he saw them approaching. A tall, big-bodied man with silver hair and a florid face, in his expensive brown tweed suit Hasbrook looked as much like a banker as he did a doctor.

"Hello, Vincent," he said without looking at Sara. "What brings you down here?"

As if he didn't know, Sara thought. The gall of the man!

Vincent glanced around the long, high-ceilinged room, which was filled with narrow beds covered with stiffly starched sheets. Most of the beds were occupied with patients, suffering from a variety of ailments. With a nod toward them, Vincent said, "Perhaps we could find some place a bit more private to talk?"

"Of course. Come with me to my office." Hasbrook hesitated, then went on with a frown, "This isn't about that case of catarrh I diagnosed earlier, is it?"

Sara couldn't stop herself from speaking up, no matter what Vincent had said earlier. "It wasn't catarrh," she insisted. "It was pneumonia."

Hasbrook looked coldly at her. "I told you that arguing with me would do you go good, Dr. Rawlings. Neither will bringing your husband back with you to plead your case; Vincent hasn't even seen the patient in question. Besides, I dismissed you not because of your misdiagnosis—that can happen to anyone—but because of your continuing attitude of insubordination to your superiors."

"Superiors?" Sara repeated, her voice rising in anger. "How can someone who knows so little be considered superior to anybody—"

"That's enough of that, Sara," Vincent said sharply. "We said we'd discuss this in Dr. Hasbrook's office, and that's what I intend to do."

Hasbrook harrumphed. "Nothing to discuss, but if you insist on having this conversation . . ."

"I do," Vincent said.

"Come along, then."

They followed him toward the double doors that led into the ward, but before they reached the entrance, the doors were abruptly thrust open by a nurse in a gray gown and white cap. "Dr. Hasbrook!" she said urgently. "That little girl who was here earlier—her parents have brought her back!"

"What for?" Hasbrook asked, looking surprised. "I prescribed a purgative for her condition, and it was administered just as I directed."

"Yes, but now her parents say her condition is much worse."

"I told you," Sara hissed. "I told you it was pneumonia, Dr. Hasbrook."

He shot an angry glance at her, then turned back to the nurse. "Where are the girl and her parents now?"

"I put them in one of the examining rooms, Doctor." The woman's expression was solemn and worried. "The little girl really did seem to be ill . . ."

"Of course she's ill," snapped Hasbrook. "She has catarrh." He looked at Sara and Vincent again. "Come with me, both of you. You can see for yourself, Vincent, that I'm correct."

"We'll both see," Sara said coldly. "But you may not like *what* we see, Doctor."

Hasbrook said nothing else as he led them down the hallway, following the nurse. She took them down a wide staircase with curving banisters on the sides, then along another corridor with doors in both walls. She paused at one of the doors, then opened it. As the nurse did so, Sara heard a hacking cough coming from within. The sound was feeble, and it made Sara's heart pound harder with alarm. The cough was that of someone who was dying.

The little girl was lying on the examining table inside the room, covered with a light sheet. Her parents stood beside her, the mother holding one of the child's hands in both of hers, the father flexing his fingers helplessly and shifting his feet. Both of the adults looked up anxiously as the door opened and the nurse stepped back to allow Hasbrook, Sara, and Vincent to precede her into the room.

"Dr. Hasbrook!" the little girl's mother cried out. "Angie's a lot worse. She just keeps gettin' sicker and sicker."

"Let me look at the child," Hasbrook said stiffly. "Please step back."

The parents moved reluctantly from the table. Hasbrook stepped up to the little girl, felt of her forehead, and then lowered the sheet to rest his hand on her thin chest. Sara watched in silence as Hasbrook continued his examination, seeing the same things she had seen earlier in the day when the parents first brought the little girl to the hospital.

The girl was blond, with slightly freckled features and slender arms. Probably somewhat malnourished, Sara thought. Both the parents were roughly dressed, and the father had the look of a common laborer about him. There would be little or no money in the household for fresh fruits and vegetables or condensed milk. Whatever milk the child got stood a good chance of being contaminated. The lack of proper food would be enough by itself to weaken her, and with the onset of pneumonia on top of that, she was truly in a perilous condition.

Hasbrook leaned over, placed his ear against the

girl's chest, and tapped over each lung with his finger-tips. Sara frowned. The procedure of auscultation and percussion had been perfectly acceptable as a diagnostic tool—in the days when her father and Vincent had first studied medicine. Now a stethoscope was much more accurate in telling a physician what was actually occurring in a patient's lungs.

She couldn't stop herself from speaking. "There's an instrument for that, Doctor," she said. "Why don't you use a stethoscope?"

Hasbrook lifted his head and glared at her. "I've been listening to patients' insides for longer than you've been alive, young lady," he said. "No piece of metal and rubber tubing is going to tell me more than these ears of mine."

"But you can hear the congestion in both lungs with a stethoscope," Sara insisted. "I tell you, the child has double pneumonia!"

"That's enough, Sara," Vincent broke in. He turned to Hasbrook. "William, I had begun using a stethoscope in my practice before I . . . retired. Surely it wouldn't hurt to listen to the girl's respiration through one."

"All right, all right," Hasbrook snapped. "But only because you and I have been friends for so long, Vincent." He looked at the nurse. "Bring a stethoscope."

"Yes, Doctor." The woman ducked out of the room and hurried back a moment later carrying one of the instruments with its pair of flexible rubber tubes and earpieces attached to a large round disk of metal.

Hasbrook took the stethoscope, placed the listening pieces in his ears, and muttered, "Damned uncomfortable contrivance." He bent over and placed the metal disk against the girl's chest.

For a long moment, as everyone else in the room looked on anxiously, Hasbrook listened to the little girl's breathing. Suddenly, another spasm of coughing struck her, and Hasbrook straightened abruptly, jerking the end of the stethoscope away from her chest.

"Well?" Sara demanded when the child's coughing had subsided again. "What did you hear, Doctor?"

Hasbrook was frowning darkly. "There does seem to be some congestion in the lungs . . ."

Vincent stepped forward and held out his hand. "Do you mind if I listen, Doctor?" he asked.

After a second's hesitation, Hasbrook placed the stethoscope in Vincent's hand. "Go ahead, if that's what you want," he said with no attempt at grace.

Vincent fitted the instrument to his ears and then repeated Hasbrook's actions, leaning over the girl and placing the other end of the stethoscope against her chest. Sara watched his face intently, but his expression was unreadable. Finally, after a few moments that seemed much longer, he straightened.

"I'd recommend immediate hospitalization for this child," he said. "She must be kept warm and given plenty of fluids, as well as the proper foods."

Sara said, "It's pneumonia, isn't it?"

"I think so," Vincent said with a nod.

Hasbrook's face had turned a bright red. "May I remind you, Doctor," he said tightly, "that you are not a member of the hospital staff. Nor is the young lady, as of approximately one-and-a-half hours ago."

"Wait a minute, Doc," said the father of the little girl. "If this fella and the gal both say Angie's got pneumonia, hadn't you ought to do somethin' about it?"

"I am," Hasbrook said. "I'm asking them to leave

this hospital immediately. I'll not tolerate being told how to do my job—especially by a young woman!"

"Hold on, William," Vincent said, putting his hand on the other doctor's arm. "There's no need to be angry. I'm sure we all just want what's best for this little girl."

"She has catarrh!" Hasbrook insisted as he jerked away from Vincent's hand. "I prescribed a purgative, and I suggest we all give it time to work." He looked at the girl's father. "Sir, I want you to take your daughter home. Keep her warm and see that she eats. She'll be better in a few days."

"She'll be dead in a few days!" Sara exclaimed. "You can't do this, Doctor! You can't sacrifice this child's life just because you're too proud to admit that you made a mistake."

Hasbrook swung around toward her, his face a dark, mottled red. "You've been dismissed from my staff, young woman, and I can promise you that none of the other hospitals in Boston will make the mistake of allowing you to practice there. Now, if you don't leave this building and stop interfering, I'll summon a constable and have you arrested!"

"Go ahead, damn you!" Sara shouted. "Go ahead and have me thrown in jail! But get that little girl the attention she needs. Otherwise she's going to die!"

For a second, Sara thought Hasbrook was going to strike her. Vincent stood by closely, his muscles tensed to get between them if necessary. He was too old and frail to do much good if the situation came down to violence, however.

But the little girl's father wasn't, and he stepped closer to Hasbrook, saying in menacing tones, "You'd better stop tryin' to boss people around and take proper care of my little girl, Doc. Sounds to me like the lady knows what she's talkin' about."

Hasbrook glanced at the man, took in his broad shoulders and powerful arms, and the physician's face paled a little under its flush. Still, he managed to summon up an indignant tone as he said, "Are you threatening me, sir?"

"I ain't goin' to stand by and watch Angie die if there's somethin' can be done about it."

In the face of that quiet statement, there was nothing Hasbrook could do except bluster for a moment, and then say, "Certainly we'll do all we can for the child. Perhaps hospitalization *would* be the best course . . ."

"And you won't mind if I come back by and pay Angie a visit or two while she's here, will you, Dr. Hasbrook?" Vincent said. At that moment, Sara felt a surge of genuine pride in her husband. Vincent had his failings, of course, but he was still a doctor, still determined to do what he could to help the sick.

"Of course not," Hasbrook muttered. He turned away and said to the nurse, "See that this child is placed in one of the wards right away. I want her to have the best care possible."

"And if the charges are more than the family can afford, have the bill sent to me," Vincent added.

The girl's father swallowed hard and stuck out his hand. "I don't know what to say, mister. Me an' the missus, we're mighty grateful to you. I guess you know what it's like tryin' to do your best for your little ones, seein' as you've got such a fine daughter yourself." He smiled at Sara.

Vincent gave a little cough of embarrassment as he shook hands with the man, but he didn't correct the man's assumption, for which Sara was grateful. Pointing out the age difference between her and her husband would have been even more embarrassing.

Taking her arm, Vincent led her out of the room. Hasbrook followed them, leaving the nurse to see to transferring the little girl to one of the children's wards. When they were in the hall and the door of the examining room was closed behind them, Hasbrook said heavily, "Don't think this changes anything."

"It's given that child a chance to recover," Sara said. "That's all I care about."

"I still don't want you on my staff." Hasbrook looked over at Vincent. "I'm sorry."

"Why don't you try apologizing to my wife?" Vincent suggested.

For a long moment, Hasbrook didn't say anything. Then he shook his head ponderously and said, "I can't do that. The fact that her diagnosis was correct in this instance doesn't excuse her continued insubordination and her efforts to undermine my authority. I have ample cause to dismiss her."

"Then you must do as you see fit," Vincent said. "But I'm afraid that our friendship is at an end, William."

"I regret that, but I won't work with your wife any longer. And I *am* still chief of staff in this hospital."

Sara was trembling with anger. This was unfair, as unfair as when she had been dismissed from her job as a nurse in the military hospitals in Washington during the war. That had come about because her supervisor, Dorothea Dix, had disliked her from the start, and Sara had been relieved of her position on trumped-up charges of neglecting her duties. She was every bit as furious now as she had been then.

And yet this situation was somewhat different, and

she acknowledged as much by saying, "I don't wish to work with *you* anymore, either, Dr. Hasbrook. I find you perfectly incompetent and am happy to end my association with Boston Memorial right here and now!"

Hasbrook glowered at her and said, "It's done, then. I'll thank you to leave now . . . *Doctor* Rawlings."

Gently, Vincent took hold of her shoulders and turned her away before she could say anything else. He steered her out of the building.

Once they were outside, she said, "That . . . that man . . ."

"I know, dear," Vincent said. "But it's over and done with now."

Sara turned to him and asked in a half wail, "What am I going to *do*, Vincent? I've already worked in every reputable hospital in Boston."

"There's still private practice. For that matter, we could always return to Pittsfield. We could sell the house we bought down here without much trouble."

Without even stopping to think about it, she shook her head adamantly. "Running back home would be like giving up, admitting that I've failed in what I set out to do. I can't do that, Vincent."

Of course, she told herself, she *had* failed. No matter how much she wanted not to admit that, even to herself, the facts were undeniable. She hadn't fit in anywhere in Boston's medical establishment.

Perhaps Vincent was right. Perhaps it was time to go home.

By the time they reached their house in Cambridge, Sara's anger had dissipated, leaving her empty and uncertain. They went inside, and Vincent said, "Why don't you sit down in the parlor for a few minutes and rest, Sara? I can see to supper tonight."

She summoned up a faint smile from somewhere deep inside. "Vincent, the only cook I know worse than myself is you. I'll take a few moments, as you said, then I'll see what I can prepare."

"Very well, if you're sure." He patted her on the shoulder, leaned toward her for a moment as if he intended to kiss her, then pulled back and said, "I'll be upstairs."

She nodded, glad that he sensed she wanted to be alone.

While he climbed the stairs slowly, she went into the parlor and walked over to the window, pulling back the curtain to look out at the gray winter day. The weather certainly matched her mood. Shadows cloaked the room behind her, and when she turned away from the window after several minutes, she went over to the chair where Vincent had been sitting earlier and lit the lamp on the table beside it. The warm yellow glow did nothing to dispel the sense of gloom that hung over her.

With a sigh, she sat down. The folded newspaper he had placed on the table earlier was still there. She picked it up and tried to force herself to concentrate on it, but her eyes didn't seem able to focus on the words. In her mind's eye, she saw her failure looming large, as if it were some sort of beast. She tossed the paper aside. It landed on the table but slid off to fall onto the floor. With an angry grimace, Sara reached down to pick it up.

That was when she saw the headlines on the story on the lower half of the front page. *REPORT ON CONDITIONS IN THE INDIAN TERRITORIES,* the first headline read, and below it in smaller type were the words *Abject Poverty and Illness Plague Cherokee Nation.*

She looked up, and for the first time in hours, her eyes shone with something besides anger.

TWELVE

"Go to the Indian Territories?" Vincent repeated in utter astonishment. "Why in heaven's name would we want to do *that*?"

"Because it's where we could do the most good," Sara said. She pointed at the newspaper story. "Look at this, Vincent. Read about the plight of these poor people and then tell me that you can turn your back on someone who so obviously needs our help."

Vincent took the paper from her, glanced at it, and said, "I read this earlier. It's a shame those Indians have to live in such poor conditions, of course, but that has nothing to do with us, Sara." He tossed the paper aside.

"You were willing to do whatever was necessary to help that little girl with pneumonia," Sara argued stubbornly, "even if it meant making an enemy out of William Hasbrook. Surely you can see that there must be dozens, perhaps even hundreds, of Indian children who need our help just as badly as little Angie. The newspaper account says that the entire tribe lives in a barren wasteland and is wracked by disease."

"And you think you could change that," Vincent said heavily.

"Anything I could do to help is worthwhile," Sara insisted. "If everyone felt as you do, Vincent, no one's lot in life would ever be improved!"

That was overstating her case somewhat, she knew, but she was also aware that it was going to take some persuasive arguing to change her husband's mind. He had lived in Massachusetts his entire life, and here she was asking him to uproot himself again, this time all the way to the southwestern desert. It would be quite an arduous journey, and Vincent was no longer a young man, by any stretch of the imagination.

But if he didn't come around to her way of thinking, she might have to make the trip by herself. She knew it was her destiny to travel to the Indian Territories and help those pathetic wretches, had known it as soon as she saw those headlines on the newspaper story. If there was one thing she had always known, it was how to follow her destiny.

Vincent was still shaking his head, however. "I just don't see how it would be possible," he said. "Our lives are here."

"You don't mean in Boston, surely. You already said we could go back to Pittsfield, so I know you don't mean to stay here forever."

"Returning to Pittsfield is one thing," he said stiffly. "Traveling to some godforsaken western wilderness is quite another!"

Sara could feel her temper slipping away from her, so she took a deep breath and ordered herself to stay calm. When she had called Vincent down from up-stairs, the plan had seemed so obvious, so right to her. Clearly, he didn't see it that way. If she pressed him

too hard, too fast, it might just make him more stubborn.

"All right," she said.

"Well, I'm glad you've finally come to your
senses."

"I didn't mean I was agreeing with you, Vincent. I
just meant we won't discuss it anymore right now. I'll
see what I can find for our supper."

"Very well. I'll be in the parlor."

Sara went into the kitchen, still trembling a bit with
anger. She knew the idea of moving to the Indian Territories was much too big to have sprung on him like
this, but her enthusiasm had carried her away. Now
she had to regroup her thoughts and find another way
to convince him.

For a moment she thought about taking him back up
to the bedroom and persuading him that way, but she
discarded the idea. Vincent was showing less and less
interest in such things these days, and besides, this
matter seemed almost too important for her to resort to
coercing him with her body. He had to be shown that
she was right, had to be won over by the evidence she
could muster for her case, not by a simple appeal to his
desire for her.

The kitchen was equipped with one of the new
iceboxes that were becoming so fashionable. Sara
took a ham from it and sliced off several thick
chunks. Her hand shook a little as she used the knife.
It might take time, she thought, but sooner or later
Vincent would see that she was right. She could afford to go slowly.

Her destiny was still out there, just waiting for her to
grasp it.

*   *   *

During the next few months, Sara learned as much as she could about the Indian Territories and the tribes that had been removed there by the government some thirty-five years earlier. There were five of them, she discovered from reading the newspapers and searching out articles in magazines like *Harper's Weekly*. The Cherokee, Choctaw, Creek, Seminole, and Chickasaw Nations had been uprooted from their native lands in the southeastern United States and taken on a forced march to a large tract of mostly uninhabited land between Texas and Kansas. Sara had heard about those places but knew little about them, other than the fact that the very names made her worry a bit. She assumed they were untracked wilderness for the most part, barren and sparsely inhabited. Savages roamed those plains, and any whites who lived there were probably little better than barbarians themselves. The idea of traveling to the Indian Territories, which were smack-dab in the middle of that frontier hell, sent a nervous shiver through her.

Yet she was still convinced that that was where she was needed. She frequented the public library and read accounts in newspapers, not only from Boston, but from New York and Philadelphia as well, of what life was like on those reservations. Evidently it was a popular subject. And without exception, all of the stories painted a bleak picture indeed. Life in the Indian lands was hard, the farming was poor, and illness ran rampant. Sara's heart went out to the Indians, especially the Cherokee, who seemed from the newspaper accounts to be in the worst shape of all.

Vincent was unmoved, however, even when she began leaving magazines lying around prominently, open to the articles concerning life in the Indian nations. He was pressing her to return to Pittsfield and go into private practice.

"Surely all this doing nothing must be getting on your nerves, darling," he said to her on more than one occasion. "I know how you like to keep busy."

"I want to make sure that when I make a decision, it's the right one," she told him. She didn't explain that she was spending much of her time researching the problems in the Indian lands. When she finally got there, she was going to be ready to help them as much as she possibly could.

Spring arrived, then summer, and Sara knew she couldn't postpone things much longer. Vincent was growing more impatient with each passing day to return to what he considered home, and he had shown absolutely no response to all her subtle—and not so subtle—prodding. Like it or not, she knew the time for a showdown was rapidly approaching.

It came on an evening late in June. The humidity that so often plagued Boston in the summer had not yet arrived this year, and when Sara suggested to Vincent that they take a walk along the Charles, he readily agreed. After dinner, they strolled arm in arm along a path beside the river as the day's light faded in the western sky.

"Vincent, I've been thinking," Sara began, a part of her wishing she didn't have to bring this up, so that she could just enjoy the evening. She knew she couldn't live with herself if she kept postponing this moment, however.

"Oh?" Vincent murmured. "What about, dear?"

"The Indian Territories," she replied flatly.

He stopped and looked over at her, a frown appearing on his face. "I thought you had gotten that wild idea out of your head," he said. "At the very least, I was hoping that was the case. Surely you must see how impossible it is, Sara."

"I see nothing of the sort. I see people desperately in need of help that I can give them. I see women and children dying from lack of proper medical care. I see something that I have to do, Vincent . . . whether you agree or not."

He put his hands on her shoulders and stared intently at her in the fading golden light. "You'd go there alone?" he asked in a hollow voice. "You'd leave me?"

"If that's my only choice."

"Just as you ran away to Washington during the war after Thomas forbade you to go."

Her chin came up defiantly. "I've always known my own mind," she said.

"Indeed you have." He released her shoulders, took a step away from her, and shook his head. "I'm sorry it's come to this. I truly am."

"Does that mean you won't go with me?" Sara tried not to let her voice tremble as she asked the question. Even though she was absolutely certain that the course she had chosen for her life was correct, the thought of setting out for the Indian Territories alone frightened her. She had become accustomed to having Vincent around, even though he was old and often annoying. Before that, there had always been someone nearby she could rely on: her father, Miles Austin, Carver Gresham . . . Seldom in her life had she ever been truly *alone*.

The long sigh of concession from her husband assured her that she would not be this time, either, making her heart give a little bound. "Very well, Sara,"

Vincent said. "As you pointed out, you've always been a woman who knows her own mind . . . and frequently the mind of everyone else around you as well."

Sara couldn't stop herself from throwing her arms around his neck. "Thank you, Vincent!" she exclaimed. "If you knew how much this means to me—"

"I think I do," he said as he smiled at her. "I recall what it was like to be a young doctor, full of hope and ambition and the desire to help others. If you're lucky, those feelings never go away entirely, although they change somewhat with time, of course."

"They'll never go away in me," she said fervently. "I'll always feel that way."

He leaned forward to press his lips lightly to hers. "I hope you're right, my dear. I sincerely hope you're right . . ."

John stared across his desk at her, a thunderous frown on his face, which was becoming more florid and rather beefy with the passage of time, even though he was still quite a handsome man. "Have you taken leave of your senses?" he demanded.

"Certainly not," Sara replied coolly. "In fact, I believe that I'm seeing things more clearly now than I ever have in my life."

"Yes, but you *always* think that!" John blew an exasperated breath out through his mustache and shook his head. "This is the most far-fetched idea yet, Sara. Traipsing off to the frontier to doctor a bunch of . . . of savages!"

"They're not savages. From everything I've read, the Cherokee are quite civilized . . . for Indians, of course."

"Of course," John repeated dryly. "Good God, Sara! What's Father going to say?"

She laughed, but it had a hollow sound. "I imagine *he'll* think I'm insane, too. But then, it wouldn't be the first time, would it?"

John stood up and began to pace back and forth across his office. "You *are* going to tell Father, aren't you?"

Sara nodded. That was something she had thought long and hard about after reaching her decision to travel to the Indian Territories. "I thought I would go back up to Handley's Mill next week, while Vincent is making preparations to sell our house in Cambridge."

"What about Vincent?" John asked. "Surely he can't think this is a good idea. The Vincent Rawlings I've always known is much too levelheaded to just go along with such madness. But of course—"

He fell silent, but he didn't need to finish the sentence for Sara to know what he meant. *But of course, he married you.* That was the thought that had gone through John's head.

"Vincent was opposed to the idea at first, but I convinced him it was the best thing for us to do."

"I don't think I want to know how you persuaded him of that."

Sara felt her face growing warm and wished she could stop the flush that was spreading across her features. Her heart thudded heavily with anger. But she didn't rise to the insult that John had just flung at her. Instead, she said, "I'm here to ask a favor of you, John."

"What do you want me to do, take over your practice? I think I can manage to work in all of the patients you'll be leaving behind."

Of all the arrogant, sarcastic . . . He knew very well that she didn't have any patients at the moment, but he didn't have to rub her face in that fact. She stood up, unable to contain her anger any longer, and said, "I'll not sit here and be insulted, especially not by my own brother. Good day, Doctor." She turned toward the door of the office.

John grimaced and lifted a hand, holding it out toward her. "Blast it, wait a minute . . . Doctor. I realize I was a bit of an ass just now." He smiled. "You've known me all my life; you ought to be used to it by now. I'm sorry, Sara."

"Well . . . all right." She sat down again. "But you should really learn to take me seriously, John."

"Oh, I do, I do," he assured her as he sank down again into his own chair. "What is it I can do to help you?"

"Will you go home with me next week to see Father and Mother?"

He frowned, the question evidently taking him by surprise. "Home," he repeated. "I haven't been back to Handley's Mill in quite some time. Over a year, in fact."

"Neither have I. I want to see how Mother's doing before I leave for the Indian Territories."

John grunted. "I can tell you how she's doing. Just as she's been doing for more than five years now. She won't know a damned thing that's going on, not really. Her mind's never been right since the war."

"No, but it could be getting worse. I just have to see her again before I go. And Father, too, of course."

"You just want me to help you defend this wild-eyed notion of yours when Father hits the roof—and you know he's going to."

"Maybe he'll surprise us," Sara said. "Perhaps he's gotten over his opposition to the idea of me being a doctor. If he can accept that, he ought to accept the plans I have."

John looked skeptical. "Thomas Black change his mind about anything? That's a sight I'd like to see."

"Then come with me," urged Sara.

Slowly, he nodded. "You know, I believe that I will. It'll be good to see the old place again. And besides, I could use a few days away from the office—and Judith."

"Are the two of you having trouble?" Sara asked quickly.

He shrugged. "Nothing we can't handle. It's rather difficult for Judith, what with two children and another on the way."

Sara nodded but didn't say anything. She wasn't sure how sympathetic she could be where the plight of her sister-in-law was concerned. True, Judith had two small children and was pregnant with a third, but the woman had a small army of servants to help her! And anyway, whose fault was it she was pregnant in the first place? As far as Sara was concerned, Judith didn't *have* to allow John to pleasure himself in her bed whenever he chose, even though society did tend to look down on a woman who shirked her wifely duties. Sara had no trouble at all telling Vincent no whenever she meant no. But many women, including Judith, weren't as strong-willed as she was, she knew.

"I thought I would take the train to Pittsfield on Monday, then rent a buggy for the drive up to Handley's Mill," she said. "Is that all right with you?"

John flipped open a thin, black, leather-bound book on his desk and studied it for a moment, then nodded.

"All right. I have a few appointments I'll have to cancel and reschedule, but nothing I can't handle. I'll be glad to go with you. I suppose we'll be back on Tuesday."

Sara nodded. "I'm not planning on spending more than one night in the old house."

"Very good. What time does the train leave?"

"Eight-thirty in the morning."

"All right, I'll pick you up about eight, then, and we'll drive together to the station in my carriage. Please be ready to leave when I get there."

"I will be," Sara promised as she stood again. "Thank you, John. I really appreciate this."

"I hope you know what you're doing," he said, almost echoing what Vincent had said to her a few nights earlier when he had agreed to go with her to the Indian Territories.

Sara nodded and smiled at him. "I do, John. If there's one thing I'm sure of, it's that I know what I'm doing."

"Like I said before, you always do." He returned her smile, but his expression was wry. She left the office, glad that once again he had agreed to do what she wanted, just as he had when they were children.

John leaned back in his chair once Sara was gone and stared broodingly, unseeingly, at the glass-fronted medicine cabinets and the shelves full of thick volumes of medical history and philosophy. Once again, his sister had hatched some unlikely scheme, the upshot of which would be to make him look bad.

He had entered the infantry during the war; Sara had run off and become first a nurse in Washington, then an angel of mercy in field hospitals across the war-torn

South. He had finished the war working in field hospitals himself, while she rode with a cavalry patrol of dashing Rebel raiders. That hadn't been by her own choice, of course; the circumstances had been forced on her. Yet strangely enough if there were any real glory to be garnered from that brutal conflict, it had been personified in those gallant Rebs, who knew their cause was lost but fought on anyway. John envied Sara even those terrible times.

And of course, after the war, he had barely scraped his way through medical school, while Sara had been at the top of her class. It didn't really matter to John that to even attend medical school in the first place she had had to virtually prostitute herself by marrying old Vincent Rawlings. Once she was there, no matter how she had gotten there, she had outshone her brother— again. As always.

And now she was going off to the frontier to care for a bunch of poor, sick, filthy savages. All the while, he would be here in Boston, tending to his wealthy, influential patients whose illnesses were imaginary nearly as often as they were real. Sara was devoting herself to yet another good cause; his only causes were making more money and bedding as many of his attractive female patients as he could. Roberta Ingersoll wasn't the only one now. There was Eunice Ralston and Pamela Dashford and Natalie Garrison and . . .

He gave a little shake of his head. There was no point in running through a mental list of his conquests. Once again, Sara was being so altruistic, so damned *noble*, that he wound up looking like a venal little snake, at least in his own mind. He was tired of it. There had to be something good *he* could do.

Miss McLowry put her head in the door of the office

and said, "Mr. Faulkner is here to see you, sir. I know he doesn't have an appointment, but—"

John stood up quickly. "That's quite all right, Miss McLowry. Mr. Faulkner is welcome here anytime. Show him right in." He had no idea what Edward wanted, but John could always make time for his father-in-law.

Only it wasn't Edward, he realized a moment later when he heard the clumping sound in the hallway. Miss McLowry swung the door open and Nathan Faulkner limped into the office, a grin on his face. "Hello, John," he said. "Haven't seen much of you lately."

"I've been pretty busy," John said as he shook the hand his brother-in-law extended across the desk. "Sit down, Nathan, sit down."

Nathan sank gratefully into the upholstered chair and stretched his crippled leg out in front of him. "That's better," he said. "Thanks."

"What brings you down here?" John asked as he sat down as well. He looked closely at Nathan, searching for the telltale signs of drunkenness. Nathan's eyes seemed clear, however; in fact, they were brighter and more alert than John had seen them in quite some time. Of course, as Nathan had pointed out, it had been a while since John had even seen him.

Nathan clasped his hands together on the knee of his good leg and said, "I've come to ask you a favor, John."

"This must be my day for it," John said with a chuckle. "Sara was just here a little while ago, and she had a request to make of me, too."

"I'm sorry," Nathan said quickly. "If you're busy—"

John waved off his question. "Don't worry about that. There's always time for family."

"Well . . . good. By the way, how is Sara? I haven't seen her in quite some time."

"She's fine," John replied a little curtly, not wanting to have to explain about her newest addle-brained scheme. "I'll be seeing her again next week, and I'll tell her you asked about her."

"Yes, please do that. I always thought Sara was a fine woman. I was sorry to hear that she's had so much trouble finding a suitable position at a hospital here in Boston."

She wouldn't have to worry about that anymore if she went through with her mad plan, John thought, but he kept the comment to himself. Instead, he said, "What's this favor of yours, Nathan?"

"I was wondering . . ." Nathan hesitated for a moment, then plunged ahead. "I was wondering if I could convince you to donate a bit of your time to a worthy cause."

John's eyes narrowed in surprise. He had just been thinking about how Sara always aligned herself with some noteworthy cause while he simply pursued wealth and women, and then here was Nathan, not half an hour later, trying to recruit him for something or other. Had his brother-in-law developed the ability to read minds? John wondered.

"What sort of worthy cause?" he asked cautiously.

"There's a . . . an orphanage in Dorchester Heights. Some of the children are sick, and I thought . . ."

As Nathan's voice trailed away, John finished the sentence for him. "You thought that I might take a look at them, see if there's anything I could do for them . . . at no charge, of course."

"Oh, no, that's not necessary," Nathan said quickly. "I could pay you myself. That's not a problem. I just need to find a good doctor to help care for the children."

Then you should go see my sister Sara, John thought. *This sounds like just the sort of thing that would appeal to her.*

But Sara had plans of her own, and John sensed that this might be an opportunity for him to do some actual good. Why allow Sara to take over every worthy cause in the world?

He was puzzled, though, and before responding to Nathan's proposition, he asked, "What's your connection with this orphanage?"

"The director and I are friends. I . . . I volunteered to try to find someone who might help take care of the place's medical needs."

John looked more closely at his brother-in-law. Not only were Nathan's eyes clear and alert, his hands were fairly steady and his features weren't as ruddy as the last time John had seen him. John frowned. Was it really possible . . . ?

Had Nathan stopped drinking?

There was one way to find out. John stood up and went over to one of the medicine cabinets. He opened the glass front and took out a bottle. It wasn't a bottle of medicine, however, except in the loosest sense. It was a bottle of the best Irish whiskey to be had in Boston, which was saying quite a bit.

"How about a drink while we talk about it?" he asked Nathan as he turned and held up the bottle.

Nathan's eyes followed the bottle like a Crusader watching the Holy Grail. His tongue came out and rasped over lips that had gone dry. But he shook his head and managed to say, "No, thanks, John."

"You're sure?"

"I'm certain."

John felt a little twinge of guilt as he replaced the bottle in the medicine cabinet. That had been cruel, he knew, and yet he had wanted to find out just what Nathan's mental state was. Evidently Nathan was clearheaded and resolved to stay that way.

When he turned back to his brother-in-law, John nodded slowly. "I think I can help you, Nathan," he said. "And you don't have to pay me. I'll donate my time to help those poor motherless children."

Nathan stood up quickly, only a little awkward on the thick peg. He grabbed John's hand and pumped it. "Thank you, John," he said effusively. "I knew I could count on you. I just knew it."

"Of course," John said, satisfied with the way this day had turned out, as unexpected as its developments might have been. Let Sara run off to the Indian Territories and tend to those damned savages. He had something even better.

He had *orphans*.

THIRTEEN

There was a high fence of black wrought-iron around the orphanage. A pair of arched gates were topped by iron letters that spelled out *ST. ANDREW'S HOME FOR BOYS AND GIRLS*. John brought his buggy to a stop in front of the gates and looked up at the sign. "A Catholic orphanage," he said. "I suppose it's run by nuns?"

Nathan, who was riding beside him, shook his head. "Nuns take care of all the instruction of the children, but the administration of the place is handled by volunteers from the local parish. That's how I became involved."

John glanced over at him in surprise. "You're not Catholic."

"No, but I guess you could say I'm one of the director's good works. I . . . I've stopped drinking, John, and I have some of the people here at the orphanage to thank for it. One person, in particular."

"Well, I'm glad to hear it," John said honestly. "I've worried about you for a long time, Nathan. I feel a certain . . . responsibility, I suppose you could say."

"Because of what you did for me during the war?"

"Because I'm your brother-in-law and I love your sister." John handed the reins to him and stepped down from the buggy. "I'll open the gates and you can drive through."

Nathan nodded in agreement. John unlatched the gates, swung them open, and stepped back to let the buggy roll past him. Then he closed the gates and climbed back up beside Nathan.

The orphanage was situated on a large lot dotted with trees and shrubbery. It was a pleasant-looking place. The building itself was a long, three-story red brick structure with a porch supported by white pillars. Quite impressive, John thought. Not at all like the grim, dark, foreboding places people usually thought orphanages were. Many, if not most, of the children's homes fit that popular image, but St. Andrew's was obviously an exception to the rule.

Still, no matter how nice the surroundings, anywhere a lot of children were gathered together, there was going to be sickness. From what Nathan had said, in that way St. Andrew's was no exception. "What sort of illnesses will I be dealing with here?" John asked as he guided the buggy up a long, curving driveway that ran in front of the porch.

"The usual sort. Grippe, skin rashes, infestations of lice, that kind of thing."

"Nothing too serious, in other words."

"Not that I know of," Nathan said. "But still, these are things that need treatment."

"Of course," John agreed readily. "I shouldn't have any trouble dealing with the problems."

He hoped that was right. Helping out here at the orphanage couldn't do anything except make him look good, but he wanted to accomplish that without having to spend too much time on his good deeds. With any luck, there wouldn't be any cases that would turn out to be medically challenging—and time-consuming.

John parked the buggy near the porch, where several other vehicles were waiting for their owners to return. There were some expensive carriages and phaetons among them.

"Who do these belong to?" John asked, nodding toward the other vehicles.

"Probably people who are here to see about arranging adoptions," Nathan replied. "St. Andrew's places quite a few children with the more well-to-do families in the city."

John nodded. The orphanage looked like a successful, thriving operation, although one could hardly judge it the same way a regular business would be judged. St. Andrew's wasn't out to make a profit.

But John was, and he began reconsidering his offer to provide medical treatment for the children at no charge. From the looks of the place, St. Andrew's could easily afford to pay him, and for that matter, Nathan Faulkner could easily afford it, too. Edward Faulkner paid his son a healthy wage for his office job, which was primarily a figurehead position. Nathan didn't have any real responsibilities.

That thought prompted John to ask a question that had occurred to him earlier. As he climbed down from the buggy, he said to Nathan, "I was wondering why you weren't at your father's offices today."

Nathan stepped down, his peg thumping heavily against the pavement of the drive. "Oh, I don't work for my father anymore," he said casually.

"You don't?" John couldn't conceal his surprise. "But I thought—"

"There was no point in it. All I ever did was shuffle papers and issue meaningless orders that everyone ignored. They all knew I was just there because my father thought he had to give me something to do." Nathan waved a hand at the orphanage. "Well, I found something better to do. Something that's really worthwhile, not just to keep me busy."

John frowned. He couldn't help but wonder what Edward Faulkner's reaction had been when Nathan announced that he was quitting. Edward couldn't have been happy about it.

"Are you still living at home?"

"Of course. What did you think, that I'd move in here at the orphanage? Although I'm sure they could find a place for me." Nathan laughed and went on, "Don't worry, John. I haven't been disowned or anything. Father was a bit upset when I told him what I wanted to do, but Mother understood, and so did Judith." He hesitated for a second, then said, "I'm surprised she didn't mention anything about it to you."

"I guess she forgot," John said, not wanting to admit to Nathan that he and Judith didn't actually talk that much anymore. They spoke when something had to be said, of course, but other than that their conversations in the evenings were usually sparse. Judith was tired from having the children underfoot all day, and John's work took a great deal out of him, so they had settled into a pattern of companionable silence for the most part.

Perhaps it wasn't that companionable anymore, John thought. Perhaps it was just that neither one of them really cared . . .

He put that train of thought out of his head with a

little grunt. Smiling at Nathan, he said, "Let's go inside and see that friend you mentioned."

Nathan had said that the director of the orphanage was not one of the nuns who taught here, so John expected some sort of hatchet-faced old-timer. Male or female, it wouldn't really matter. The demeanor of this person would probably be pursed-lip sanctimony.

Nathan led him through the heavy wooden double doors of the entrance and across a high-ceilinged lobby that echoed with the sound of their footsteps on the tiled floor. Several overstuffed armchairs and divans were scattered around the room, along with some potted plants. The lobby looked more like that of a hotel than an orphanage, and John wondered if this building had originally been constructed for some other purpose. On the far side of the lobby was a polished hardwood counter. A black-robed nun stood on the other side of it.

She greeted them with a smile. "Hello, Nathan," she said. "I take it this is your brother-in-law?"

"Yes, Sister Agnes. This is Dr. John Black."

"Pleased to meet you, Sister," John said, tipping his low-crowned beaver hat.

"I thought I'd introduce John to Miss Caine, then take him upstairs to meet the children," Nathan went on.

"An excellent idea," the nun agreed. She smiled at John and said, "Thank you for coming today, Dr. Black. Your generosity in lending your medical skills to us will be amply rewarded in heaven, I'm sure."

"Thank you, Sister. One can only hope."

"And pray," Sister Agnes added.

"Yes, of course."

Nathan put a hand on John's arm and steered him toward a closed door. "Miss Caine's the director of the orphanage," he explained. "A volunteer, like the rest of us. She does a wonderful job."

"I'm sure she does," John murmured, wanting to meet this harridan and get it over with. Nathan opened the door and motioned for John to go in first.

John stepped into the room, holding his hat in his right hand, and stopped short as a beautiful young woman with shining brown hair stood up from behind a desk cluttered with papers. A brilliant smile appeared on her face, but it was directed past John and aimed at Nathan instead. Nathan came into the room, shut the door, and then stepped around the still-startled John to go over to the desk. He put out a hand and said, "Hello, Victoria."

The young woman took his hand and squeezed it briefly. "Nathan," she said.

John blinked, trying to take in what he was seeing. The two of them might be trying to be proper about this meeting, but he recognized the look in their eyes. Handshakes aside, Nathan and Miss Victoria Caine would have much rather been in each other's arms right now, lips pressed together in a passionate kiss.

John cleared his throat.

With a slightly embarrassed laugh, Nathan turned and gestured toward John. "Victoria, this is the man I told you about, my brother-in-law, Dr. John Black."

Victoria Caine moved out from behind the desk and came toward John. She was slender, her bosom a gentle curve in the plain, high-necked brown dress she wore. Her hair was worn loose, falling around her shoulders. Sunlight came in through the window behind the desk and struck golden highlights from the brown strands. Her eyes were a fabulous green and sparkled as she held out her hand to John.

He put his hat in his left hand, along with his medical bag, then took her hand, resisting the impulse to bend over and kiss the back of it. He said, "I'm very pleased to meet you, Miss Caine. Nathan has told me a great deal about you."

"I have?" Nathan said.

"Of course you have," John snapped.

Victoria smiled at him. "You don't have to exaggerate on my account, Dr. Black. Nathan knows my work here is intended merely to help the children, not to gather any sort of glory to my name."

Just like Sara, John thought as he let go of her hand. *Another do-gooder. But a lovely one.*

"I suppose that's why I'm here, too," he said. "To help the children, I mean. Are there many who are sick?"

"Oh, no, only a few. It won't take long for you to examine them. Can you do it now?"

He hefted the black bag in his left hand. "I'm ready whenever you are, Miss Caine."

"Very well. If you'll come with me, Dr. Black . . ."

She led John out of the office and up a curving staircase, followed by Nathan. He wondered where all the children were, and when they reached the second floor he got the answer to his question. Victoria took them through a tall, arched doorway into a long, barracks-like room with bunks on both sides. The room was filled with noise as children ran, laughed, and played under the watchful eyes of several nuns, but the entire place fell silent as the trio of adults entered. All the children stopped whatever they were doing and stood up straight, almost like soldiers standing at attention.

The whole thing reminded John of his days in the army, except that the bunks here in this big room looked more comfortable than the rickety cots on which he had spent many a miserable night. The children—all boys, John saw now—wore uniforms, too, although in this case they consisted of dark trousers and white shirts, rather than the blue shirts and pants of the Union Army. Most of the lads were ten to twelve years old, he judged, although there were a few younger and a few older.

Victoria lifted her voice and said, "Hello, boys."

The answer that came back from them was loud and echoing in the big room. "Hello, Miss Caine."

She turned and indicated John. "This is Dr. Black. He's come to pay us a visit, and any of you who are sick should line up now to see him. Don't be ashamed to step forward. Dr. Black is here to help."

Yes, that was true, John thought, but somehow he hadn't expected there to be this many children. And this was only one group of them, he told himself. There was probably another big room full of girls, and the third floor might hold even more children.

As about a dozen of the youngsters lined up to be examined, Nathan stepped up beside John and said in a low voice, "I can't thank you enough for this."

"Don't worry, I'll think of a way you can pay me back," John said with a rather nervous chuckle. "I can see why you volunteered my services."

"To help the children, you mean?"

"No, I'm talking about the impression you've made on Miss Caine. I'm proud of you, Nathan. It's about time. I suppose she's the reason you gave up drinking?"

Nathan flushed deeply. "I never could have done it

without Victoria. But you're wrong about me and her, John—"

"Save it," John said with a grin. "I know a couple of lovebirds when I see them. Now, let me get to work. Here come the first of my patients."

For the next couple of hours, which took well into the evening, he peered down throats, felt for swollen glands, listened to heartbeats and respiration, examined rashes and sprained ankles, and passed out both advice and medications from his bag. There were four of the large rooms in the orphanage, two on the second floor, two on the third, plus a smaller room on the first floor where the infants and toddlers lived.

When John had finally seen all of the orphans who needed medical attention—and none of them was seriously ill, thank goodness—he closed up his bag and sighed wearily. Victoria Caine said quickly, "I'm sorry, Dr. Black. That took a lot longer than I said it would, didn't it?"

"Nothing to worry about, Miss Caine," he assured her. "At least none of the little tykes required hospitalization. In fact, they should all be fine in a few days. If you ever need me to come by and take a look at any of them again—"

She broke in with a surprised frown. "Oh, didn't Nathan tell you?"

John's eyes narrowed as he shot a glance at his brother-in-law. "Tell me what?"

"Well, John, we were hoping . . . Victoria and I . . . I mean, Miss Caine and I . . . we were hoping that you'd come by every week and do this."

"By next week, these children may be well," Victoria said, "but there will be others who are sick. With this many children it's inevitable."

"Yes, I imagine it is," John said, still frowning. "Every week, eh? I'm not sure I have the time . . ."

Victoria put a hand on his arm. "Please, Dr. Black. At least for a while. It would mean so much to us."

He took a deep breath, mentally kicking himself for allowing a pair of green eyes, some thick brown hair, and a graciously curved body to sway his judgment. Then he said, "I've never been able to say no to a beautiful woman, Miss Caine. I can't promise to continue indefinitely, but I suppose I can come back next week . . . and for a while after that."

"Thank you, Doctor," she said, not gushing but instead rather solemn in her gratitude. She stepped forward and gave him a quick hug. "God bless you."

"I'm sure He already has," John said dryly. "Well, I had better get home. I'm sure my wife is wondering what's become of me." He wasn't certain of that at all, but he wasn't about to admit that Judith might not have even noticed that he was late. "Are you coming, Nathan?"

"Yes, I suppose so." Nathan clasped Victoria's hand again, still the proper gentleman. "Good evening, Miss Caine."

"Good evening, Mr. Faulkner," she murmured. "And good evening to you, too, Dr. Black."

When they were back in the buggy, rolling through the streets of Dorchester Heights toward Boston, John said, "Miss Caine is quite a lovely woman, isn't she?"

"Yes, she is," Nathan replied, keeping his gaze turned straight ahead. The shadows of twilight were too thick for John to tell, but he would have been willing to bet that Nathan was blushing again.

"How in the world did you wind up getting involved with her and all those orphans?"

"She's also a volunteer in the, ah, temperance movement."

John laughed. "So you met when she and some of her cohorts busted up a tavern, eh?"

"Something like that," Nathan admitted uncomfortably. "I'm not sure why she took a personal interest in me, unless she felt sorry for me. Because I'm a cripple and all, I mean."

"I know what you mean," John said. "Take my word for it, Nathan, that woman wasn't looking at you like you were some poor cripple that she pitied."

"Victoria and I have become . . . closer friends since then," Nathan said carefully.

"Well, more power to you, old boy. I'm glad to see it, glad that you're not wallowing in the bottom of a bottle of whiskey anymore."

"You never tried to stop me from doing that."

"I looked out for you more than you know," John said, letting an edge creep into his voice. "Besides, you're a grown man. I figured you were responsible for making your own decisions in life. That's what you did by quitting that job of your father's, isn't it?"

Nathan nodded slowly. "Yes, I suppose so. And you're right: it was up to me to quit drinking. But Victoria gave me a reason to after all these years."

"Lucky man," John said softly.

Nathan looked down at the peg on the end of his right leg. "I never really considered myself so before . . . but I think now that you're right." He gave a little laugh and changed the subject by saying, "Thank you again for coming today, John."

"Glad to do it."

"I'm still willing to pay you . . ."

Somewhat to his own surprise, John found himself

shaking his head. "Not necessary," he said. "Good works are their own reward. Isn't that what people say?"

"Yes. Yes, that's right."

And besides, John thought as he guided the buggy team, if he went back to the orphanage the next week, he would have the opportunity to see Victoria Caine again . . .

Sara felt a peculiar breathlessness as she stepped down from the train in the Pittsfield station. The town had never been her home, of course, except for the short time she had lived there with Vincent, but Handley's Mill was only an hour's buggy ride away. Soon she would be seeing her father and mother again—perhaps for the last time. Thomas and Clarissa were both getting on in years, and it was possible that both of them would have passed away by the time Sara came back from the Indian Territories, if indeed she *ever* came back. She didn't like to think about that possibility, but it remained stubbornly in the back of her mind.

John climbed down from the train and stood beside Sara on the platform. "What do we do now?" he asked. "You're in charge of this little expedition."

"You have our bags?" she asked, turning toward him.

He hefted the carpetbags, one in each hand. "Right here."

"Then I suppose we should hire a buggy. There's a stable just down the street where we can rent one."

The train trip from Boston to Pittsfield, which had taken several hours, had been uneventful. John had talked some about an orphanage in Dorchester Heights where he was evidently volunteering some of his time.

Sara had been surprised by that generous gesture on his part, but she hadn't really given it much thought. Her mind was full of her own plans, as well as the impending reunion with their parents.

For his part, John was well aware that his sister had listened to him with only half an ear, and he was seething with frustration. What would a few words of praise have cost her? Nothing. But as usual, Sara was too wrapped up in her own plans and schemes to give anyone else credit where it was due.

Ah, well, he hadn't become involved with the St. Andrew's orphanage solely to impress Sara. His first visit had been primarily as a favor to Nathan Faulkner.

He had his own reasons for planning to go back.

Sara led the way down the street to the stable and wagon yard, out in front as always, and she negotiated the rental of the buggy that would take them to Handley's Mill. Once the price had been agreed on, she turned to John, who put the carpetbags down and dug some money out of his pocket to give to the stable owner. It took only a few minutes to hitch up the team, and then they were rolling northward out of Pittsfield with John handling the reins.

"I couldn't help but notice," he said as he guided the two horses along the hard-packed dirt of the wide road, "that I paid for the rental of this buggy, just as I paid for our train tickets."

"With all the wealthy patients you have, surely you can afford the expense," Sara said. "Vincent and I are using our savings to finance the journey to the Indian Territories."

"Yes, of course you are," John said, not bothering to be gracious about it. "We wouldn't want anything to stand in the way of your plans, especially not something as crass as money."

Sara glared at him. "You don't have to be rude."

"Sorry," John muttered, but he didn't sound very sincere about it.

Let him sulk, Sara thought. She wasn't quite sure what he was upset about, but she had more important things to worry about now. It wouldn't be long until they reached Handley's Mill.

The place seemed to grow more each time she visited it. Originally, the town had been a cluster of buildings around the village green, with some outlying farms in the area that were also considered part of the community. Now there were half a dozen or more streets crisscrossing each other around the green. New buildings were everywhere, and the outskirts of town extended almost as far as the first of those farms. From the hill overlooking the valley where the town was located, Sara could see the Daulton house, which was built on land that had originally belonged to her family. Thirty years earlier, when she was a baby, that land had been out in the country. Now it was on the edge of town.

She sighed as the buggy started down the hill. "The settlement is so big now. It's almost a city like Pittsfield."

"It's got a ways to go yet," John said. "And it's nothing at all like Boston and never will be." He shook his head. "I'd hate to move back here. I'd never be happy in a village like this anymore."

"No, I don't suppose I would, either."

He looked over at her. "The place you're going may be even smaller."

Sara shrugged her shoulders. "Perhaps. But I won't

have Dr. Thomas Black looking over my shoulder at everything I do."

"True enough."

Quite a few people waved and called greetings to them as John maneuvered the buggy through the streets of Handley's Mill. They were still well known in the village, even though neither of them had lived there for quite some time. A few minutes later, John brought the buggy to a stop in front of the white picket fence around the yard where he and Sara had played as children. The grass was rather overgrown, he noticed, and the fence—as well as the house itself—could have used a fresh coat of whitewash. Obviously, it was getting more difficult for Thomas to keep the place up at his age. John decided to talk to his father about hiring someone to help out more around the house. Thomas's pride might not like that idea, but as far as John could see, such a step was inevitable. But first there was the matter of his sister's latest wild-eyed idea to get through.

Sara didn't even notice the slightly rundown appearance of her old home. Her heart was beating fast as she climbed down from the buggy without waiting for John to help her. She opened the gate in the picket fence and hurried up the flagstone walk to the porch. She hadn't tried to let her father know that she and John were coming for this visit, and as she stepped onto the porch, she realized what a disappointment it would be if Thomas weren't even here. For all she knew, he might be off making a call at some outlying farmhouse. He had always been willing to drop everything and go wherever he was needed.

But a few moments after Sara knocked on the door, it swung open to reveal the startled face of her father.

Thomas's hair and mustache were completely white now, and his features were lined and weathered, but they lit up in a smile at the sight of his daughter standing there on the porch.

"Sara!" he exclaimed. "What in the world—? And John! Come in, come in, both of you."

He seemed hale and hearty enough, Sara thought as she stepped forward to embrace him for a moment before going on into the house. John came up the walk behind her, and he set down one of the carpetbags long enough to shake hands with his father. "Hello, sir. It's good to see you."

Thomas returned the handshake, then threw his arms around John and hugged him. John looked vaguely embarrassed, but he managed to pat Thomas on the back affectionately.

The three of them went into the parlor. Thomas was in his shirtsleeves, although he wore vest, tie, and sleeve garters and needed only to slip into his coat to be dressed for any patients who might come to see him. He told John to put the carpetbags down and then asked, "Can I get you something to drink? There's lemonade in the kitchen . . ."

"No, Father, that's all right," Sara told him. "Why don't you sit down? Don't tire yourself out fussing over us."

"If a man can't fuss over his children, who can he fuss over?" demanded Thomas. But then he smiled and said, "All right, all right. Sit down, both of you. Are you just here for a visit . . . or is there a reason for both of you showing up together?"

Sara sat down next to her father on a divan, while John took off his hat and settled himself in an over-stuffed armchair across the room. Gathering up her courage, Sara said, "I've come to tell you something, Father. John came with me so I wouldn't have to travel alone."

A frown suddenly appeared on Thomas's face. "What is it?" he asked. "Has something happened to Vincent? Is that why John had to come with you?"

Quickly, Sara shook her head. "Vincent is fine. He's back in Boston getting ready for our journey."

"Journey?" Thomas repeated. "I don't understand, Sara. Where are you going?"

She took a deep breath. There was no point in postponing this. "Vincent and I are going to the Indian Territories. I'm going to set up a practice there and try to help those poor people."

For a long moment, Thomas just stared at her, and Sara braced herself for the angry explosion she was certain was coming. The silence stretched out for so long that John finally felt compelled to ask, "Father, did you hear what Sara said?"

Slowly, Thomas nodded. "I heard her," he said. He reached out and caught hold of Sara's hands with both of his, his gnarled fingers closing around her slender ones. "If my blessing is what you've come here for," he said, "then you have it, Sara. I wish you Godspeed on your journey and the best of fortune when you get there."

The only thing Sara could do for several seconds was stare at him in astonishment. Finally, she was able to say, "You . . . you're not upset, Father?"

Thomas sighed and smiled wearily at her. "I've long since learned, my dear Sara, that you have a mind of your own and that you're not going to hesitate in expressing it. I'm sure you have your reasons for what you're doing, and they must seem like good ones to you. It wouldn't do any good for me to argue with you, would it?"

"None at all," she said, returning his smile. Her surprise at his reaction had been replaced by a feeling of gratitude and relief.

"Well, then, why waste time being upset?" Thomas put his arms around her and hugged her again. "I love you, Sara, you know that. No matter where you go or what you do."

For an instant, she felt a sharp pang of guilt. Her father was such a good man, and he was being so understanding about this. Perhaps she should have given more thought to returning here to Handley's Mill to stay, she told herself. She was sure that would have pleased him so much . . .

And yet he had told her just now that she had to follow her own destiny. For years, she had been trying to make him realize that, and now he finally did. She was glad of that, glad that she could head west with a clear conscience. She knew she couldn't turn her back on her dream.

"Well, this is much more touching than I expected it to be," John said dryly from the other side of the room. "By the way, Father, where's Mother?"

Thomas took his arms away from Sara's shoulders and turned to face his son. His eyes were shining a bit with moisture behind his spectacles. "She's upstairs resting," he said. "I'll go and get her in a moment. I'm sure she'll be so glad to see both of you."

Sara wasn't as certain of that. Chances were, her mother wouldn't even recognize her or John. But that was all right. For a short time . . . for this night, anyway . . . the family would be together again under one roof. All four of them together, perhaps for the last time. She was going to savor this visit and try to imprint every detail of it on her mind, so that she could carry it with her in her memory always.

The time would come soon enough, as it always did, to say good-bye.

BOOK FOUR

This day we fashion Destiny, our web of Fate we spin.

> —JOHN GREENLEAF WHITTIER

Where your treasure is there will your heart be also.

> —LUKE 12:34

FOURTEEN

Indian Territory, 1872

Sara watched the gentle hills with their lush grass and thick woods rolling past the window beside her and wondered when the train was going to reach the Indian Territories. It seemed as if she and Vincent had been traveling for a long time, more than long enough to have reached their destination. If she had to endure many more days of rocking along in this uncomfortable coach, breathing the smoke and cinders that drifted in through the open windows, she wasn't sure if she could stand it or not.

Still, what was a little discomfort if that was all that stood between her and her dream? She could endure whatever she had to endure if it meant realizing her ambition.

The past six months had been incredibly frustrating. First there had been the unexpected delays in finding a buyer for their house in Cambridge, and once that had finally been taken care of, Vincent had unexpectedly fallen ill with a hacking cough brought on, so he claimed, by the excessively high humidity of the Boston area. Since he was too sick to travel and their house had already been sold, they were forced once

again to rent a place to stay, until Vincent had recuperated enough to make the journey. Each day that passed
during that interval grated fiercely on Sara's nerves.

Finally, Vincent had recovered sufficiently to make
the trip, even though he was still seized from time to
time by spasms of coughing that left him shaken and
gasping for breath. They boarded a South Mountain
and Boston Railroad train in Boston and headed west.

That had been the beginning of what seemed like an
interminable journey, as they frequently had to change
trains and even lay over a night or two a couple of
times as they waited to make connections with a line
that would carry them farther west. Vincent grew more
haggard, and Sara's mouth was tight with impatience.
A trip that should have taken no more than a week
stretched into ten days and then two weeks due to
delay after delay. At long last, they turned south at
Kansas City, connecting with the Missouri, Kansas,
and Texas Railroad, which would carry them into the
Indian Territories. They were still riding in one of the
passenger cars of what Sara had heard a porter refer to
as the Katy Railroad, after the last two initials of its
name.

The blue-uniformed conductor came through the
car, drawing Sara's attention away from the landscape
outside by calling, "Downingville! Downingville station coming up, folks!"

Sara nudged her husband in the seat beside her and
said, "Vincent, stop the conductor. I want to ask him a
question."

Obligingly, as the conductor passed Vincent raised a
hand and said, "Excuse me?"

The conductor stopped. "Yes, sir, Dr. Rawlings,
what can I do for you?"

Vincent began, "My wife wants to know—"

"When will we be in the Indian Territories?" Sara broke in. "Surely it won't be much longer."

"The Indian Territory, ma'am?" the conductor said with a puzzled frown. "Why, we're in it now. Have been for the past twenty miles. We're coming up on Downingville, and that'll be our first stop in the Nations."

Sara frowned right back at the man. "But that can't be," she protested. She gestured through the window beside her at the lush grass, the plowed fields full of crops, the stretches of thick woods. "I understood that the Indian Territories were nothing but barren desert. This land is abounding with life!"

"Yes, ma'am," the conductor said dryly. "I reckon you must've been misinformed, because we're sure enough across the line in the Nations." He reached up, tugged on the brim of his cap, and gave her a pleasant nod before moving on down the aisle of the car, calling out the approaching station.

"I don't understand it," Sara said, as much to herself as to Vincent. "All the articles I read in newspapers and magazines back east made this part of the country sound like a terrible place to live!"

"I imagine that reporters sometimes tend to, uh, exaggerate for dramatic purposes," Vincent said. "That must be the explanation."

"I suppose so." Sara leaned back against her seat, still frowning. She paid even more attention to the farmhouses they passed, most of which were large and built of logs and appeared to be solid structures. She didn't see a single one she would have considered a hovel.

Downingville was a good-sized village with quite a

few buildings along its central street, including the railroad station. While the train was stopped there, Sara sought out the conductor again and asked him what their next stop would be.

"Muskogee, ma'am," the man replied. "If I remember right, that's where your tickets run out. Course, if you and Dr. Rawlings want to ride on, you can pay for your passage once we get there."

"Muskogee," Sara repeated. "Is that in the Cherokee lands?"

"No, ma'am, it's just over the line in the Creek Nation. But there's regular stage service over to Fort Gibson and Tahlequah. That's the capital of the Cherokee Nation."

"You mean we'll have to ride a stagecoach to reach this place . . . what did you call it? . . . Tahlequah?"

"Yes, ma'am. The stages run ever' day, though, and it's not far. You won't have any trouble getting there." The conductor was getting a bit impatient with Sara's questions. "Now, if you'll excuse me, ma'am, I got to make sure there's no more freight or passengers we got to pick up."

Sara nodded distractedly and called out a thank-you to the man as he bustled off. If Tahlequah was the capital of the Cherokee Nation, she supposed that was where she should go. She had intended from the first to seek out the federal Indian agent in charge of the tribe and offer her services as a doctor through him. His office was no doubt located in Tahlequah.

She went back to her seat. Vincent was dozing, but he roused as she sat down beside him. "Did you find out what you wanted to know?" he asked.

"I suppose so," Sara said. "This certainly isn't how I expected to find things down here, though. Why, from the looks of this town and the other houses we've passed, there might as well be white men living here!"

"The Cherokee are known as one of the Civilized Tribes, my dear," Vincent pointed out.

"Yes, but the reporters all said they were savages—!" Sara broke off with a sigh. Obviously, she had put a bit too much faith in what she had read.

Late that afternoon, the train reached Muskogee, which was even larger than Downingville. The town looked newly built but already prosperous, and it was surrounded by more of the rolling hills. Sara inquired at the ticket window in the station and was told that the next stagecoach heading over into the Cherokee Nation wouldn't leave until morning. The railroad agent explained to her that the stage station was just down the street and also recommended a hotel where she and Vincent could spend the night. A porter unloaded their bags from the baggage car, and it was no problem to find a man with a wagon who for a quarter was willing to take the bags over to the hotel.

The hotel, while certainly not as luxurious as what she would have expected to find back east, was comfortable enough. Sara didn't sleep much, though, and it wasn't Vincent lying beside her, snoring and coughing, that kept her awake. Instead, she stared at the darkened ceiling of the room and wondered just what other misjudgments she had made about this place. Perhaps they didn't even need doctors. She assumed that most of the people she had seen on the streets of Muskogee were Indians—Creeks, according to the conductor—and they had looked fairly healthy.

Maybe it was different over in the Cherokee lands, she told herself before she finally dozed off, far into the night. Once they reached Tahlequah, perhaps she would find that conditions really were as bad as the eastern writers had made them sound. She was no longer quite sure what to expect.

She just hoped that this long, arduous trip had not been for nothing.

Sara had ridden in a few stagecoaches back in Massachusetts, but those trips had done nothing to prepare her for the ride from Muskogee to Tahlequah. The red-painted Concord coach was an old one that rocked violently on wide leather thoroughbraces that had lost some of their flexibility over the years. Dust boiled up from the hooves of the six-horse hitch and billowed in through the windows of the coach. The canvas coverings over the windows did little or nothing to stop the dust. Vincent coughed almost constantly, and Sara found herself coughing, too. Her eyes felt gritty, even though they watered heavily, and her stomach was queasy from the rocking motion.

Their bags had been stowed away in the boot on the back of the stagecoach, along with the baggage of the other passengers. There were four other people riding inside the coach: a Cherokee woman with two small children, and a man who was evidently a drummer of some sort, judging by his garish suit and his sample case. Unlike most traveling salesmen, though, this man wasn't the least bit talkative about himself or whatever he was selling. Instead he sat in silence, with a dour expression on his face. He probably saved up all his affability for potential customers, Sara thought as she studied her fellow passengers, desperate for something to take her mind off the miserable traveling conditions. Another passenger was riding up on the seat with the driver, a young man wearing a wide-brimmed hat on his head and a heavy revolver strapped around his waist. Sara had seen him climb atop the stagecoach and shake hands with the driver back at the station in Muskogee.

The woman and her children appeared to Sara to be full-blooded Indians, although the clothing they wore might have been worn by any white woman and her youngsters. She couldn't tell about the drummer, but the driver and the young man up on the box looked to her as much white as they did Cherokee. Not once so far had she seen anyone wearing buckskins and feathers, or any man with his head shaved so that only a scalp lock remained, such as in the magazine illustrations she had seen. She struggled with a surprising sense of disappointment—along with the nausea from the bucketing coach.

The stop at Fort Gibson was a welcome one, even though it only lasted long enough for the hostlers at the stage stations to change teams. Sara was grateful for the chance to get out of the coach and stretch her legs. She was able to breathe air that wasn't clogged with dust, too.

Vincent's face was pale as he climbed out of the coach after her. Sara put her hand on his arm and asked, "Are you going to be all right?"

He nodded, saying, "Don't worry about me, dear. I'm sure that I'll be fine once we get away from this blasted dust."

Sara caught her bottom lip between her teeth as she felt a wave of guilt go through her. Vincent wouldn't have been there aggravating his already fragile condition if it hadn't been for her insistence that they come on this journey.

"Excuse me, ma'am."

The voice came from beside her and made her look around quickly to see who had spoken to her. It was the young man who had been riding with the driver. He had his hat in his hands, revealing a thatch of rumpled black hair. His eyes were a deep brown, and they held an expression of concern as he looked at her. He went on, "I couldn't help noticing that your father's having a hard time of it. Is there anything I can do to help?"

"No, thank you, we're quite all right," Sara said stiffly. "And this is my husband, not my father."

"Oh." The young man looked embarrassed. "Sorry, sir."

Vincent waved a thin, veined hand and summoned up a smile. "No need to be, sir. I'm well aware of my advanced age."

"Well, if there's anything I can do—"

"Thank you," Sara said again. "We'll be fine."

The young man nodded and walked off, putting his hat on again. Sara watched him go, wondering why she had been so short with him. True, the journey had taken quite a bit out of her, but that was no excuse for being rude. She was about to call out to the young man and apologize to him when another man spoke to him first, walking up and saying, "*'Siyo*, Will."

"*'Siyo*," the young man called Will responded. "How you doing, Tom?"

"All right, I reckon. *Nihina?*"

"Just fine. On my way over to Tahlequah."

The second man nodded. He was rather fearsome-looking, Sara thought. He had a short dark beard and was dressed in worn, patched clothes and down-at-the-heel boots. There was nothing shabby about the guns he carried, though. A Winchester rifle was cradled in

his left arm, and a pair of revolvers were stuck behind
his belt, one on each side. The gun barrels gleamed as
if from a recent cleaning. The man looked as if he
knew how to use the weapons, too.

Sara repressed a shudder as she turned away. The
second man looked like some sort of outlaw, and if he
was that friendly with the young man called Will, then
Will might be an outlaw, too, despite his earlier polite-
ness. Even though Sara's reading had concentrated on
the condition of the Indians who lived down here, she
had scanned enough articles about the West to know
that the frontier was thick with desperadoes of the
worst possible stripe, men who murdered and robbed
and raped without a second thought. Will and Tom
might be members of a gang of such men. They might
even be in rival gangs. Sara put her hand on Vincent's
arm and led him around to the other side of the stagecoach. She felt a little better once she had the body of
the vehicle between them and the two men. Now they
would have at least some protection if gunplay broke
out.

The stop at Fort Gibson—which was less of a fort
now than a settlement surrounding what had once been
a good-sized military installation—passed peacefully,
however, and soon the coach was rolling down the
road to Tahlequah once again. Will had climbed back
onto the seat next to the driver. Sara was glad that the
man called Tom seemed to have moved on. She had
been worried that he would board the coach, too.

Thankfully, it wasn't far from Fort Gibson to Tahlequah. Vincent was struck by another fit of coughing
during this final leg of the journey. His face was gray
when the stage arrived in Tahlequah, and it wasn't just
from the layer of dust that had settled on his features,

Sara knew. She helped him from the coach, only to find that the young man was standing there, having evidently waited for them to disembark after he hopped down from the box.

"Heard your husband coughing in there, ma'am," he said to Sara. "Sounds like he's not well. Maybe you ought to find a doctor for him."

Sara's earlier resolve to be more polite to Will had long since evaporated in her concern for Vincent and the weariness that gripped every muscle in her body. "I'm a doctor," she snapped, "and so is my husband. Now, I'll thank you not to bother us."

Will looked more surprised than offended. "You're a doctor, ma'am?" he said.

"Yes, I am, if it's any of your business." She had hold of Vincent's arm and was about to turn away when a thought occurred to her. To Will, she said, "If you really want to help, you can tell me where I'll find the man in charge around here." She was referring to the federal Indian agent.

"Sure, I can do that," Will replied without hesitation. He pointed to an impressive, two-story, red brick building up the street. "See that building yonder? Just go in there and ask to talk to Lewis Downing."

"Thank you," Sara said. "I'll do that directly. Right now I want to find a place to stay so that Vincent can rest."

"Hotel's right over there, ma'am," Will said. He was holding his hat again, but he clapped it on his head and stepped quickly over to the boot. "If you'll show me which ones are your bags, I'll get 'em out and take them over there for you."

Sara hesitated. Even though she hadn't meant to, she was still talking to this young man. Not only that, but she had somehow wound up accepting his help after all. But the rough-looking man called Tom wasn't around here in Tahlequah, and she found that she was less frightened of Will than she had been. Perhaps it wouldn't hurt anything to allow Will to give them a hand.

He fetched the bags from the boot of the stagecoach and carried them across the street to the hotel, a solid-looking frame structure. Sara followed, her hand on Vincent's arm. "I . . . I'm sorry to be such a bother," he said, still a little breathless from the earlier coughing jag. "I thought I was over this before we left Boston."

"Obviously we rushed our departure too much," Sara said. "You still have some respiratory irritation, and the dust down here makes it worse."

"I'll be all right now that we're off the stagecoach. You can go on and do whatever you need to once we're settled in at the hotel."

"I will. Don't worry about that," Sara promised. "I won't allow our trip down here to have been wasted."

Once or twice during the conversation, she caught curious glances that Will threw over his shoulder. He had to wonder what two white physicians were doing here. But he didn't ask any questions, and Sara was grateful for that. She didn't want to have to explain their presence to a complete stranger. She would have to do that very thing soon enough when she met this fellow Lewis Downing, the Indian agent.

There were several people in the lobby of the hotel, and Sara noticed that some of the men greeted Will by name. Others, however, turned quickly away from him, leading her to suspect that he had something of a reputation around here as a badman. From the clerk behind the counter, she rented a room on the ground floor, then she took the bags from a protesting Will.

"I can handle things from here quite well, thank you," she said to him. "I suppose I should give you some money . . ."

His features hardened, and for the first time, he really looked like that ruthless desperado Sara thought he might be. "That's not necessary," he said. He tugged on the brim of his hat. "Be seeing you, ma'am."

Briefly, Sara regretted offending him, but there wasn't time to worry about something like that. She carried the bags into the room and got Vincent stretched out on the bed, his shoes off and his collar loosened. She opened the window to let a fresh breeze into the room. The curtains moved a little as the wind puffed against them.

"You're certain you'll be all right here?" she asked.

"Positive. You go ahead and talk to that Indian agent. Find out where our services are needed the most and how to get there."

Sara nodded, leaned over, and kissed his forehead. Since his eyes had slid closed, she grimaced at the taste of dust on his skin.

She left him there and went out through the lobby. As she stepped off the porch and into the street, she was surprised to find someone walking beside her. She looked over and saw Will.

"What are you doing?" she asked sharply.

He shrugged. "Thought you might need somebody to walk with you where you're going."

"Are you afraid I won't be safe because I'm white?"

"You'll be safe enough whether I'm with you or not, ma'am. Not many folks around here would ever bother a woman, white or Indian, and they sure wouldn't do it right here in the middle of Muskogee Avenue. But I wouldn't want you to get run down by somebody not watching where he was driving his wagon, either."

Sara looked down the street, which was indeed rather busy. Wagons rolled along in both directions, and horseback riders and pedestrians weaved their way among the vehicles. "It does look a bit intimidating," she admitted.

Will grinned. "Come on. I'll get you there." He reached out, as if he intended to take her arm, then stopped short in the motion and dropped his hand instead.

Sara pretended not to notice as she started walking alongside him toward the red brick building. "We haven't been properly introduced," she said.

"No, ma'am, I reckon we haven't. I'm Will Sixkiller."

"That's an . . . unusual name."

"Not for a Cherokee, it's not. There's Sixkillers all over these parts, and I reckon I'm related to most of them."

"You're a Cherokee, then?"

"Mostly. One of my grandmothers was white."

"You don't really *look* like an Indian."

Will's grin widened. "Maybe not to you. You were expecting a bunch of savages, right?"

Sara felt her face growing warm, and she knew it wasn't from the afternoon sun. She said, "In all the magazine and newspaper stories I read—"

"You don't have to explain. I know what you mean." He put a hand on his chest. "Lo, the poor Indian. The noble redman. I've read those stories, too. Never put much stock in 'em, though. You didn't get around to telling me your name."

His mocking tone and the sudden change of subject put her off-balance. "It's Sara," she said without thinking. "Sara Rawlings. *Doctor* Sara Rawlings."

"Well, I'm pleased to meet you, Doctor."

Curious, she asked, "Is that what your people call a physician?"

"What should we call you, something like 'medicine woman'?" Will shook his head. "I reckon Dr. Rawlings'll do just fine. What brings you down here?"

The way he kept making fun of her, Sara wasn't sure if she wanted to continue this conversation or not. There was still over a block to go before they reached the red brick building, though, so she said, "My husband and I came to the Indian Territories to—"

"Territory," Will said.

"I beg your pardon?"

"It's Indian Territory, not Territories. There's just one, although it's divided up into five main nations and quite a few smaller ones. This is the Cherokee Nation we're in now."

"Yes, I know that," Sara said, "and if you'll let me answer your question without interrupting me—"

"Just setting the record straight, Doctor."

Sara swallowed her exasperation and went on, "We came here to offer our services to your tribe."

"As doctors, you mean?"

"Of course. What else?"

Will looked solemn for a change as he nodded. "That's mighty nice of you. We've got some doctors of our own, of course, as well as some healers who follow the old ways. But one thing there's never enough of on the frontier is medical knowledge. You talk to Lewis Downing. He'll tell you what to do."

They had reached their destination. The building

had a well-cared-for lawn around it, and there were several benches on the grass. Some old men were sitting on the benches, drinking up the warmth of the sun. Sara remembered old-timers in Handley's Mill doing the same; she supposed some things never changed, no matter where you were.

She paused at the beginning of the paved walk that led to the entrance of the building. "Are you coming in?" she asked Will.

"Me?" For the first time, the self-confident air about him appeared somewhat shaken. "What for? I got no business in there. I better not go in."

Sara frowned. Was he *afraid* to go in? She had almost forgotten her suspicions that he might be an outlaw, but his reaction to her suggestion brought them back to her. A man in some sort of trouble with the law wouldn't want to go into a government building, that was certain. She found herself edging away from him.

"Thank you for walking with me, Mr. Sixkiller. I'm sure I'll be fine now."

He touched the brim of his hat and nodded to her. "All right then. I'm sure I'll be seeing you, Doctor. Good day to you."

He turned and strode off. Sara watched him for a moment, then took a deep breath and walked into the building.

A Cherokee man in an office on the first floor directed her to a larger office on the second floor when she asked him where she could find Lewis Downing. The man who answered her knock on the door, by calling out for her to come in, looked like a successful politician. Sara supposed an Indian agent had to be exactly that. She smiled and said, "Mr. Downing?"

"Yes, ma'am," he said as he rose from his chair behind a desk cluttered with papers. "What can I do for you?"

"I take it you are the Indian agent for this district?"

A frown appeared on Downing's face. "Well, no, ma'am, I'm not."

"But . . . but I was told that you were in charge in this area . . ." Dear God, Sara thought, what else could go wrong?

"I suppose I am," Downing said. "I'm the principal chief of the Cherokee Nation, Miss . . . ?"

"Rawlings. But it's Mrs. Rawlings. Actually, Dr. Rawlings is correct."

"You're a physician?" Downing sounded surprised.

"Yes. My husband and I are both doctors, and we've come to offer our services to the Cherokee tribe."

"Well." Downing still looked surprised, but intrigued at the same time. He gestured to a chair in front of the desk. "Please sit down, Dr. Rawlings, and tell me exactly what you have in mind."

He sat down as well and listened intently as Sara ran through an abbreviated version of the circumstances that had brought her and Vincent here. She saw a smile tugging at the corners of Downing's mouth as she explained about the articles she had read in newspapers and magazines like *Harper's Weekly*. Embarrassed, she said, "I realize now that most of what I read was highly exaggerated."

"Not completely," Downing said. "When the Cherokee Nation was removed from its native lands and brought out here to Indian Territory by the U.S. government, there were a great many hardships, both along the way and after we got here. That march was given a name that fits it very well."

"The Trail of Tears," Sara said. "I know."

Downing's face was solemn as he continued, "Anything you've read about that part of our history probably wasn't exaggerated, no matter how bad the writers made it sound. Because it *was* bad, very bad. And it took a long time and a great deal of unrest after we got here before our lives settled down into something approaching what they once were." He gestured toward the window and the city of Tahlequah outside the glass. "As you can see for yourself, though, we've become a nation that is, if not exactly thriving, at least surviving quite nicely. But that doesn't mean we can't use some help. There's always a shortage of doctors on the frontier."

Sara nodded, thinking about Will Sixkiller. "Yes, someone just told me the same thing not long ago."

"Well, whoever told you that was right. Normally, we require at least some Cherokee ancestry to live here, but in the case of you and your husband, we may be able to make an exception, if you're serious about staying here to help tend to our medical needs."

"We're very serious about it, Mr. Downing," Sara said without hesitation.

He nodded. "Very well. I'll take the matter up with the council. Until then, you're certainly welcome to stay here in Tahlequah. You have a room at the hotel?"

"Yes. It seems to be quite comfortable."

"It's not as fancy as Boston, I'm sure," Downing said. "If there's anything I can do to help you . . ."

Sara stood up. "I'm grateful for everything you've done already, Chief Downing."

"All I did was listen and promise to talk to the council."

"Yes, but I appreciate it." Sara paused, then admitted, "I was afraid you'd tell me that my husband and I had to turn around and start back east. I thought our trip had been for nothing."

"I don't think that will turn out to be the case, Doctor," Downing told her. "I've got a feeling that coming out here is going to be good for you and your husband . . . and for the Cherokee Nation."

Sara hoped fervently that he was right.

FIFTEEN

Boston, 1872

"There are the Ingersolls," Judith said as she pushed the baby carriage along the path that led around the Common. "Shouldn't we go over and say hello to them?"

John sighed. "I suppose we should." The last thing in the world he really wanted to do, however, was to be confronted with Roberta Ingersoll.

Still, she was his patient and they were friends of the family, so it would look bad if he were impolite to them. As Judith angled the carriage in which Theodore rode so that their path would intersect that of the Ingersolls, John shifted Rosemary a little in his left arm. Harvey, the oldest of the three children, walked alongside John, his hand tucked securely in his father's hand. They made a near-perfect picture of a family on a Sunday outing, John thought.

But pictures could lie.

John thought he saw a slight hesitation on the part of both Roberta and Michael Ingersoll as they caught sight of him and his family. Michael had never forgotten the indelicate nature of the complaint that had brought him to John's office the year before, and it was only natural that Roberta would be somewhat uncomfortable around John and his wife and children. After all, she was still his mistress.

Appearances were every bit as important to the Ingersolls as they were to John and Judith, however, so there were smiles and pleasant greetings all around. Michael shook hands with John and asked, "How have you been, Doctor?"

"Never better," John lied. "How about you, Michael?"

Putting his arm around his wife's shoulders, Michael said with a hint of defiance in his voice, "We're fine, just fine."

John wondered if he suspected Roberta was having an affair. That was possible, although John was convinced that no one could have even a hint that he and Roberta were romantically involved. They had been too careful for that. At least, he *hoped* he wasn't just deceiving himself with false optimism.

"Your children are lovely," Roberta told Judith. "And so well behaved. Michael and I were never blessed with children."

"They *are* a blessing," Judith said with a little laugh. "But they can be rather tiring at times."

"I would imagine so. I'm afraid the responsibility of raising children would be a bit too much for me."

"It's like training horses or dogs," John said. "Just a matter of discovering the proper mixture of discipline and affection."

Judith shot him a quick glare. "I wouldn't compare children to horses or dogs," she said.

"Well, that wasn't exactly what I was doing—" John began, then decided that dropping the subject might be the best course of action. Whenever Judith

was looking for a fight, she could manufacture one out
of thin air with no difficulty. There was no point in
making her task any easier.

"I've been meaning to come see you again, Doctor,"
Roberta said into the awkward silence. "I've got a pain
I can't seem to shake."

"Of course," John said. "Why don't you come by tomorrow afternoon? I believe I have some time free
then."

"All right, I'll do that. Thank you, Doctor."

The exchange seemed perfectly innocent, John
thought. Michael didn't look suspicious, and neither
did Judith.

All the same, he wasn't looking forward to the encounter. Roberta had become more and more jealous
over the past months, and while she was well aware
that he was not going to leave Judith for her, she had
insisted that his only affair be with her. The idea of a
man "cheating" on his mistress seemed faintly ludicrous to John, but that was the way Roberta seemed to
view the situation. She demanded fidelity—of a sort.

At first John had been inclined to ignore her veiled
threats, but then he grew convinced that she was having him watched, probably by private detectives. It
hadn't taken him long to realize that the prudent thing
to do was to go along with Roberta's demands. She
possessed the power to ruin him if she chose to do so.
None of his other relationships had been serious; it
was easy enough to break them off. That left him with
only his wife and his mistress, but he could live with
that . . . for a while.

After saying good-bye to the Ingersolls, John and
Judith moved on with their children. John put Rosemary down and let her toddle along with him holding

her hands. He felt a twinge of guilt as he did so. Here he was, playing at being the devoted husband and father, when in reality all he could think about was another woman—and that other woman wasn't even his mistress! In fact, he had never kissed her, never laid a hand on her.

Victoria.

Her name sprang unbidden into his head, and he could see her lovely image in his mind's eye. He had known Victoria Caine for over six months now and had seen her nearly every week during that time. But he still felt a tiny shock go through him every time he saw her. He could not imagine any woman ever being more beautiful.

Neither could Nathan Faulkner, obviously. Nathan was as infatuated with Victoria as ever and had confessed as much to John on numerous occasions. But although Victoria seemed to return Nathan's affection, at least to a certain extent, John sensed there was no real love affair going on between the two of them. He had decided that he had misjudged Victoria's attitude during his initial meeting with her. Nathan was in love; Victoria perhaps *wanted* to be, but she wasn't sure.

And that made things very interesting indeed to John.

"Come along, you two," Judith said impatiently to John and Rosemary, who were trailing along behind. "I want to get home."

"Yes, dear," John said as he scooped Rosemary up into his arms and took several long strides that brought him alongside Judith and the carriage again. Harvey had run ahead and startled some birds that had been pecking through the grass of the Common in search of insects. The birds rose into the air, wheeled around, and flew off rapidly.

John found his gaze following them, and he realized he envied them. It would be wonderful to have the ability to take wing like that and fly away, leaving everything behind, slipping the bonds that held him to the earth—to his wife and family—to his job. To be able to soar through the air above everything and find a better place, a place where he really wanted to be . . .

"Come *on*, John. You're lagging behind again."

"I'm sorry," he said. "I suppose I am."

The next morning, John was still somewhat distracted as he saw the patients who had come for appointments. The professional part of his brain was able to put aside his personal problems and concentrate on what he was doing, but in the back of his mind were the three women who occupied so many of his thoughts these days: Judith, the woman he had loved and married; Roberta, the woman he had lusted after and seduced; and Victoria . . . the woman he now wanted almost more than life itself.

He hoped Roberta wasn't coming to the office that afternoon to issue another ultimatum. He got so tired of her demands. If not for the fact that making love with her was still exciting and satisfying, he wouldn't have had anything more to do with her. Maybe that was all she wanted, he thought as he ushered out his final patient of the morning.

To his surprise, he found Michael Ingersoll coming down the hallway, trailed by Miss McLowry. John stopped in his tracks. There was a solemn expression on Michael's rugged face, and for an instant, John thought that the man must have discovered the affair he and Roberta were having. But then Michael nodded pleasantly enough and said, "Good morning, Doctor. I was wondering if I could trouble you for a few minutes of your time."

"I told Mr. Ingersoll that you were about to go to lunch, Dr. Black," the nurse began.

John held up a hand to stop her. "That's quite all right, Miss McLowry. I always have time for a friend like Mr. Ingersoll. Come in, Michael, come in."

Michael hesitated. "Actually, I was thinking that perhaps you could come out, Doctor. How about having lunch with me at the club?"

Both men belonged to one of the most exclusive clubs in the city, Ingersoll because of the wealth he had accumulated, John because of his social standing as a member by marriage of the Faulkner family. John often lunched there anyway, so he nodded in agreement to Michael's suggestion, although it took him by surprise. "That sounds like an excellent idea to me."

Michael had his hat in his hands. He put it on and said, "My carriage is out front. I'll wait for you there."

"I'll join you in just a moment," John promised.

He went back into his office and got his own hat and walking stick. "I should be back in time for my afternoon appointments, Miss McLowry," he said to the nurse. "If I'm late, the delay won't be very long."

"Very good, Doctor."

John put his hat on, gripped his silver-headed cane, and strode out to join Michael Ingersoll in a well-appointed carriage pulled by a team of glossy black horses. A coachman sat on the high seat of the vehicle with a short whip in his hand.

Michael opened the door from inside, and John climbed into the carriage. It was every bit as luxurious and comfortable inside as he had expected. As the coachman cracked his whip and the carriage began moving through the streets of Boston, Michael said from the seat opposite John, "I appreciate you joining me like this, Doctor. I have something important to discuss with you."

"Oh?" John said, feeling a tingle of apprehension again. Michael might be merely playing with him before springing some sort of trap, especially if he knew about the affair. He was a bad man to have for an enemy, John knew. Forcing himself to sound much calmer than he felt, John went on, "What do you want to talk about, Michael?"

The other man waved a hand casually. "As I said, the matter is an important one, but it's nothing that can't wait until after we've eaten. I prefer not to deal with anything unpleasant before a meal."

John swallowed. "Quite a sound policy," he said. His nervousness was growing rapidly now.

But Ingersoll couldn't attempt any sort of reprisal for the affair as long as he and John were in the middle of the crowded club, so John told himself to relax. He just wouldn't leave the club with Michael if he sensed any sort of trouble brewing. That was the most logical solution.

Michael made small talk the rest of the way to the club. John tried hard to join in, but it took quite an effort. He was glad when the carriage pulled up in front of the gray edifice that housed the club.

Inside, the place was dark and rather stuffy, as befitted most of its members. A butler in livery took their hats and sticks, then showed them to a table in the dining room. Evidently they were expected, because their food arrived only a few moments later.

The mutton was superb, as always, if a bit heavy for John's taste. Michael continued to chat idly, indulging in some low-voiced gossip about other members of the club who were also in the dining room. Under ordinary circumstances, John would have enjoyed the meal and the conversation, but he was unable to stop reminding himself that he was sitting across the table from the man he had cuckolded on countless occasions during the past few years. He found himself looking at the food and the wine and wondering if he should have employed the services of a professional taster, as the kings of old had done to ward off poisoning attempts. But Michael was not handling the food and drink, and John doubted if he could have bribed the chef or the waiters to slip anything into the meal.

Finally they were done, and Michael patted his lips with a linen napkin as he leaned back in his chair. "Excellent," he murmured.

"Indeed," John said. He couldn't contain his curiosity and his anxiety any longer. "You said there was something else you wanted to discuss, Michael . . . ?"

"Yes. Very important matter." Michael laid his napkin aside and leaned forward, his voice dropping even more into a conspiratorial tone. "I find myself in need of some discreet assistance, John."

That didn't sound too threatening, John thought. But his instincts were still warning him to be cautious as he said, "I'm sure I'll be glad to do whatever I can."

"Good. Because you're the only man I'd trust with this, John. The only one. After what you did for me that other time . . ."

Suddenly John had an idea what this might be about. He said, "You haven't picked up something you shouldn't have, have you, Michael?"

"Well, not exactly." The man was looking distinctly more uncomfortable now. "But the problem *is* related, I suppose you could say. You see, there's a young lady involved, and she . . . well, she has a certain condition—"

"A disease?"

Michael shook his head vehemently. "No, it's more of a . . . blessed condition . . ."

"She's with child," John guessed, the light dawning in his head. "And you're the father."

Michael nodded miserably.

John fought down the impulse to throw back his head and laugh madly. This was not at all what he had expected. And yet it wasn't a surprise. Michael Ingersoll evidently preferred women of the gutter to his own wife, and now one of them had a swollen belly thanks to him. Trying to sound properly solemn and sympathetic, John said, "I'm sorry, Michael. But what can I do to help you?"

"You can . . . take care of the situation. The young woman doesn't want to have the child."

Now John really was serious as he frowned at Michael and started to shake his head. "I can't do that—" he began.

Michael leaned forward even more and hissed, "You have to! You're the only doctor I can trust! She . . . she's threatened to go to Roberta and demand money if I don't do something."

"And you don't want that, do you?"

"Of course not!" Michael took a deep breath and pulled a handkerchief from his vest pocket. He patted away some of the fine beads of sweat that had begun to sheen on his forehead. "If it was just a matter of . . . of losing Roberta, I might be able to stand that.

She and I haven't been close for years. But the scandal would ruin me, John! I'm not a Catholic, but many of the people I deal with are. They'd never forgive me."

John felt anger washing through him. He wasn't a Catholic, either, but he didn't like what Ingersoll was asking of him. "I'm sorry, Michael, but I just can't—"

"It would be worth a great deal of money for me to have this burden taken off my shoulders. I don't want to know anything about it, you understand. I want to walk away from the situation as if it never happened. I realize that's going to take a pretty price."

For a long moment, John didn't say anything. Michael obviously regarded him as a man who would do almost anything for money. And that assessment had never been very far wrong, John had to admit. He closed his eyes and lifted a hand to his face, pinched the bridge of his nose together between two fingers as he thought. Then, finally, he sighed and looked across the table at Michael again.

"I'll need two thousand dollars," he said flatly.

"You'll have it," Michael replied without hesitation.

"And the girl's name and where to find her, of course."

"Of course," Michael said eagerly. "I can have the money and the information delivered to your office later this afternoon."

"All right," John said with a nod.

"I can't thank you enough. I have faith in you, John. I know you'll do right by me."

"And you had nowhere else to turn, did you?" John asked dryly.

"No. No, I really didn't. You were my last hope." Ingersoll reached across the table and clasped John's arm. "You're a good friend, John, a good friend indeed."

John just smiled thinly and thought that he was going to take particular pleasure in the act the next time he made love to this man's wife.

John was whistling a tune as he walked into the lobby of St. Andrew's a couple of weeks later. Things had begun to look up in his life recently, he thought. The way he had dealt with Michael Ingersoll's problem, his affair with Roberta, even the mood Judith had been in at home—all of those things were working out quite well as far as he was concerned.

And today he got to see Victoria Caine again. That was enough to brighten the world for him right there.

Yet, when he entered her office a moment later, breezing in after a perfunctory knock, his spirits suddenly plummeted.

Victoria's face was tear-streaked as she looked up from behind her desk. She had a handkerchief in her hands and used it to dab at her eyes as she stood up and fumbled, "John! I . . . I forgot this was your day for the children—"

"That's all right, Victoria," he said as he crossed the room toward her, a frown of surprise and concern on his face. "What's wrong? Why are you upset?"

He had already glanced around the room and seen that she had been alone until he came in. Obviously, she had been sitting in here sobbing about something, and he wanted to know what it was.

"It . . . it's nothing," she said with a shake of her head.

"It must have been something, to make you cry like

that," he insisted. "I'd like to help, Victoria, but I can't if you don't tell me what's wrong."

She summoned up a smile as she wiped away the tears and looked at him. "You're more than a good doctor, you know that?" she said. "You're a good man, John Black. A very good man."

John wasn't so sure about that. In fact, he was certain that he *wasn't* a good man. The many women he had bedded, the corners he cut in his business dealings, the very way he lived his life were proof enough of his nature. But he still didn't like to see Victoria so upset. Especially not Victoria . . .

"You're so wonderful with the children," she went on.

A bunch of runny-nosed brats, for the most part, he thought. But he did what he could for them, and in the time he had been coming here to the orphanage, none of them had come down with a serious illness.

"But no matter how good you are," Victoria went on, "there's nothing you can do about this."

He set his medical bag on the desk. "Why don't you tell me about it, and then we'll decide if there's anything I can do."

"Well . . . all right. If you're sure you want to know."

"Of course I want to know!"

She took a deep breath. "The orphanage may be forced to close."

John blinked in surprise. "But why? I thought it was doing quite well."

"This isn't a profitable organization, John," she pointed out gently.

"No, of course not. But I thought there was plenty

of money to continue operating the place. I've given you donations myself—"

"And you've been very generous," she said with a smile.

"—and I know other people have donated money as well, in addition to what the Church provides."

"The Church doesn't own this land and this house, though."

That surprised John as well. "Then who does?"

"The heirs of a man named Edgar Morrison."

The name meant nothing to John. He shook his head in bafflement.

"Mr. Morrison was a very kindhearted man who loved children, even though he had none of his own," Victoria went on. "He provided this estate for the orphanage, for as long as he lived. He made his fortune in the fishing industry, and his home was up in Maine."

"But now he's passed away," John guessed.

Victoria nodded wordlessly.

"And his heirs don't want to continue the arrangement?"

"That's right. They're going to sell the estate, and they've given us until the end of the month to vacate it."

"But that's insane!" John exclaimed. "Didn't you have any sort of lease with Morrison, something that would continue in force even though he's dead?"

Victoria shook her head, and fresh tears glistened in her eyes. "Mr. Morrison never really trusted lawyers. He said he didn't want to have anything to do with them. So there was no lease, and he left no will stating his wishes. There's nothing we can do."

John slumped into one of the chairs, shaking his

head. An idea occurred to him, and he looked up. "Perhaps the Church could buy this property."

"I already thought of that and spoke to the monsignor. He said it's not possible right now." She smiled faintly. "Despite what you may think, the Church doesn't have all the money in the world, John. And this institution is not nearly as well off financially as it might appear. So much of the work is done by volunteers."

"But you're cash poor," John finished. "I understand things are not always as they seem. But surely *something* can be done . . ."

"Not unless you want to buy the property for us. Can you afford that, John?"

Now, that was a thought . . . but not a feasible one, he realized. He made a good living at his practice, a very good living indeed, but an estate of this size would cost many thousands of dollars. And it took quite a bit of money just to maintain the style of life to which Judith was accustomed. John might have been able to scrape up enough cash to purchase the orphanage, but it would have meant going into debt and living very frugally for years in order to pay off what he owed. Judith would never have stood for that.

Nor could he turn to Edward Faulkner for the money, although the banker could readily have provided it. Edward would demand to know what John's interest in the place was, and John didn't want to do anything that might lead to suspicion of the way he really felt about Victoria. He couldn't take that risk.

But, he suddenly realized, he knew someone else who had more money than he knew what to do with . . .

John stood up sharply. "I'm going to take care of

this for you, Victoria," he said. "I can't buy the place myself, but I know someone who can, and I'm certain he'll let you continue to use it for as long as you like. We'll even have papers drawn up giving you that right, so that something like this can never happen again."

A glimmer of hope appeared in her red, swollen eyes. "Are . . . are you sure about this, John?"

"I'm certain." He stepped over to her and put a hand on her shoulder. "Just wait here, and don't tell anyone else about this. There's no point in upsetting anyone over something that won't ever happen."

"If you can really do this, I . . . I can never repay you."

"Don't worry about that. Just concentrate on taking care of the children."

She smiled up at him. "As I said before, you're a good man, John Black."

Then she raised herself on her toes and abruptly pressed her mouth to his.

John was stunned by the kiss, but his instincts took over and his arms went around her. He drew her into an embrace and thrilled to the feel of her body molding against his. Her lips were as warm and moist and sweet as he had dreamed they would be. He feasted on them, as he had done previously only in his imagination.

But the feast was short-lived, as Victoria suddenly broke the kiss and drew back from him, a shocked look on her face. "I . . . I'm sorry," she stammered. "I don't know why . . . why I did that!"

"It's all right," John told her, his voice a little shaky from the tremors running through him. "We'll talk about that later. Right now we have to think about the orphanage." Making an effort to calm the storm raging inside him, he reached for his hat and his medical bag. "I'll see the children another day. Right now I have to pay a visit to someone else."

Victoria nodded without looking at him.

"I'll be back," John promised.

"I'll be here," she said quietly.

He turned and left the room, clapping his hat on his head as he strode resolutely out of the building. He wanted to turn around and run back to her, but he didn't dare. There were too many other important things he had to do now. Besides, he felt the sharp teeth of guilt gnawing at his belly. Nathan Faulkner, his brother-in-law and probably his best friend, was in love with Victoria Caine.

And yet, John thought, mere moments ago she had been in *his* arms, not Nathan's, her mouth pressed to his mouth in a kiss that had shaken John all the way to his core.

Something was definitely going to have to be done about this.

But not until after he had seen Michael Ingersoll.

John had never been to the offices of Michael's shipping line, but he knew where they were. He found Michael there, and the tycoon looked up in surprise from behind his desk as a secretary ushered John into the room. Since the meal they had shared at the club a couple of weeks earlier, the two men had seen each other only briefly, and that was so John could report that the situation troubling Michael had been taken care of satisfactorily. That was all Michael wanted to know; the details, he said, were best left unspoken.

But today, if necessary, they *would* be spoken of.

"Hello, John," Michael said as he pushed aside

some of the papers on the desk. "What brings you down here to the docks? This is a bit out of your usual haunts, isn't it?"

"A bit," John agreed with a nod. The offices were located in a building less than a block from the harbor. "But it was important that I talk to you right away, Michael, so I took a chance on finding you here."

"Sit down, sit down. Tell me what's on your mind. What's this important matter you mentioned?"

John put his hat and bag on one of the chairs in front of the desk, then settled himself in the other one. "Well, Michael," he began, "I find myself in something of a troubling situation, similar in a way to the circumstances in which you found yourself not too long ago."

A worried look appeared on Ingersoll's face. "You're speaking of—"

"Exactly," John broke in. "We both know what I'm talking about, so there's no need to go into detail. However, there's more than one child involved this time. In fact, there's an entire orphanage full of them."

Michael's frown deepened. "I'm afraid I don't understand."

"You will," John said. Quickly, he described the predicament in which St. Andrew's found itself.

When he was finished, Michael shook his head. "That's a shame, but I don't see what it has to do with me."

"Someone with your fortune could easily buy that property and allow the orphanage to remain there."

Michael leaned back in his chair. "Why in the world would I want to do *that*?" he demanded.

"Out of the goodness of your heart?" suggested John.

Michael gave a snort of contempt. "I'm a business-man, not a philanthropist. I may feel sorry for a bunch of orphans, but I'm not going to buy an estate like that for them!"

"You're sure you can't bring yourself to volunteer?"

"I suppose I could give you a donation that might help them out, say a hundred dollars or so," Michael replied with a sigh. "But that's all I can do."

"I'm sorry to hear you say that," John said with a shake of his head. "I truly am."

Ingersoll shrugged and pulled the documents back in front of him. "If that's all—"

"It's not," John said. "There's still the matter of that street girl whose child you paid me to get rid of."

Michael grimaced and said, "I thought we weren't going to speak of that."

"We wouldn't have—if you had found it in your heart to help my friends without being forced to."

"Forced to?" Michael stared at John for a long moment, then said, "My God, are you attempting to blackmail me?"

"Not attempting. I'm doing it."

Michael's hands clenched into fists. "Well, you can go to hell!" he said angrily. "You've no proof of any-thing. I paid you cash, and the child is gone—"

"No," John said quietly.

Ingersoll came up out of his chair. "What did you say?" he demanded in a taut, thin voice.

"The girl is still with child. It'll be born in a few months, and it'll be *your* bastard, Michael. Isn't it amazing how the birth of a tiny baby can utterly ruin a rich, powerful man like you?"

"But I paid you—"

"And I took the money and gave it to the girl so that

she could go away, establish herself somewhere else as
a widow, and make a new start after she has the baby.
She was very grateful for your generosity, Michael,
and after I explained how you really wanted her to
have the child, she changed her mind about getting rid
of it."

"You bastard," Michael whispered. "You goddamned bastard . . ."

John shrugged and smiled a little. "It seemed the
best way to handle an unpleasant situation. And now
I'm glad I made that decision. I know where the girl
is. I can bring her back to Boston in a few months,
after the baby is born, and introduce the child to his father. I'm sure Roberta and all your cronies would be
very interested to meet them, too."

"I'll deny the child is mine!" Michael raged. "The
girl's a slut! She has no way of proving that I'm the father."

"She convinced you before. Who's to say who else
she might convince? Besides, the gossip alone would
be enough to damage your business a great deal."

"Oh, God." Michael slumped back into his seat.
"How can you do this to me? I always thought we
were friends, John."

"Not really . . . although we might have more in
common than you suspect. But all of this messy affair
can be avoided, Michael. Just . . . invest . . . in a certain property. You already have other investments,
don't you?"

Michael nodded bleakly.

"Then look at this as just another business deal,"
John went on. "No one will think twice about it. I can
certainly promise that I'll keep quiet about it."

"Like you've kept quiet about that other matter?" Michael growled.

"I haven't told anyone about it. You and I and the girl are the only ones who know. The only ones who ever have to know. You can afford the money, Michael. You can't afford the notoriety."

For a long moment, Michael didn't say anything. Then, with a sigh of defeat, he looked at John and said, "You're a son of a bitch, you know that?"

"Well aware of the fact, old boy, well aware."

"All right, your damned orphans will still have a place to live. Give me the details, and I'll take care of it."

John leaned forward. "I'm glad you saw the light of reason, Michael. I really am."

"Just don't ever cross me again, Black. If you do, you'll live to regret it." Ingersoll snorted again. "Hell, you may live to regret *this*."

"I'll take that chance," John said.

For Victoria Caine, he would risk almost anything.

SIXTEEN

Cherokee Nation, 1872

Sara was humming to herself as she hung up the week's washing to dry on the line strung between two oak trees behind the house she and Vincent shared. It was a beautiful autumn day; the air was crisp yet the sun was still warm. Sara knew from talking to the Cherokees who had lived here since the Trail of Tears that winter would come soon enough, bringing with it occasional ice and snow and many days of cold, steady rain. For now, though, she was going to enjoy the weather here in Indian Territory.

During the months she and Vincent had been here, Sara had grown to love this place. The house was large, with plenty of room for her medical practice. A farming family with numerous children had lived here originally, Chief Lewis Downing explained to Sara, after he had located the house and made arrangements for them to live in it. A fever had wiped out the family, however, leaving some of their relatives to work the land but no one to live in the house. Since private ownership of property was forbidden by Cherokee law and custom, people were allowed to hold what land they could use, and it hadn't taken much persuading on the part of the chief to convince the relatives of the original settlers that Sara and Vincent could put the house to good use. Initially, there had been some resentment from the people around here due to the fact that neither she nor Vincent had any Cherokee blood, but Downing, politician that he was, had been able to smooth over that, too. Though Downing himself was a full-blood and the party that had elected him was dominated by full-bloods, he was also a practical man, motivated primarily by what would be best for his people.

And once the Cherokee saw that Sara and Vincent wanted only to help them, that helped, too. As Downing and Will Sixkiller had both said, competent medical practitioners were often hard to come by on the frontier.

The house was on the road between Tahlequah and the village of Park Hill, which was some three-and-a-half miles southeast of the capital city. That made it convenient for people to drop by whenever they had some medical complaint. Sara's patients came from both towns, as well as the numerous farms around the area. She found that the mixed-bloods were more likely to seek out her services; the full-bloods tended more often to follow the old Cherokee ways. But even some of them came to see her when they were sick, and with every week that passed, she sensed that her acceptance in the Cherokee Nation was growing.

Finished with hanging up the wash, she carried the big wicker basket back inside and found Vincent in the parlor smoking his pipe and reading a copy of the *Cherokee Advocate*. The newspaper was published in Tahlequah and contained stories printed in both English and the Cherokee syllabary devised by Sequoyah.

Sara had tried to master the Cherokee writing, but so far she had had little success.

"I see that the army's still trying to find all of those white settlers who came over the line, and force them to leave," Vincent commented as he rattled the paper.

"They won't try to make us leave, will they?" asked Sara.

"I certainly wouldn't think so. We're here with the permission and sponsorship of the principal chief of the Cherokee Nation. Our rights are—" Vincent broke off and coughed several times before resuming. "Our rights are clear."

Sara frowned as she looked at her husband. Although his condition had improved somewhat since their arrival in Indian Territory, he was still subject to these occasional coughing fits, and his features were still gaunt and often haggard. At his age, Sara knew, it was doubtful that he would ever completely recover from the illness that had laid him low back in Boston. From a medical standpoint, Sara knew the odds against that.

But he was still her husband, and she couldn't help but worry about him. She had grown quite fond of Vincent over the years, especially since he had lost most of his interest in coming to her bed.

"I hope you're right," she told him now. "I'd hate to have to leave after we've established ourselves here."

The sound of a wagon pulling up in front of the house caught her attention, and she went to see who their visitors were. As she expected, there were patients to see: a couple of Cherokee children with bad stomachaches. Sara gave them both a tonic to soothe them and assured the worried parents that the youngsters would probably be all right. By the time she was finished with that, she had another patient waiting, a farmer with a bloodstained bandage wrapped around his leg. The head of his ax had flown off the handle while he was chopping wood, he explained, striking him in the leg and leaving an ugly gash. Sara unwrapped the wound, cleaned it, stitched it up, and bandaged it again. When she was finished, the man paid her a dime, as had the parents of her previous patients, and thanked her profusely, with his gaze fastened on the floor the entire time. Sara had learned enough about Cherokee customs by this time to know that he was showing his respect for her; it was considered improper for a Cherokee to stare directly at someone.

The rest of the day passed in similar fashion as she treated half a dozen more patients, none of them with illnesses or injuries that were particularly serious. By and large, these people seemed to be quite healthy, she had discovered, although there were always accidents and childhood illnesses to be dealt with.

As evening settled down, Sara lit the lamps in the house. The wind had picked up, rattling the leaves that had not yet fallen from the trees on the property. That wind signaled a change in the weather, Sara thought. It was going to get cooler now.

They had eaten their supper and were sitting in the parlor again when the wind began blowing even harder. Sara was threading sutures onto needles, but she looked up from what she was doing as the wind buffeted the windows of the house. Vincent was still reading the newspaper, but he lowered it and said, "Sounds like there may be a storm coming."

"I hope not," Sara said. She tried to go back to her work, but it was hard to concentrate with the wind howling that way outside.

There was so much noise, in fact, that she almost didn't hear the sudden pounding of hoofbeats on the road. She looked up again as the faint noise drifted to her ears. When the sounds stopped abruptly right outside the house, she frowned.

Who would come calling with a storm approaching? she wondered. Of course, from the urgent sound of the hoofbeats, she knew that whoever was out there in the night wasn't here on a social visit.

She glanced at her husband, who seemed not to have noticed the noises from outside. As she set the threaded needles aside, she said, "Someone just rode up, Vincent. I'll see who it—"

Before she could finish her sentence or get up from her chair, there was a terrific pounding on the front door. "My God!" Vincent exclaimed as he sat up sharply and put his newspaper aside. "Who can that be?"

Sara stood up and started toward the door. The pounding slacked off for a second, then started up again, as fierce as before. "I'll see who's there," Sara said over the racket.

"Wait!" Vincent suddenly said. "You know there are outlaws in this territory, Sara. It's after dark, you can't just go opening the door to everyone who knocks on it."

"But it could be someone who's hurt—"

She was interrupted by a man's voice bawling from the other side of the panel, "Open up in there! I got a wounded man out here!"

Sara cast a look at Vincent. "You see? I'm a doctor, I have to help."

Without waiting for him to argue any more, she strode to the door, grasped the latch, and opened it.

The flames in the lamps flickered and wavered as wind swirled into the room, casting crazy shadows on the walls and ceiling. Sara stepped back and gasped as she saw the two men standing on the porch of her house. One of them was standing, that is; the other was being held up by his companion. Sara recognized the man who stood straight, but it took her a moment to place him. He was the man called Tom, she realized, the man whose rough appearance had frightened her when she saw him in Fort Gibson months earlier, the day after she and Vincent arrived in Indian Territory.

Months ago, the first time she had seen him, he had been talking to Will Sixkiller, Sara recalled.

And now Will was beside Tom, slumped against him, Tom's arm around his waist to support him. Will's head lolled loosely on his shoulders, and the front of his shirt was soaked with blood.

"Dear Lord!" Sara said in a voice that was little more than a hoarse whisper. "What happened to him?"

"We ran into some ol' boys we shouldn't have," Tom said simply. "*Yonegs* put a bullet in Will here."

Sara had picked up enough Cherokee words in her time here to know that *yonegs* meant white men. But knowing who had shot Will Sixkiller wasn't nearly as important now as the fact that he had been shot. Sara knew she could think about the implications of that later. Right now, she had to deal with the medical emergency. "Bring him in," she said. "Be careful with him."

Tom grunted and steered Will into the house, half-carrying him. Vincent stood to one side of the door, looking flustered. Sara felt rather shaken herself, but she was determined to stay calm and cool-headed.

That might be the only way to save Will Sixkiller's life.

"Take him in there," she said, pointing to the door leading into the former bedchamber where they had set up their main examining room. "See if you can get him up on that table."

A Cherokee carpenter had built the examining table for Sara in return for her treatment of a sick child. It was higher and narrower than a regular table. To cover it Sara had made a pad that was stuffed with goose down, and the pad was covered in turn by thick sheets. A couple of lamps had been hung from the ceiling over the table to provide plenty of light, and Sara lit them as she said to Vincent, "Close the front door, please."

He did as she asked, cutting off the flow of chilly air into the house. Will was going to need to be kept warm, since he had lost so much blood. One way Sara could tell that he was still alive was the fact that he was shivering as Tom laid him down on the table.

For such a big, rough-looking man, Tom handled his friend gently. Will's coat fell open even more than it already had been, revealing the walnut-butted revolver holstered on his right hip. A small leather thong was looped over the hammer of the gun, holding it in the holster. Sara repressed a shudder as she looked at the weapon.

"Could you . . . could you take that away, please?" she said to Tom as she pointed at the revolver.

"Sure." Tom unfastened the thong and slid the gun out of the holster. He tucked it behind his belt as he stepped back to give Sara more room next to the table.

"*Wado,*" she murmured, using the Cherokee expression of gratitude without even thinking about it.

Vincent moved up on the other side of the table and asked, "What can I do to help?"

"I'll need that shirt cut off of him," Sara replied as she searched out Will's pulse with her fingers in his neck. It was fast but fairly steady, which was encouraging. His eyes were closed, but he wasn't completely unconscious. His lips moved and he muttered something. Sara leaned closer, trying to make out what he was saying. He seemed to be repeating one word over and over, but it was in Cherokee and it wasn't one of the words she knew.

She turned her head to look at Tom. "What's he saying?"

"*Unaligohi.* Means partner. He's calling me." Tom stepped forward again and reached out to grasp one of Will's hands. "I'm here, Will, right here. I brought you to the doctor's house, just like you wanted."

That seemed to calm Will down a bit, and his muttering subsided. By this time, Vincent had pulled his coat aside and cut away most of the blood-soaked shirt. Sara was able to see the ugly, black-rimmed hole just below Will's left shoulder.

She looked at Tom again. "Did the bullet go through?"

He shook his head and said, "Don't think so. Didn't see any blood on his back."

"Neither do I," Sara said, as much to herself as to Tom. "I don't want to roll him all the way over to check. Tom, come around on this other side of the table. I want you to lift Will just enough for me to slip my hand underneath him, inside his shirt."

"Yes, ma'am." As Tom positioned himself, he went on, "We ain't really been introduced, I reckon. I'm Tom Whitson."

"I'm pleased to meet you, Tom, although I can't help but wish it had been under better circumstances." Now that she had been around him more, he didn't seem quite so frightening—although he still looked like something from a story a mother would use to scare her child into going to bed. She hadn't forgotten, either, what he had said about Will getting shot when the two of them encountered some white men.

The only white men Sara knew of who were moving around the Territory were soldiers and deputy United States marshals from Fort Smith, Arkansas. If Will and Tom were really outlaws, as she had suspected, they wouldn't want to run into representatives of either group.

But again, such worries could wait for another time. When Tom lifted Will as she directed, she leaned over and slipped her hand inside the back of his shirt, running her fingertips quickly across the skin that was stretched over his shoulderblade. There was no exit wound, and she couldn't feel any telltale lumps underneath the skin that would mark the location of the bullet. She had seen wounds like this in which the slug had almost completely penetrated the body, stopping just under the skin on the far side from the entrance wound. In a case like that, it was easier to remove the bullet from that side.

The bullet that had struck Will hadn't gone that deep, though, so she would have to go in through the wound to find it. She nodded to Tom and said, "Lower him carefully."

Will let out a little groan as Tom eased him down flat on the table again. Sara looked up at Vincent and said, "I'll need a probe and a pair of forceps."

He nodded. "I'll clean them with carbolic while you're getting some of that blood off the field."

Tom stepped back again and watched in wonder as Sara and Vincent worked quickly, calmly, and efficiently. Sara cleaned away the blood around the wound, some of which had already begun to dry, while Vincent prepared the instruments needed to remove the bullet. When everything was ready, Sara took the probe and leaned over Will's body, easing the tip of it into the bullet hole and working it gradually into the wound. She breathed shallowly, not wanting to increase the chances of infecting the wound. Her face was a study in concentration, and her red hair and green eyes stood out sharply in contrast to her taut, pale features.

"I've got it," she said after a few moments. There was no triumph or relief in her voice; it was still too early for that. Instead it was a simple statement of fact. She held the probe in position with her left hand while extending the right to Vincent. "Forceps."

He put the instrument in her hand. She slid the forceps down over the probe, letting the slender shaft of metal guide them into position.

God, how often have I done this! she thought. She had lost count of the number of bullets she had removed from riddled bodies. Most of them had been during the war, when she was riding with Carver Gresham's patrol of Confederate raiders, but there had been other occasions, too, while she was working in the hospitals in Boston. Just because Massachusetts was a civilized place didn't mean nobody ever got shot. At any rate, this was far from the first bullet hole in which she had gone exploring, seeking the ugly lumps of misshapen lead that could mean death if they were not removed.

When the forceps were in position, she withdrew the probe, got a good grip on the slug, and began slowly to work it out. Will groaned and shuddered, and Sara said sharply, "Hold onto him, please! We don't want him jumping up off the table."

"I got him," Tom said, stepping forward quickly to grasp Will's shoulders.

It took only a moment for Sara to pry the bullet from Will's body with practiced ease. She straightened, feeling a twinge of pain go through her back as she did so, a protest from muscles that had grown stiff from standing hunched over for too long. Vincent held out an empty basin, and she dropped the bullet into it. There was a clang and a rattle as the slug landed and rolled around a little.

Will heaved a long, ragged sigh and visibly relaxed once the bullet was out of him. Tom sighed as well and said, "Reckon the worst is over now, huh?"

"Not necessarily," Sara said. "More people who have been shot die from blood poisoning and festering wounds than they do from the bullet itself. I have to clean this wound thoroughly, inside and out."

For that she used wads of cotton soaked in carbolic acid held in the pincers of the forceps. As a final measure, she said to Vincent, "Bring that bottle of whiskey from the other room."

Tom's eyes widened. "Whiskey?" he repeated. "You ain't supposed to have any whiskey around here. It's against the law."

"It's for medicinal purposes only," Sara snapped. "Besides, after what I've done for your friend here, I don't think you'd turn me in, would you, Tom?"

"Well, no, I reckon not," he said slowly. "Besides, it ain't like there aren't bootleggers all over these parts already, not to mention the fellas who bring the stuff in from Arkansas and sell it on the sly. I don't reckon there's any need to say anything about one bottle."

"Thank you," Sara said. Vincent came back into the room with the dark brown glass bottle in his hand. He gave it to Sara and she said, "All right, hold him down again."

Will's body bucked and heaved as Sara carefully poured the fiery liquor into the bullet hole. Corded muscles bunched underneath Tom's coat as he held his friend down on the table. Will's eyes flew open and he gasped for breath. After a moment, his struggles subsided and his eyes slid closed again. A shudder went through him and then he lay still, his chest rising and falling steadily.

Sara placed a thick pad over the wound, which was still oozing blood, then tied it tightly in place with strips of cloth. "There," she said, unable to keep a note of satisfaction out of her voice. "With any luck, that should heal cleanly. His shoulder will be very sore for a while, of course, and there may be some stiffness for a long time, perhaps forever."

"But he won't die?" Tom asked.

"Not from this gunshot wound. At least I don't think so, and I've seen quite a few of them."

More than she liked to remember, she thought.

"I sure do thank you, ma'am—" Tom began, then the sound of more hoofbeats outside made him fall silent. He turned toward the door, and his hand moved toward the butt of one of the revolvers tucked behind his belt, as if it was acting on instinct.

"What's wrong?" Sara asked, surprised by his reaction.

"Those *yonegs* who shot Will, they maybe followed us here," Tom said, his bearded jaw clenched tight. "You folks better stay back—"

"No," Vincent said suddenly. "Stay here, both of you. I'll handle this."

"Wait, Vincent," Sara said, clutching at his arm as he started toward the door of the room. "I'm going with you."

He looked as if he wanted to argue with her, but there was no time for that. A man's voice shouted from outside the house, "Hello in there! Anybody home?"

"Let me do the talking," Vincent hissed at Sara as they left the examining room. Sara cast a glance over her shoulder at the window. The shutter was closed and the curtain was drawn tightly over the inside, and she was thankful for that. No one would be able to peer in from outside.

Vincent went to the front door and opened it, and immediately the wind plucked at his thin hair and swept into the room. He stepped out onto the porch and Sara followed, her own hair whipping around her head in the stiff breeze. She lifted a hand to push the long red strands out of her face.

The light from inside the house spilled out to reveal half a dozen men on horseback. Sara couldn't see their faces well enough to know if they were white or Cherokee, but the man who spoke *sounded* white as he said, "Howdy, folks. Sorry to bother you on a night like this, but we got to find out if you've seen a couple of men come through here in the past few minutes."

"What sort of men?" Vincent asked, raising his

voice so that it could be heard over the wind. "Indians?"

"Yes, sir, a couple of them damn Cherokee bucks."

"I take it you men are the authorities?"

A couple of the strangers laughed, but the spokesman glared at them and made them fall silent. He looked back at Vincent and said, "That's right. Deputy U.S. marshals out of Fort Smith. We got warrants on them bucks."

Vincent glanced over at Sara, clearly uncertain what he should do next. He had always been a law-abiding man, certainly not the type to shelter fugitives from the law.

But Sara remembered how Will had tried to befriend them during the stage ride from Muskogee to Tahlequah, and he *had* been helpful in directing her to Chief Lewis Downing, even though she had actually been trying to locate the federal Indian agent at the time. Everything had worked out for the best, though, and Will Sixkiller was partially responsible for that.

Besides, he was severely wounded, and if these men slung him on a horse and took him to Fort Smith tonight, the trip would kill him. Sara was sure of that.

Her voice was firm as she said, "I'm sorry, sir, but we've had no visitors tonight—until now."

The spokesman reached up and tugged on the brim of his hat. "Good evenin' to you, ma'am," he said. "You mind if we take a look around your place? Them Cherokee could be hidin' somewheres."

Sara's mind worked rapidly. She had already looked around the front of the house and seen no sign of the horses on which Will and Tom had arrived. She couldn't figure out where they might be, but at least they weren't in plain sight. They would have to risk a search, though; so far the man who had spoken had been polite, but Sara sensed an undercurrent of steely determination in his voice. If she and Vincent refused to let them look around, the men would do it anyway and would be more suspicious to boot. She caught Vincent's eye and gave a tiny nod.

"By all means, go ahead and look around," Vincent told the men. "If there are criminals hiding around here, we want them found and captured as much as you gentlemen do. Probably more, because I'm alone here with my wife." He slipped an arm around Sara's shoulders.

Don't overplay it, she cautioned him silently. She was grateful, at least, that he had followed her lead, although he had to be wondering why she had chosen to conceal the fact that Will and Tom were here.

The spokesman for the group gestured to his men, and several of them spread out to ride around the house in both directions. Sara and Vincent waited anxiously until they returned a few minutes later. "No sign of 'em, Lew," one of the men said to the spokesman, who was obviously the leader of the group.

The man grunted. "We're wastin' time around here, then." He looked at Vincent and Sara again and went on, "If you do see any sign of them fugitives, you better steer clear of 'em, folks. They're mighty dangerous men. Kill you as soon as look at you."

"I assure you, sir, we want no part of them," Vincent said.

The man called Lew frowned a little as he looked at them. "You ain't Cherokee, neither one of you, are you?"

"No, sir. I'm Dr. Vincent Rawlings, and this is my wife, Sara."

"Doctor, huh? One of those bucks might be carryin' a slug in him. If they know you're a sawbones, they might come here lookin' for help. Could be I ought to leave a man here, just to keep an eye on the place."

Sara felt a cold tingle of fear go through her at that suggestion. Before she could say anything, Vincent tightened his arm around her and declared, "Thank you, but that won't be necessary. I have a loaded rifle inside, as well as a shotgun. I assure you, Marshal, if anyone comes up here tonight who is unknown to me, he'll find a .44 slug or a faceful of buckshot waiting for him."

Lew chuckled, a harsh, ugly sound. "You sound mighty fierce for a pill-roller, Doc, but I believe you. Still, if we don't run them boys to ground, we might stop back by here later, just to check on you."

"That would be fine," Vincent said.

Lew lifted an arm and waved his men into motion. As they rode away, he called out, "Good night, folks."

Vincent lifted his free hand in farewell, then waited until the men were well out of earshot—which wasn't too far in this howling wind—before saying, "My God, Sara, what have we gotten into?"

"I don't know," she replied tightly, "but I've got a patient to check on, and that's all I'm going to worry about right now."

She turned and walked quickly into the house, only to stop short as she saw Tom standing in the doorway of the examining room, a revolver in each hand. "They gone?" he asked quietly.

Sara nodded. "They are. Now, put those away. I don't like guns being waved around in my house."

Will's voice came from the other room. "Tom," it called faintly. "Tom, give me a hand here."

The big Cherokee shoved his guns behind his belt again and turned to go back into the examining room. Sara and Vincent followed closely behind him, and Sara frowned when she saw that Will was sitting up on the table.

"You shouldn't be doing that," she told him sharply. "You need to rest."

"Can't . . . can't do that," he said. "Tom told me Lew . . . Lew Stoddard was just here . . . looking for us. You've done enough for us . . . already, Doctor. Can't be bringing trouble down on . . . your heads. We got to . . . get out of here."

"But you're in no shape to travel!" Vincent protested. "You lost a great deal of blood. You're weak, and that wound could easily become infected."

"Got to take that chance," Tom said. "Will's right. We got to be goin'."

"Your horses aren't out there," Sara told him. "They must have wandered off."

"Nope. I slapped 'em both on the rump when I got Will off his saddle. Didn't want 'em standin' out in front of your house in case Stoddard came along— which is just what happened. Those *soghwilis* won't have gone far. I can whistle 'em right back up."

Will reached over with his right hand and pulled his coat back over his left shoulder. His shirt was in tatters, and there was no point in worrying about salvaging it. "Give me a hand, partner," he said. "And while you're at it, I'll have my gun back, too."

Tom's bearded face split in a grin as he took Will's gun from behind his belt and put it back in the other man's holster. Sara watched, hands on hips, as Tom helped Will down from the table. Will grimaced in pain, but he didn't make a sound.

"You're insane, both of you," she said with a sigh, "but I suppose you're right. You can't stay here."

"Glad you understand, Doctor," Will said. His voice sounded a little stronger now. "The longer we're here, the more danger you folks are in. Come on, Tom."

Vincent sighed and nodded in acceptance of the decision. "Keep that wound clean," he advised. "Check the dressing every day and change it when you need to."

"Make sure you use clean cloth," Sara added. "That's the most important thing. That and rest."

Tom had one arm around Will again, supporting him as he had done when they arrived. With the other hand, he dug in his pocket. "I reckon we better pay you," he said.

Vincent waved off the offer. "That's not necessary. We don't need to take money from outlaws."

"Outlaws?" Tom repeated with a frown. "What—"

"Marshal Stoddard told us about the warrants he and his men have on you two," Sara said. "I don't know what you did—and I don't want to know."

"But, ma'am—" Tom began.

"Let it go, Tom." Will stopped him. "I want to be . . . long gone from here . . . before Stoddard comes back."

Tom nodded. "I reckon you're right. Come on."

The two of them moved slowly through the front room of the house. Sara went ahead of them and opened the door, holding it tightly against the wind that tried to jerk it out of her hands. Will and Tom moved through the door quickly and off to the side, and Sara realized their actions were those of men who habitually avoided being silhouetted by a light behind them.

They didn't want to be targets.

Will turned his head and called something that might have been *"Wado,"* but Sara couldn't tell for sure what he said. The wind caught his voice, shredded it, carried it away. For a moment she could still see them, a moving patch of shadow deeper than the darkness around them, but then they were gone, vanished into the night.

"Why didn't you want to turn them over to the marshals?" Vincent asked from behind her.

"I don't know," Sara replied honestly. "Somehow, I . . . I just don't think they were really bad men. But that man Stoddard—I wasn't so sure about him."

"I know what you mean. Something seemed wrong to me, too." Vincent sighed. "We're on the frontier now. I suppose such violence is common. Perhaps one grows accustomed to it."

Sara thought back to the war, to all the blood and death she had seen then, and she shook her head and said, "No. You never get used to it. Not if you're lucky . . ."

SEVENTEEN

Boston, 1873

After the first time, it was astoundingly easy. During the months following John's confrontation with Michael Ingersoll, he wondered why more people didn't resort to blackmail to get what they wanted—especially doctors.

As a physician, he was privy to all sorts of secrets besides Ingersoll's bastard child. He knew other wealthy men whom he had treated for conditions that a gentleman didn't pick up in polite, proper society. He heard business confidences from women who were distraught about their husbands' financial affairs. He knew a well-to-do widow who had never been legally married because she and the lover whose will had left her so rich were both actually men. He knew which daughters of wealthy families who had gone on the so-called Grand Tour of Europe had departed Boston because they were actually pregnant, one of them by her own brother.

In short, if there was a dirty little secret of any sort among the upper crust he moved in, John Black did his very best to ferret it out.

And the donations began to roll into St. Andrew's at

a greater rate than they ever had before. Michael Ingersoll had given the orphanage a permanent, unbreakable lease on the property it occupied, and the coffers of the establishment were full once more. All in all, good work for half a year's time, John thought more than once in his reflective moments.

Now, if the problem of what to do about Victoria Caine could be settled as easily . . .

She was thrilled at all the good fortune coming the way of the orphanage, and it would have been easy enough for John to tell her that he was responsible for it. At one time, that was exactly what he had planned to do. But although Victoria treated him in a friendly enough manner, there was a certain reserve about her, a wall that had not been there before. She seldom saw him when Nathan Faulkner wasn't around, and John had to wonder if that was by accident or design. It was as if she regretted that impulsive kiss in her office and was determined not to give such a thing the chance to happen again.

Very well, John decided, if that was the way she wanted it, that was the way things would be, at least for the moment. He would continue his clandestine good works on behalf of the orphanage, making sure not to put too large a bite on any one of his victims. His approaches were always couched in vague language as he suggested that it might be a good thing to make a donation to St. Andrew's, and some of the people probably never even realized that he was subtly blackmailing them. That was all right with John. Once the initial crisis had been averted, he could afford to work slowly and be patient.

He had time. He had all the time in the world.

But his patience was wearing thin. He wanted to

sweep Victoria into his arms, wanted to proclaim to her that he—*he alone*—was responsible for the orphanage's continued success.

Of course, he couldn't do that, and he knew it. Victoria was a morally upright young woman, or at least she tried to be. If he ever admitted his crimes to her, she would despise him.

No, he would have to win her over without telling her all the things he had done.

He tied his carriage in front of the building on a cool, damp spring day, and walked inside, his medical bag in hand. It had been a wet, dreary winter, but despite the continuing overcast and occasional drizzle, there were now breaks in the clouds at times, allowing the sun to shine through with a hint of the warmth to come.

John's footsteps echoed off the high ceiling of the lobby as he crossed it, nodding to the nuns he passed. One of them smiled at him and said, "Miss Caine is in her office, Dr. Black."

"Thank you, Sister."

John went to the door of the office and knocked lightly on it, then opened it without waiting for Victoria to tell him to come in. She looked up from her desk, a little frown of annoyance on her face.

"What is— Oh, it's you, John. Come in. I'm sorry I almost snapped at you." She smiled wearily.

"That's all right," he said. "Is there something troubling you?"

"No, not really. Everything seems to be running quite smoothly for a change. Our luck has really turned over the past few months, as we've discussed before."

John nodded, feeling a glow of satisfaction go

through him. No one except him knew the true extent of his contributions to this place, but that would have to be enough.

"I'm just a bit tired," Victoria continued. "Even when things are going well, there's still a great deal to do to keep them that way."

"Indeed," John murmured. "And I know what you need."

He set his medical bag on the desk, and without really thinking about the decision he had suddenly reached, he went behind her chair.

"What are you doing?" she asked, twisting her neck around so that she could look up and back at him.

"Turn around, sit back, and try to relax," he told her. "You push yourself too hard, my dear. The strain of your life is overwhelming you."

"Someone has to keep up with everything," she said, but she did as he told her and leaned back against the chair in which she sat.

"Close your eyes," John said quietly as he placed his hands on her shoulders.

Instead she jerked upright a little and looked around at him again. "Really, Dr. Black, I'm not sure this is proper—" she began.

"Of course it is. You said yourself that I'm a doctor. There's nothing improper about me touching you. I'm just trying to help you, Miss Caine."

And that was almost certainly a bald-faced lie, he thought. He had his hands on Victoria because he could no longer keep them off of her. Desire for her was welling up inside him, an irresistible tide. It was enough that his good deeds had to go unrecognized; no longer was he going to deny what he felt for her, too!

His fingers began to caress her shoulders, massaging and digging deeply into the tense flesh. Victoria gave a little cry, a sound of mingled surprise, pain, and pleasure, then closed her eyes, tilted her head back, and uttered a soft moan. She rolled her head around on her shoulders. "That . . . that feels so *good*," she said in a voice that was little more than a husky whisper.

"I know," John said, his own voice equally hushed. "I know."

Then he leaned over her as she turned her head, and her lips were right there, almost touching his. All he had to do was move forward slightly. He could feel the warmth of her breath on his mouth.

There was no turning back now. He kissed her.

Victoria responded eagerly, passionately, as if all the reserve she had demonstrated over the past months had never even existed. It had all been a sham, John knew now. She had denied her feelings for him, probably because she knew he was married. Her sympathy for Nathan probably had something to do with it, too. She had felt some genuine affection for Nathan, John was sure of that, and if he had never met Victoria, that affection might have grown into something deeper.

But he *had* met her, and everything had changed for both of them, and now there was no turning back. *He* was the one kissing Victoria, not Nathan Faulkner, and as far as he was concerned, that was the way it would be from now on.

His tongue slipped into Victoria's mouth and found her tongue. She stiffened a little, then her lips melted even more into his as she met his thrusts with darting jabs of her own, participating fully in the sensuous duel. Was this the first time she had ever experienced such a sensation?

They were so caught up in what they were doing, so

awash in the delicious ecstasy of it, that neither of them noticed the door opening again.

"My God!" Nathan exclaimed. He took an involuntary step backward as if he had been struck, his peg thumping heavily against the floor.

John jerked away from Victoria and straightened. She cried out, "Nathan!"

Nathan's mouth worked soundlessly for a few seconds before he got out, "John . . . what . . . what are you *doing*?"

"I think you know that, Nathan," John replied coolly, much more coolly than he really felt. "You're not a total innocent. I've seen evidence of that with my own eyes. Or have you forgotten about all those tavern doxies?"

"That . . . that's no tavern doxy you're kissing! That's Victoria!"

"I'm right here in the room, Nathan," she reminded him, a flash of anger warring with the shame in her quaking voice. "If you have anything to say, you can say it to me."

"How . . ." Nathan took several steps into the room and lifted a hand to point at John. "How could you do such a thing with *him*? John's a married man! He's married to my sister!"

"I know that," Victoria said. "And you have to believe me, Nathan, when I tell you that I never intended for this to happen."

"She's telling you the truth, Nathan," John said. "Neither one of us expected this."

That was right. It had been totally unexpected. But not unwanted, at least not on his part. He had dreamed for months about kissing Victoria again. But this was not the moment to reveal such a thing to Nathan.

"I can't believe it," Nathan said, shaking his head. "I just can't believe it. The woman I love . . . and my brother-in-law!"

John felt a sudden surge of impatience. "Let's not couch this in the terms of some melodramatic tragedy put on by a troupe of hack actors. Things like this happen, Nathan. You might as well accept them."

"No. I can't . . . I can't . . ."

With that, he turned and almost ran out of the room, moving as fast as he could on his crippled leg. Victoria shot up out of her chair and cried, "Nathan!" but he ignored her. She swung toward John and said, "Well? Go after him!"

John hesitated, then shook his head. "I don't think that would be a good idea. Nathan has to come to grips with this himself, and the sooner he does it, the better." After a moment, he added, "It won't be easy for him. He's been in love with you for a long time, I think, ever since you helped him stop drinking."

"And what about you?" she asked.

"Me? I've loved you since the first moment I saw you. You're the only woman I've ever really loved."

A simple declaration, he realized, but a true one. He had desired many women, he had even felt a certain level of affection for Judith that he had thought was love at the time, but now he knew better. Only one woman had ever filled all the empty spaces in his being, and that woman was Victoria Caine.

But she was shaking her head and backing away from him.

John took a step toward her. She put her hands up, palms toward him. "No!" she cried. "Stay back! This isn't right, John. You can't ever touch me again."

"Wait," he said miserably. "You can't mean that. I

kissed you, you kissed me . . . I know you feel the same way I do. I could tell. You love me, too, Victoria!"

"No! Yes! It doesn't matter!" She had her back against the wall and couldn't go any farther. He could step up to her, draw her into his arms, make her his forever. But something held him back, the sheer force of her will, perhaps. "It doesn't matter," she repeated, more quietly now. "You're married. There could never be anything real between us."

"I'll leave Judith." The words came out of his mouth, surprising him. He had never seriously thought about ending his marriage. That would take away everything he had fought so hard to win over the years.

But the only prize he really wanted anymore was standing in front of him, her lovely face twisted by doubt and fear and perhaps even a little loathing.

"I'm a Catholic. I could never marry you, John, even if you left your wife. *Especially* if you left your wife. You know that."

"But . . . but what *can* we do?"

She took a deep, ragged breath. "Go on about our lives. Tend to the work of this orphanage. Try to make Nathan understand. Perhaps one day he . . . he'll forgive both of us."

"No!" John practically roared the word. "If I can't have you . . . if you deny what we feel for each other . . . then I can't stay here, Victoria. I *won't* stay here." His hand shaking, he reached out and snagged the handle of his medical bag.

"But what about the children?"

"Damn the children!" Now he was shouting, but he couldn't help it. "The only reason I kept coming back here was because of you, not because of those little bastards! They can all rot, for all I care!"

John had no idea where the venom that spewed out of his mouth came from. None of it was true, not really. He *had* grown to care for the children. He wanted the best for them. He never would have gone to so much trouble over the past months simply for Victoria's sake. Deep down, he knew that. But he was gripped with an uncontrollable desire to hurt her at this moment, the way she had just hurt him by denying their love a chance to exist. As her face crumpled into tears under his words, he felt a fierce surge of satisfaction.

Followed by an even stronger wave of guilt.

Trembling all over, he took a step toward her, saying, "I . . . I didn't mean . . . I'm sorry, Victoria . . ."

"Just leave!" she cried without looking at him. "Please, John, just get out of here."

He stopped where he was and swallowed hard. Aware suddenly that he was being watched, he turned his head and saw several of the nuns clustered in the doorway of Victoria's office, drawn no doubt by the shouting and the way Nathan had left so hurriedly. He felt a sharp pang of regret, knowing that the sisters must have overheard enough to realize how he felt about Victoria. He could rely on them not to gossip, but had the revelation damaged Victoria in their eyes? He hoped not; he had done enough harm without that.

"All right," he said hoarsely. "I'm going. But if you change your mind, Victoria . . ."

The wordless stare she gave him as tears rolled down her cheeks told him just how unlikely—how impossible—it was that such a thing would ever happen.

Without saying anything else, he turned and walked

out, past the nuns, who drew back hurriedly to give him room. He didn't look behind him as he left the orphanage. The gray clouds in the sky had closed ranks again, shutting off any hope of the sun shining again soon. John paused by his buggy and looked up, and felt the first drops of a fresh wave of cold rain strike his face.

The sky was cold and gray, he thought, but no colder and grayer than what was left of his soul.

"John!" Roberta Ingersoll exclaimed as he pushed past her into the foyer of her house. "What are you doing here?"

"It's Wednesday afternoon, Roberta," he said grimly. "I've visited you here before, remember? The servants all have the afternoon off, of course, and Michael is at his offices, as always." He put his hat and medical bag on a small side table, then reached out and grasped her arms to jerk her against him. She gasped in surprise. John demanded, "Don't tell me you've forgotten what we used to do on Wednesday afternoons!"

Then he crushed his mouth down on hers.

It had been several months since he had come to her house like this. He had begun visiting the orphanage on Wednesday afternoons, using that as an excuse to Roberta, telling her that was the time the administrator of the place preferred he make his examination of the children. Actually, of course, he had been looking for a way to wean himself away from Roberta, who had grown more and more demanding since the beginning of their affair. But today, after leaving the orphanage in a state of shock and anger and despair, he had remembered what day it was and known that she would be here alone in the big house. And right now, he needed someone, needed a release from all the emotions swirling around inside his head. He needed to forget, to lose himself in the feel of soft, warm, creamy flesh . . .

She *was* alone, wasn't she?

What if he had miscalculated?

He pulled his lips away from hers and asked anxiously, "My God, Michael's not here, is he?"

"No," Roberta said, sounding a little breathless. "Michael's not here, and neither are the servants. Your memory has served you well, John." Her arms were around his neck, and her fingers snaked through the hair on the back of his head. She hissed, "And it's about time, damn it!"

She pulled his mouth back down to hers.

There was a desperate urgency, a savage need, to the kiss. Neither of them wanted to take the time to go upstairs to her bed chamber. The parlor was nearby, and they moved toward it awkwardly, their lips still melded together. John put his hand on her left breast, cupping it through her expensive dress, kneading the mound of soft flesh almost brutally. Her fingers pawed at him. She moaned, deep in her throat.

Somehow, they wound up on the long, heavily upholstered divan. Clothes were strewn around the parlor, some of them lying on the thick rug, others draped where they had been tossed over expensive, elegant furniture. Neither of them was completely nude. Roberta still wore her shift, although it was bunched up around her waist and pulled down so that her breasts were bared. John had his shirt and socks on, and he supposed he looked rather ludicrous. At the moment, he didn't give a damn about that.

He loomed over her as she lay back. His head

swooped from one breast to the other as he took each nipple into his mouth in turn. He sucked hard on the brown, pebbled nubs, running his tongue around them while Roberta held onto his head and panted heavily. That was all the preliminaries either of them wanted or needed. John lifted himself above her and she clutched him tightly, guiding him into her. He gave a fierce grunt of satisfaction as he entered her.

The pace was harsh, demanding. They matched each other thrust for thrust, want for want. It was all strangely impersonal, John realized dimly in the back of his mind. He was awash with sensation, but he knew he didn't really give a damn about Roberta—any more than she really gave a damn about him. They needed each other, but all they were interested in was their own satisfaction.

That was the way it had always been between them, he recognized now. Just a slaking of a physical need. It wasn't an expression of love . . .

As it would have been with Victoria.

He pushed any thoughts of her out of his head ruthlessly. There was no room in there for her. All he wanted to think about now was the moment: the heat, the flesh, the soft scream that came from Roberta's mouth as he drove into her again and again and finally emptied himself in long, shuddering spasms. Perhaps it *was* just pure and simple rutting, like a pair of animals. It was what he needed right now.

And as always, what he needed, he took.

He groaned and rolled off of her, sated, then sat up at the end of the divan. His chest heaved as he drew in great drafts of air. Roberta was breathing heavily, too, as she lay back, hair in a wild tangle around her face, her thighs still splayed open. She said, "My God . . . my God . . ." over and over.

John's head dropped into his hands. He trembled. It hadn't done any good, he realized. *It hadn't done any good!* He still saw Victoria's face, sad and hurt and beautiful. She filled his thoughts, overwhelmed the fleeting sensations of lust. The spear of loss that spiked into him was as painful as ever.

"John . . . ?" Roberta said in a near-whisper.

He lowered his hands away from his face and turned his head to look at her. Her eyes widened, and he could only imagine what she saw in his features. Utter despair, he supposed. The look of a man who had thought himself to be alive, only to discover that he was really dead all along.

"John . . . I'm sorry . . ."

The front door of the house slammed open.

John's head jerked around in that direction, and moving more out of instinct than anything else, he grabbed for his clothes and started trying to yank them on. It was too late, much too late. He fell back against the divan and looked up into the face of his wife.

Judith's features were a hard, expressionless mask as she stalked into the parlor. Roberta screamed and lunged toward her discarded gown, trying to cover herself with it. Judith paid no attention to her. All of her attention was focused on John.

"I wanted to believe it wasn't true," Judith said, her voice cold and empty. "Even though I knew it was, I didn't want to believe it. How could you . . . how could you do this to me, John?" For an instant, the facade she had thrown up over her emotions cracked, and John caught a glimpse of the pain inside her.

"I'm sorry," he said, quietly, uselessly. He knew it

wouldn't do any good, but he said it again anyway. "I'm sorry, Judith."

Roberta scrambled up off the sofa and ran from the room, leaving the two of them to look at each other.

John scrubbed a shaking hand across his face, then asked, "How long have you known?"

"Oh . . . a long time. I suspected, and then I knew. I had you followed. I had your office watched. You weren't nearly as . . . discreet . . . as you must have thought you were."

"I . . . I don't understand . . ."

"You don't have to," Judith said sharply. "But for what it's worth to you, you never paid enough attention to the woman you really should have paid attention to, John. She was more than happy to tell me what you were up to, although I suspect she never would have betrayed you if you had only given her some of what you were giving all those other women."

"Miss McLowry?" John breathed in amazement.

"Miss McLowry," Judith said. "She told me about the Ingersoll woman, and after that it was easy enough to find out about all the others." She smiled faintly. "There are some very good detective agencies for hire in this city. You didn't present much of a challenge to the one I settled on."

Even though his entire world seemed to have crumbled around him today, John still had his wits about him enough to ask, "Why now? Why did you choose to confront me today, of all days?"

"It seemed fitting after Nathan came to me and told me about what he saw at that orphanage. I'm a little surprised at you, John. A slut like Roberta Ingersoll I can almost understand. But an innocent young Catholic girl like that Miss Caine?" Judith's voice shook a little as she went on, "You must have really enjoyed corrupting her, turning her into a tramp like Roberta."

Anger shot through John, enabling him to shake off the air of defeat and despair that had enveloped him. He stood up, buttoning his trousers as he did so. "You can't speak like that about Victoria," he said sharply. "She's not to blame for any of this. There was never anything between us. Nothing, I swear."

For a moment, Judith looked up at him intently, then she said, "You know, I believe you. About Miss Caine, anyway. But nothing else, and I'll never believe you again, John. It's over between us."

"It doesn't have to be," he said, urgency and desperation gripping him now. "I haven't seen any of those other women in months. You must know that if you've had me followed. And Roberta . . ." He waved a hand to show how insignificant she was to him. "She doesn't mean anything. She never did. I'll never see her again, Judith, you have my word—"

"Shut up!" she cried, the mask slipping again. "I don't want to hear that! I don't want to hear a lot of empty promises that don't mean any more than what you said to me on our wedding day. The vows you took then—they were lies, all lies! I hate you! I hate you!"

She started to throw herself at him, her hands balled into fists, and John began to lift his arms to ward off her attack. But she stopped herself and stepped back, trembling.

"I don't want to touch you again, even to strike you," she said. "It would be all right with me if I never saw you again. But I will. I'll see you in court, when I finish the job of destroying you. Good-bye, John." She turned toward the door.

"Wait!" he cried. "Where . . . where are you going?"

"Far away from you," she said contemptuously. "You can go home if you want, John. The children and I won't be there."

"You're going back to your father's house," he accused.

"It doesn't matter to you any longer where I go. But I'd stay away from my father if I were you. He might not wait for the lawyers to settle everything. He might just shoot you down like the dog you are."

"I . . . I saved your brother's life during the war," he said.

"Oh, God," Judith whispered, staring at him. "Don't play that card, John. Don't ever even think about it again."

He stood there, shoulders slumped, as she walked into the foyer.

She made it all the way to the front door before she paused and looked back through the arched entrance to the parlor at him. "By the way," she said, "it's possible you'll want to think about getting out of here. I sent a message to Michael Ingersoll's office telling him that he might want to come home and see what his wife was doing, and he should be here any minute."

John stared at her in horror, unable to speak as she opened the door and swept out of the house. Michael Ingersoll was a hard, brutal, ruthless man. He could probably kill someone with his bare hands if he wanted to badly enough.

With a jerk, John came out of his reverie and lunged for the rest of his clothes.

He was pulling his coat on hurriedly as he went

through the foyer. Roberta, fully dressed again, came running out of the hall that led toward the rear of the house and clutched at his sleeve. "John, wait!" she cried. "Where are you going?"

"Away from here," he said curtly.

"I . . . I heard what your wife said. You can't leave me here to face Michael alone! What will I tell him? You know what kind of man he is!"

"That's why I'm getting out of here," he snapped. "Judith didn't say she told him about us. She was deliberately cryptic in the message she sent. So I'd suggest that when your husband gets here, you do the same thing you've been doing all along."

"What . . . what do you mean?"

"Lie your sweet little behind off, darling," he said.

Then he jerked away from her, slapped the door open, and got out of there as fast as he could.

EIGHTEEN

Cherokee Nation, 1873

It was several months before Sara saw Will Sixkiller again, and when she did, it was on the streets of Tahlequah. She and Vincent had come in to pick up some supplies, and they were on the porch in front of the general store, watching while sacks of flour and salt were loaded into the back of their wagon, when some commotion broke out down the street. Sara glanced curiously in that direction and saw a group of men on horseback moving along the street, heading toward the capitol building. Small children and dogs ran alongside the horses, the children shouting, the dogs barking, all of them sounding excited. Men walking along the street called out to the riders. Sara frowned a little and said to Vincent, "I wonder what's going on."

Instead of her husband, one of the white-aproned clerks on the porch answered her. "I heard a couple of deputies were bringing in some *yoneg* bootleggers this morning. I suppose that's them now."

Vincent nodded, knowing that liquor—*wisgi,* as the Cherokee called it—was illegal to possess or sell in Indian Territory. Sara was watching the group of riders as they approached, and she stiffened abruptly as she recognized two of them. Will Sixkiller, looking fully recovered from his wound, and his big ugly friend Tom were riding in the rear of the group. For an instant, Sara thought that they must be part of the bootlegging gang that had been captured.

Then she realized that couldn't be. The clerk had referred to the bootleggers as white men. Besides, both Will and Tom were armed, and that wouldn't have been the case if they were prisoners. In fact, both of them were carrying rifles pointed in the general direction of the half dozen men riding in front of them, as if Will and Tom were the captors, not the captives. But that would make them—

Deputies, the talkative clerk had said. A couple of deputies were bringing in some captured bootleggers.

They weren't outlaws at all, Sara realized with a shock. Will and Tom were lawmen.

"I say!" Vincent exclaimed as the group of horsemen came nearer. "Isn't that—"

"Yes, it is," Sara said. "It seems as if we misjudged them, Vincent."

The clerk looked over at them. "You know some of those fellas?"

"The two in the back," Vincent said.

"Oh," the clerk said, visibly relaxing. "You mean Deputy Sixkiller and Deputy Whitson. Thought for a second you were talking about those bootleggers. They're some of the Stoddard gang, from what I hear. Sixkiller and Whitson have been trying to break them up for nigh onto a year now."

"Stoddard, you said?" Vincent asked, glancing over at Sara.

The talkative clerk nodded. "Yeah, Lew Stoddard's

the leader of the bunch. He's a mean one. They call him *Tseg'sgin* sometimes."

"Devil," Sara said quietly, her eyes still on Will and Tom.

"Yes, ma'am. And I reckon ol' Stoddard lives up to the name."

The riders were abreast of the store now. Will Sixkiller glanced over at them and smiled suddenly as he saw Sara and Vincent. He spoke in a low voice to Tom, who looked over as well and gave them a polite nod. The group moved on, but not before Sara thought she recognized some of the prisoners as men who had been with Lew Stoddard that night in front of their house some months earlier. Men she had taken to be federal marshals, it now appeared were actually vicious criminals instead. That was one of the troubles with this frontier land, Sara thought. It was sometimes hard to tell the truth of something just by looking at it.

The clerks finished loading the supplies, and Vincent went inside the store to settle up with the owner. Sara climbed onto the seat of the wagon and watched the men dismount in front of the capitol building up the street. She knew that the sheriff of this district had his office in the capitol and that the lockup was there, too. That was obviously where the prisoners were headed. Will and Tom herded them inside at riflepoint.

She wanted to speak to Will, find out how his wound had healed, but Vincent emerged from the store and was ready to go. If he was curious about Will, evidently he wasn't enough so to prompt him to delay. He took up the reins and got the team of horses moving.

Sara looked back once as the wagon rolled out of Tahlequah, but of course there was nothing to see.

* * *

A couple of weeks passed, and during that time Sara found herself thinking quite often about Will Sixkiller. Even at their first meeting, there had been something about him that made her nervous, an edgy quality of suppressed violence that led her to believe he was an outlaw. His friend Tom had seemed even more dangerous. Now she understood that feeling a lot better. Men like Will and Tom *had* to be on the alert all the time, had to be ready for trouble. But instead of breaking the law, as Sara had supposed, they were upholding it. She felt guilty now for jumping to conclusions about them.

She would have liked a chance to explain that to Will, to apologize for the things she had thought about him. He and Tom must have thought she and Vincent had lost their minds when they started talking about Marshal Stoddard. She could clear up all the misunderstanding, Sara knew, if she just had the opportunity to talk to Will again.

That was on her mind as she walked, a bucket in each hand, toward the small creek that ran about fifty yards behind the house. It was a beautiful spring morning, and Sara was on her way to fetch water back to the house, as she did every morning about this time. There was a well-trod path leading from the house to the creek.

The path cut through a gap in the cottonwoods and bushes that lined the banks of the stream, and as Sara stepped through the opening, she froze in her tracks in surprise. A man on a big horse was beside the creek, sitting calmly in his saddle while the horse dipped its muzzle into the water and drank.

He was Will Sixkiller.

He smiled at her and lifted a finger to the brim of his hat. "*Siyo,* Dr. Rawlings. Good to see you again."

Sara took a deep breath, willing her racing heartbeat to slow down. It was pounding so hard, she told herself, only because his presence here had surprised her. She gave him a curt nod and said, "Good morning, Mr. Sixkiller. You look well."

"Thanks to you, I reckon I am." Will's smile widened into a grin. "You did a good job digging that slug out of me. Tom told me all about it. I'm afraid I don't remember much about that night."

"I'm not surprised. You were badly injured." She made her legs work again and stepped down to the bank of the creek. The horse lifted its nose and skittishly moved back a little. Will clucked to it, calming it.

"Yep, Tom told me all about it," Will went on. "Even the part about how Marshal Stoddard came there looking for us."

Sara felt herself flushing as she knelt by the stream. Sunlight reflected off the water, striking the places where the dappled shadows of the cottonwoods didn't fall. She said, "You don't have to make fun of me. I know now that I was wrong about you and your friend. You're both lawmen, and Stoddard is a bootlegger and an outlaw."

"That's right. But you helped us anyway, even when you thought we were owlhoots. Why is that, Doctor?"

She didn't look up at him, didn't trust herself to study whatever expression was on his face. "I had just patched up that bullet hole in your shoulder," she said. "I didn't want to see you taken back to Fort Smith and hanged."

"So it was pity, then."

"I didn't say that." Something compelled her to be

honest with him. "I just didn't think you were a bad man, and for some reason, I didn't trust Stoddard."

Will grunted. "Glad you decided to put some faith in your instincts. Stoddard would've killed Tom and me if he'd known we were there. It was him or one of his men who put that bullet in me earlier that night, when we tried to stop one of his whiskey convoys. But Tom and me are paid by the Cherokee Nation to take those risks. You and your husband aren't."

"Are you saying Stoddard would have hurt us, too?" She had to look at him now.

Will nodded grimly and said, "I'm sure he would have gunned down the two of you when he was done with us. Lew Stoddard doesn't like to leave any witnesses behind. He's killed plenty; two more wouldn't have mattered. That's why they call him Devil."

A shudder ran through Sara. The water buckets, filled now, sat at her feet, forgotten. "When we saw you in Tahlequah, you had captured some of his men . . ."

"We raided one of his camps. Got lucky and took the men there by surprise, so we got the drop on them and didn't have to kill any of them. Stoddard wasn't there, though, worse luck. But if he had been, there would've been shooting. He's not the kind to let himself be taken alive."

"But you're still looking for him anyway."

"It's our job," Will said with a little shrug. "It's illegal to sell *wisgi* here in the Territory, and Stoddard brews and sells a bunch of it. When we raid his stills and bust them up, he just brings the stuff in from Arkansas until he can set up more stills. He's making a lot of money, and he doesn't want to give that up."

"Those men of his you captured . . . what happened to them?"

"The sheriff held them in Tahlequah until some U.S. marshals—some *real* U.S. marshals—could come over from Fort Smith and pick them up. The federal boys have jurisdiction over white criminals, even when they're breaking the law in Indian Territory. Most of 'em will wind up behind bars over there, but some will end up on the gallows, the ones who were wanted for murder or other crimes."

"I didn't realize when Vincent and I came out here that this was such a . . . a lawless place to live! Nothing has been as I thought it would be."

Will rested his hands on his saddlehorn and leaned forward. He looked at her intently and said, "I guess you could always go back east where you came from."

Sara took a deep breath and shook her head. "No. No, that's not what I want. I came out here to help people, and I think I have, even though I didn't really know what it would be like."

"You've helped people, all right," Will said quietly. "I might be dead now if it wasn't for you. And I've heard folks talk about all the other people you've helped, all the good you've done. There are plenty of us who are glad you decided to come out here, Dr. Rawlings . . . Sara."

She felt a surprisingly strong tingle of pleasure go through her at the sound of her name on his lips. She wasn't sure how to respond to what he had said—wasn't sure, in fact, of the emotions suddenly coursing through her—so she said nothing.

"I've been keeping an eye on your place whenever I can," he went on after a moment. "That's how I knew you come down here to the creek every morning. Stoddard's still around these parts, and if he ever figures out that you and your husband helped me that night, he's liable to pay you a visit. He doesn't like being lied to."

"You mean we're in danger?"

"Probably not, but it never hurts to be careful. You have some guns?"

"A rifle and a shotgun," she told him.

"Keep 'em loaded, and keep 'em handy," Will said. "Can you handle a gun if you have to?"

Her mind went back to the days when Carver had taught her how to shoot, during those all too rare periods of calm between raids. She nodded and said, "I can shoot."

"Well, let's hope you never have to." He paused, then went on, "You're a healer, Sara, not a destroyer. You build things up instead of tearing them down. I'd like for you to be able to stay that way."

Abruptly, he wheeled his horse and started it in a trot along the creek bank, before she could say anything. Turning in the saddle, he lifted a hand in farewell and called back to her, "I'll be seeing you."

She raised her hand but didn't call after him. As she stood and watched, he rounded a bend in the creek and was lost in the thick shadows of the overhanging tree branches. Then and only then did Sara take a deep breath and reach down for the water buckets.

He had been watching out for them, he had said. There was some danger, however slight, from Lew Stoddard. Knowing that made a shiver of fear go through her. But there was more than that to what she was feeling, she knew. If Will had been keeping an eye on the place, that meant he would be back. She found herself liking that idea very much.

Too much, she told herself.

Spring moved relentlessly toward summer, and Sara thought it was the most beautiful season she had ever seen. After the cold, dreary winter, the sunny days with their warm south breezes were like the beginning of a whole new life. Wildflowers spread a lovely carpet over the hills, the grass turned a lush green once again, and the trees were thickly covered with leaves. It wasn't just the beauty of nature that made Sara so happy, however.

Will Sixkiller came to see her nearly every week.

She never knew for sure when he would be there, standing beside the creek and letting his horse drink. His duties as a lawman made it impossible for him to stick to any sort of regular schedule. But he came when he could, and Sara's heart leaped every time she stepped through the gap in the brush and saw him there. There was a grassy verge along the creek bank, and they would sit there and talk, Will telling her about the old Cherokee legends, Sara answering his questions about life back east. There was never enough time, because Vincent would begin to get suspicious if it took her too long to fetch water, but the conversations, short though they might be, came to mean a great deal to Sara. She might have gone so far as to say that her life now revolved around the meetings with Will.

She was no fool. She knew what was happening. And Will did, too, unless he was totally blind. Unfortunately, nothing was ever quite that simple, Sara knew. In life, there were always . . . other considerations.

Such as her husband.

Vincent had not weathered the winter very well. His cough had grown worse during the cold, wet months. Sara nursed him along as best she could, of course, tending to him as she would have one of her Cherokee patients. But it was certain now that he would never fully recover. His lungs were in bad shape, and sometimes he coughed up blood. She had hoped that his condition would improve when the warmer weather set in, but so far it hadn't. A change in climate might help, Sara reflected, recalling some of the articles she had read in the medical journals she had sent to her every so often on the stagecoach into Tahlequah. But that would mean leaving Indian Territory and probably heading farther west.

She wasn't sure she could bring herself to do that. In her most ungenerous moments, moments that shamed her greatly when she thought about them later, she told herself that if Vincent would just go ahead and die—

She always banished those thoughts as soon as they sprang into her head. But they were becoming more and more persistent . . .

In May, she received a letter from her brother John, surprising her because it was the first time she had heard from him in months. The news was unhappy, however: Judith had left him, taking the children with her, and the courts had granted her a divorce. John didn't go into detail about the reasons behind the breakup, but Sara knew her brother well enough to make an educated guess. Other women must have played some part in it. John's medical practice was floundering, no doubt due to having his former wife's influential family turn against him, and he hinted in his letter that he might have to close his practice in Boston and return to Handley's Mill.

That might not be such a bad thing, Sara decided. Her father and mother were well along in years now, and Thomas's health had been declining for quite some time. It would be good for them to have their son back close to home.

Sara had already come to the conclusion that she would never return to Handley's Mill, or Pittsfield, or Boston. She had never been happy in the east, and although she couldn't pinpoint the reason for that dissatisfaction, it was undeniable.

The frontier, with all its drawbacks, was her home now.

The morning after the letter from John arrived, Will was there when Sara went to the creek for water. He greeted her as pleasantly as ever, then frowned slightly and said, "What's wrong, Sara? You look like something's bothering you."

"I had a letter from my brother," she said, surprising herself. She had intended to keep the story of John's troubles to herself, but instead she found it pouring out of her. Will nodded solemnly as she spoke, and Sara concluded, "I just feel sorry for John. He's looked so hard for happiness in his life, and he just can't seem to find it."

"Maybe that's the problem. He's looking too hard."

Sara shook her head. "I don't understand."

"Life is what happens to you, Sara." Will pointed up into one of the cottonwoods. "Look there. That *saloli* doesn't go looking for happiness."

She saw a squirrel bounding along one of the limbs, high in the tree, and knew that was what Will was talking about. "He's just a squirrel," she said. "It's not the same thing at all."

"Watch him, though. Look at the way he leaps from

branch to branch. Watch the way his tail whips around while he eats that nut he found. Don't you think he looks happy?"

"It's all instinct," Sara said. "He's a dumb animal."

The chittering of the squirrel drifted down to them.

"Maybe not so dumb," Will said. "When he finishes eating, he's going to go running off through the trees until he finds a lady squirrel. Or a bobcat'll get him, or an owl. Until what happens, happens, the *saloli* doesn't care either way, and he doesn't waste a second worrying about it. He just lives his life."

"I still say it's different. Human beings have to worry. We have to strive. Otherwise nothing ever gets done, and . . . and when we die, there are no accomplishments for us to look back on."

"You're dead either way," Will pointed out.

She sighed in frustration. Perhaps there was something to his argument, but he wasn't completely right. If he was, then there would never be any point in anything except living for the moment, like that squirrel. Which had now vanished, she saw as she glanced up into the towering cottonwood again. With a twitch of his tail, he had bounded off and disappeared.

"I have to get back," Sara said. She started to bend over to dip the buckets in the creek.

"Let me do that for you," Will said hurriedly. He reached out, intending to grasp the handle of one of the buckets, but his fingers closed over Sara's hand instead. She froze, feeling the warmth of his strong fingers against her skin.

Well, maybe that squirrel *did* have the right idea, she found herself thinking.

She dropped the water bucket and turned her head to look into Will's dark eyes, only inches from hers.

She was never quite sure how she found herself in his arms, his mouth pressed hungrily to hers. It was what she wanted, what she had wanted for so long a time, but she had sworn to herself that she would never take that step. She had been faithful to Vincent, even though he touched her in a loving way only occasionally. The vows she had taken meant something to her.

But not as much as the waves of passion cascading through her as she kissed Will Sixkiller and felt his embrace tightening, molding her body to the lean lines of his. This was wrong, completely wrong, but she couldn't stop herself. She gave herself over to the moment as totally as that squirrel did as he leaped from branch to branch a hundred feet above the ground, never experiencing a second's doubt or fear that he would fall. Sara knew she wouldn't fall, either.

Will was there to catch her.

She had forgotten what it was like, but the feelings all came rushing back to her, and as she lay there half an hour later on the blanket Will had taken from his saddlebags and spread on the ground, she swore that she would never again cut herself off from experiencing life. For too long, she had dedicated her existence to medicine . . .

Never realizing that the one most in need of healing was herself.

She turned to him, and no longer was there anything particularly sensuous in the feeling of skin against skin. But it was human, so very human, and as he held her she began to cry, great sobs that wracked her body, and the tears were for herself and Carver Gresham and her parents and her brother John and even for Vincent . . . for everyone who had lost love—or never found it . . .

Her reaction took Will by surprise, and he said hurriedly, "I'm sorry, Sara. It's all my fault . . . I never should have—"

"No!" she cried through her sobs. "Don't be sorry! Don't ever be sorry! Just hold me, Will. Hold me! . . ."

So he did, until they both heard the sudden crackling in the brush along the creek bank.

Will's head jerked up at the sound. His hand darted instinctively toward the butt of the holstered revolver that lay on the ground only a couple of feet away, the shell belt coiled around the holster.

Sara's instincts made her move, too, away from Will. *Vincent!* Her husband's name thundered inside her head. Vincent must have grown concerned about the time it was taking her to bring water from the creek, and he had come looking for her. In a moment, he would find her naked, practically in the arms of Will Sixkiller. She had no idea how he would react to such a sight, but she was sure it wouldn't be pleasant.

Only it wasn't Vincent who appeared, pushing through the brush with a crackling of branches. As Will sat up and Sara snatched up his coat to wrap it around her nudity, a figure on horseback appeared. There was a drop-off of a few feet from the surrounding landscape to the actual bank of the creek, and as the rider paused there at the edge, the higher ground made him look even more looming and ominous from where Sara was. Then, suddenly, she recognized him, and her fear went away to be replaced by a flood of shame.

Tom Whitson sat there in his saddle, a grim look on his craggy, bearded face.

Will had grabbed up his pants and flung them over his lap. He glared up at his partner and said, "Damn it, Tom—"

The other deputy broke into Will's angry protest to say in a hoarse voice, "Sorry, Will. I . . . I never would've bothered you if . . . if . . . Stoddard . . ."

Something was wrong, Sara realized. Tom's voice was weak and erratic, and she could see now how pale his face was under the beard. Abruptly, he swayed in the saddle and clutched at the horn, trying to steady himself. His fingers slipped off the smooth leather, though, and he fell.

"Tom!" Will cried as he lunged to his feet, his nudity forgotten now, the revolver held tightly in his hand.

Tom tumbled down the short slope and came to rest practically at Will's feet. He was either passed out—or dead. Sara scrambled up, her hands going to her mouth in horror as she saw all the blood on Tom's clothes.

"Stoddard," Will Sixkiller said, and although his voice was quiet, it was also cold.

As cold as the grave, Sara thought.

Then she knelt beside the wounded man to see if there was anything she could do to help him, and there was no more time for thoughts of Stoddard, no time for anything except doing all she could to save Tom Whitson's life.

NINETEEN

The Cherokee word for blood was *gi-ga,* and Sara saw plenty of it that morning. Tom had bullet wounds in his left arm, his left side, and his right leg. Sara wasn't sure how any man who had lost that much blood could still be alive, let alone how he could have escaped from the gang of bootleggers that had ambushed him and then ridden all the way to the creek to find Will. Tom had known, of course, that that was where his partner would be.

Sara had slowed down the bleeding as best she could by tearing strips from her dress and binding them around the wounds, then she and Will had hurriedly thrown their clothes on, lifted Tom into his bloody saddle, and taken him back to the house. Vincent had dozed off in a chair, which explained why he had never noticed that Sara had been gone so long, but when they carried Tom in, he woke up and pitched in to help as much as possible.

Will raged around the room until Sara told him in a sharp voice to get out. Tending to the injured was *her* job, not his, and if he couldn't shut up, he could damn well get out and let her get on about it. After that, he settled down, as Sara had hoped he would, because she didn't really want him to go.

By that night, once all of Tom's wounds had been cleaned and bandaged, and she saw that he was still alive, Sara began to hope that he would survive after all. He was conscious again by late the next morning, and able to tell them about the trap Stoddard's men had laid for him. He had gotten a tip, no doubt planted by Stoddard, about a new still the bootlegger had set up. He had gone to scout out the location, intending to return later with Will.

"Only they were waitin' for me," Tom explained as he lay propped up in the spare bedroom, pillows behind him, his torso crisscrossed with bandages. "I had to go through a little gully to get to the place, and they were on both sides. They opened up on me 'fore I could get through."

Will stood at the foot of the bed, a cup of coffee in his hand. "You're lucky you made it out of there alive."

"I didn't figure to," admitted Tom. "I got my gun out and started blazin' back at 'em while I kicked the tar out of that *soghwili* of mine. Not sure what happened after that. I just pointed that hoss's nose toward the doctor's place. After that, I don't remember a thing."

Sara wasn't sure if he was telling the truth or just trying to spare her feelings. His phrasing made it sound as if he had come here looking for medical help, instead of searching for his partner. And that was a feasible enough explanation, she thought. But it also served the purpose of not giving anything away to Vincent about what was going on between her and Will.

Vincent was sitting on one side of the bed while Sara stood on the other. He reached out and patted Tom on the shoulder. "You just rest now, friend. That's what you need more than anything."

"That's what I intend to do, Doc," Tom replied. "At least, I will in a minute. First I got to find out what that partner of mine intends to do."

"What do you think I'm going to do?" Will asked. "I'm going to find Lew Stoddard and kill the man."

"Now, that ain't what I wanted to hear. Goin' after Stoddard's a two-man job, at the very least. If you go lookin' for him, you'll just get yourself killed, Will."

"Tom's right," Sara said quietly. "Please listen to him."

Will looked at her, his eyes hooded, his expression unreadable. Sara met his gaze squarely. Things were different between them now. After what had happened the day before, they would never be the same. Whether that was good or bad, it was too soon to tell, but Sara knew she had a greater stake in Will's well-being now than ever before.

"I won't make any promises except to be careful," Will finally said. "And to come back here to see how you're doing, partner."

With that, he drained the last of the coffee, turned toward the door, and walked out.

Sara wanted to go after him and plead with him not to do this. She couldn't make her muscles work, though. She couldn't run after him like that in front of Vincent.

But if he tried to track down Lew Stoddard's gang by himself, it might cost him his life . . .

Sara's indecision cost her the chance to go after

him. Vincent stood up and said, "I'll see Deputy Sixkiller off." He left the room.

Sara stood there and looked down at Tom, wondering if her expression was as bleak as she felt. After a moment he said, "Don't worry 'bout Will, Doctor. He can take care of himself. There's nobody better at that."

"I hope you're right, Tom." She forced herself to smile. "My father's name is Thomas. I don't believe I ever told you that, did I?"

"No, ma'am, you didn't. Your father, is he a doctor, too?"

"Yes, he is. He's always followed what he calls the healer's road."

"Then I reckon it's natural you do, too," Tom said.

She nodded. She had followed the healer's road over all sorts of obstacles, but she had always been confident that sooner or later it would lead her into a land full of light.

Now it seemed to be leading her into a land cloaked with shadows and uncertainty . . .

For the next two weeks, as Tom Whitson recuperated from his wounds at the Rawlings house, Sara lived in fear. Not fear for herself, but for Will Sixkiller, who, local gossip said, was ranging far and wide across the Cherokee Nation in search of Lew Stoddard. Will's authority as a deputy extended only to a single district, but he wasn't letting that stop him. The stories Sara heard in Tahlequah had him traveling as far north as Nowata and as far south as Sallisaw. His crusade was the talk of the capital city. Principal Chief Lewis Downing, who had been so helpful to Sara and Vincent when they were getting established here in Indian Territory, had died unexpectedly the previous winter after a bout of pneumonia, and the new chief, William Ross, had spoken to the district sheriff about reining Will in. All that had brought from Will was a threat to quit his deputy's job and go after Stoddard as a private citizen of the Nation. The sheriff didn't want that, so he had been trying to soothe the ruffled feathers of Chief Ross and the lawmen from the other districts who complained about Will encroaching on their stomping grounds.

Will wasn't having much luck finding the head of the bootlegging gang, but that didn't mean his quest had been entirely unsuccessful. Sara had heard about the stills he had located and broken up, the shipments of liquor he had disrupted, the whiskey runners he had captured—or killed, when he had no other choice. Each time she heard about one of the gun battles, the icy feeling along Sara's spine grew a little colder.

Will never spoke of such things when he came to visit Tom, however. Instead he grinned and tried to make a joke out of the whole thing, but Sara knew there was no laughter in his eyes. She could see that for herself.

With the benefit of plenty of rest and good food, Tom's iron constitution soon asserted itself, and he quickly grew stronger. Within two weeks, he was getting around the place with the aid of a cane. Sara thought he would soon be walking normally again. Luck had played a part in his survival and recovery, of course, but Sara liked to think that good doctoring had had something to do with it, too.

Tom was sitting in the rocking chair in the front room of the house one evening, reading the parts of the *Cherokee Advocate* that were printed in the Cherokee language. Vincent was dozing in another chair, as he spent more and more time doing these days. The coughing fits that came on him from time to time drained his strength so that he was able to do little else. Sara was seated at the table, going through a packet of medical journals that had come into Tahlequah on the stage the day before.

She looked up from an article concerning the relationship between microorganisms and human disease, in particular what the writer referred to as the anthrax bacillus, and was about to ask Vincent his opinion about it when the sound of a horse outside drifted through the open window. Vincent appeared not to notice, but Tom was instantly more alert and exchanged a glance with Sara. Both of his revolvers were tucked behind his belt, and a loaded Winchester was leaning against the wall near the door. A moment later, a knock sounded on that door.

"Better let me answer it," Tom grunted. He got to his feet, using his left arm awkwardly to balance him with the cane while his right was wrapped around the butt of one of the pistols. "Who is it?" he called.

"Just me, *unaligohi*," came back the reply. It was Will's voice, and Sara and Tom both relaxed. So did Vincent, who had started awake at the sound of the knock.

Sara got up and opened the door, then gasped and stepped back suddenly. Will came into the room, grinning, and said, "I didn't think it looked *that* bad."

There was a bullet burn on his left cheek, an ugly red furrow that showed how close the slug had come to boring through his face and into his brain. The wound seemed to be several days old. Sara stepped toward him and lifted a hand as if to touch the injury, then stopped the motion.

"What happened to you?" she demanded.

Will shrugged. "The same thing. Another run-in with some of Stoddard's men."

"You catch him this time?" asked Tom.

Will shook his head as he closed the door behind him. "I'm afraid not. Didn't even see him. But I'm cutting his gang down, a little at a time. If I keep this up, sooner or later he's not going to have anybody left to brew that *wisgi* or sell it for him."

Tom snorted. "Don't you believe it. He can always get more no-account *yoneg* gunmen from over in Arkansas. I think that's all they've got over there. The Cherokee would be a lot better off if we could just build a nice tall fence all along the border so that nobody from Arkansas could get in here."

Will's grin widened as he came over to his partner and shook Tom's hand. "You must be feeling better," he said. "You're getting more and more proddy every time I see you."

"Yeah, and I'll be able to ride pretty soon, so why don't you quit gallivantin' all over the country and gettin' in shoot-outs with Stoddard's boys? You're ruinin' all the fun for me."

"Don't worry about it, Tom. There's plenty of 'em to go around."

Will sat down at the table and eagerly ate the supper Sara offered him. Evidently he had been riding for a long time, because he was tired. Sara could see it in the way he held himself. He was pushing too hard, trying to do too much. Sooner or later, his weariness would lead him to make a mistake.

A mistake that could be fatal . . .

Evidently he was willing to spend the night, though, and Sara was grateful he had decided to slow down for that long. He and Tom spent the evening talking about places and people Sara didn't know, and several times Will changed the subject abruptly, as if the conversation were about to lead into things he didn't want her to hear. More tales of gunfights he'd had with the bootleggers, she thought. That was all right. She didn't want to hear about it, didn't even want to think about it.

Vincent, tired as always, went to bed while Will and Tom were still talking. Sara stayed up, unwilling to waste even this opportunity to be with Will, even though they weren't alone. Finally, though, Will was all talked out, and he stood up and stretched.

"Think I'll go out to the barn and get some sleep," he said.

"There's a perfectly good sofa," Sara said quickly. She didn't want him leaving the house tonight. He might take it into his head to ride off and start looking for Stoddard again. "You can sleep there."

"Or I reckon there's room to bunk down with me," Tom offered.

Will chuckled. "No, thanks. I've slept with you before, partner—or at least tried to. Remember that hotel in Muskogee when we had to go over there on that errand for the sheriff? I thought your snoring was going to rattle the walls right down!"

"You imagined the whole thing," Tom said, drawing himself up in wounded dignity. "I ain't never snored in my life."

"Then I reckon it must've been an earthquake I heard." Will turned to Sara. "Thanks for the meal and the hospitality, Doctor. The barn'll do fine for me."

"Well, if you insist," Sara said, a new idea occurring to her. "But I want to take some blankets out there for you."

"I can—" Will began, then stopped. He nodded. "Much obliged, ma'am."

Tom pushed himself to his feet, having evidently not seen—or having chosen to ignore—the look that had passed between the two of them. "I'm turnin' in," he said. "See you in the morning, Will."

"I'll be here," promised Will.

While Tom limped off to the spare bedroom, Sara got a couple of blankets from the cedar chest she had bought in Tahlequah the previous autumn. Will came up behind her and said quietly, "I really can take those if you want me to, Sara."

She shook her head without looking at him. "No. I want to do this." She took a deep breath, then turned and said, "Let's go."

They slipped out the rear door of the house and walked side by side toward the small barn where the horses that pulled the buggy and the wagon were kept. Stars shone brightly in the black velvet sky overhead, and a thin slice of moon was visible as well. Will swung the barn door open. After they had stepped inside, he dug a lucifer out of his pocket and scraped it into life. Sara squinted her eyes against the sudden brightness of the flame. Will held it to the wick of a lantern hanging on a peg driven into the wall near the entrance.

"Are you sure you'll be comfortable out here?" she asked him.

"I'm sure. I'll go get my horse and tend to him while you . . . do whatever it is you're going to do with those blankets."

Sara knew very well what she was going to do. She spread the blankets on some freshly thrown hay in an empty stall, then reached for the buttons of her blouse.

She listened to him, enjoying the sound of his movements as he led his horse into the barn, unsaddled it, and made sure it had grain and fresh water. Then, as he stepped around the corner of the stall where Sara was waiting for him, she lifted the corner of the lightweight blanket she had thrown over herself. A smile pulled at the corners of his mouth as he looked down at what he could see of her nude body—an arm, a shoulder, a bared breast with the nipple hard with desire and need.

"I love you, Sara," he whispered.

"And I love you, Will Sixkiller."

He came to her, and it was as good as the first time, the weariness that both of them felt slipping away, purged by the fires that ignited inside them. In the dim, flickering light of the lantern, they explored each other with hands and mouths, finally molding together in a surge of want that would no longer be denied.

Sometime during their lovemaking, a vagrant breeze curled into the barn, through the door that Will had left open an inch or so, and the draft sucked out the flame in the lantern.

Neither of them noticed the darkness.

Sara woke to the sound of thunder and thought that a summer storm had moved in.

Then, an instant later, she knew it wasn't thunder she heard at all.

The gunshots kept slamming through the night, and in the darkness she felt Will roll away from her sud-

denly, heard the startled exclamation that came from
him. He must have been asleep, too, she thought.

But he came awake with the instant alertness of a
wild animal—or a man who lives constantly with danger. Light—a red, garish, flickering light that made
Sara think of hellfire and brimstone—suddenly
washed into the barn, through the big door that had
been jerked open, and she saw that Will was on his
feet, struggling to pull his pants on. A man's voice
shouted, "There's somebody in the barn!"

Another man yelled back, "Then kill 'em!"

Sara knew the second voice, recognized it even as
Will threw himself to the side, his hand reaching out
for the gun rig he had hung on a post at the head of the
stall. The man who had issued the order to kill was
Lew Stoddard. Sara was as certain of that as she had
ever been of anything in her life, even though she had
only heard Stoddard's voice on one previous occasion,
and that months in the past.

There was another gunshot, close by this time, and
Sara bit back a scream as she grabbed for her dress.
Out of the corner of her eye she saw Will spin around
with his gun in his hand and fling himself forward into
the hard-packed dirt runway in the center of the barn.
Flame blossomed from the muzzle of his gun as it
bucked twice in his hand. Somewhere near the front of
the barn, a man grunted in pain, then gave a soft, bubbling cry.

Will scrambled to his feet and ducked into the stall.
He grabbed Sara's arm and said urgently, "Out the
back! You've got to get out the back! Now!"

He pulled her out of the stall and gave her a push in
that direction, then spun toward the entrance again.
Sara almost lost her balance and fell, but she caught

herself and looked toward the entrance, seeing Will silhouetted against the leaping flames that were consuming her house.

Vincent. Vincent was probably still in there.

She knew without even thinking about it what was happening. Lew Stoddard, tired of the damage that Will was doing to his gang, had tracked the deputy here some way, and now he intended to put an end to the trouble Will was causing. At the same time, as an object lesson to everyone else in the area, he would wipe out the friends who had dared to help Will.

That was why her house was enveloped in flames, and that was why gunshots and savage yelling filled the night. That was the hell Will Sixkiller was charging right into, armed only with a pistol that already had two chambers empty.

Sara dashed into the corner of the barn and felt around in the darkness for the pitchfork she knew was there. Will wouldn't like it if he knew she planned to disobey his orders, but she couldn't help that. She wasn't going to let him fight this battle alone. He had been doing too much of that. Besides, she wouldn't be fighting just for him. There were Vincent and Tom to consider, too, and if they hadn't managed to get out of the house yet, they might be trapped in that inferno.

Her fingers closed over the smooth wood of the pitchfork handle. She snatched it up and ran out of the barn. Will had gone to one knee and was firing at several men on horseback who were fighting to control their skittish mounts near the blazing house. Sara saw orange muzzle flashes as the men returned Will's fire.

Suddenly, a huge shape loomed up to her right, and when she twisted her head in that direction she saw another rider who had evidently just come around the barn. He wore a long duster that was flapping behind him, and in the light from the fire, Sara saw that he had a bandanna tied over the lower half of his face. There was a rifle in his left hand. He didn't seem to have noticed her, because he pointed his horse right toward Will, evidently intent on riding him down from behind.

Sara stepped toward the man and thrust the pitchfork up and out as hard as she could.

The tines slammed into his side with an impact that tore the fork from Sara's fingers and left her hands and arms tingling. The man let out a scream and slid to the far side of his saddle, toppling out of it as he let go of the reins and the Winchester to clutch futilely at the pitchfork embedded in his belly. He crashed to the ground and lay still, either dead or knocked out from the fall. At the moment, Sara didn't care which. She wasn't a healer any longer. She was a woman fighting for her own life and the lives of those she loved.

She ran toward the man as Will threw a glance over his shoulder and then finished emptying his revolver at the raiders. Sara bent to scoop up the rifle the man had dropped, then ran on to tug the revolver out of his holster. She spun around and headed toward Will.

She cried out, "Will!", and as he spun toward her, she threw the heavy Winchester with all of her strength. The rifle cartwheeled through the air for a dizzying instant before the stock and the breech slapped into Will Sixkiller's outstretched hands. Instantly, he was whirling back to face the raiders, the rifle spitting death as he fired as fast as he could work the lever and jack fresh cartridges into the chamber.

At the same moment, the back door of the burning house burst outward and two figures stumbled into the night, one large and brawny, the other frail and much smaller. Tom Whitson had one arm around Vincent, half-dragging him. Flames licked at the clothes of both men, but there was no time to extinguish them. As soon as they were clear of the blaze, Tom let go of Vincent, and the older man slumped to the ground. Tom already had a gun in one fist; now he jerked another one from behind his belt. Shots rolled from the revolvers in a hail of fire and lead.

The bootleggers had counted too much on the element of surprise. And they had underestimated the resistance that the Cherokee lawmen would put up as well. Several of the men, all wearing dusters and bandannas, went spinning from their saddles as the fierce volley from Will and Tom took its toll. Others managed to stay aboard their horses, but they hunched over and screamed in agony as bullets bored into them. Sara had meant to join in the fight with the pistol she held tightly in both hands, but it didn't appear to be necessary. Almost as one, the surviving raiders wheeled their horses and lit out in a gallop, wanting nothing more than to get away from here with their lives.

All except one man, who came around the other side of the house and rode toward Will, bellowing curses at the top of his lungs as he fired the long-barreled pistol in his hand.

"Will!" Sara screamed.

She knew somehow the last man was Lew Stoddard, knew that the leader of the bootleggers wouldn't flee until Will, at least, was dead. She lifted the gun, pulling back the hammer with her thumbs.

Will tried to twist around to meet the new threat, but the first of the slugs smashed into him when he was only halfway there. Sara saw him stagger, saw the dark stain that suddenly flowered on his side. The impact of the bullet knocked him all the way around so that he was facing the onrushing Stoddard, who fired again. The bullet caught Will in the chest this time, but somehow he stayed on his feet and even tried to bring the rifle up so that he could fire.

Sara pointed the barrel of the gun she held at Stoddard and pulled the trigger. The concussion was enormous, more even than she expected, and the recoil almost tore the weapon out of her hands. She held on to it, though, and saw as she squinted through the clouds of powdersmoke floating in the air that Stoddard was still coming. Half-deafened from the explosions, her arms and shoulders throbbing from the weight of the gun and the recoil of the first shot, she looped her thumbs over the hammer and hauled it back again.

Stoddard fired before she could, and Sara saw Will's head jolt back. A huge sob welled up inside her, and tears filled her eyes, which were already burning from the smoke. She couldn't think about what she had just seen, couldn't think about anything except lining up the blade of the sight with Lew Stoddard's chest . . .

She fired, and on the other side of the clearing between the barn and the burning house, Tom Whitson's two guns blasted at the same time. All three slugs slammed into Stoddard, jerking him straight up in the saddle. The galloping horse ran out from under him, leaving him to seemingly hang in midair for an instant, blood welling from his wounds and turning his light-colored duster dark. Then he crashed to the earth and lay still.

But no more motionless than Will, who was sprawled unmoving on the ground nearby. Sara dropped the gun, sobbed his name, and ran toward him. She fell to her knees beside him, just as she had fallen to her knees beside another motionless body a little more than eight years earlier. She had cried out Carver's name then, just as she screamed Will's now.

But now, as then, it was too late. Her physician's eye had seen the hole in the center of Will's forehead. She knew what the back of his skull would look like where the bullet had blasted its way out. He was dead, had died instantly.

Strong hands took hold of her shoulders, pulled her up and away from Will's body. Tom folded her against him, and as Sara buried her face against his broad chest and let the wracking sobs roll through her, she was vaguely aware that she had seen Vincent standing nearby, apparently all right. She knew she should be glad of that, but right now she couldn't bring herself to care. She couldn't do anything except mourn, and her wails blended with the crackle of flames that roared up even louder as the roof of the house collapsed.

This—*this!*—was where the healer's road had led her again. Standing over the body of the man she had loved. Powerless to do anything as her world was destroyed.

The shadows had closed in around her, and this time she didn't think they would ever go away.

EPILOGUE

Sara looked down at the piece of paper in her hand. Her mind could comprehend the words, but her heart had trouble grasping them.

The news came as no real surprise. A heart attack, John's letter said. Only the Almighty knew how much pain Thomas Black had been in when he died, but at least the end had been mercifully swift. John had handled everything, and Thomas had been laid to rest there in Handley's Mill. John was staying to take care of Clarissa and try to rebuild his own life. The letter was dated three weeks earlier, and it had arrived in Tahlequah just in time for the local postmaster to catch Sara and give it to her. The wagon, loaded with supplies for the journey, was ready to roll.

Vincent stood beside her, reading over her shoulder, and he put a hand on her arm as he said, "I'm sorry, my dear, so sorry. Thomas Black was . . . was the finest man I ever knew."

"Yes," Sara said softly in agreement. But she had known other fine men, now lying beneath the earth in eternal rest, too.

Carver Gresham. Will Sixkiller.

How many more men would she love . . . and lose?

Never again, she vowed. Never again would she allow herself to feel what she had felt with Carver and Will. That part of her life was over.

But she knew that wasn't true. Not with the new life that was growing inside her. Will's child . . . She was going to have to tell Vincent about that—one of these days. But not yet. Not yet.

First she wanted to put Indian Territory behind her forever.

The decision had been a simple one. Lew Stoddard was dead, his gang scattered. But someday the bootleggers might get together again and want to come after the people who had killed their leader. It would be much safer for Sara and Vincent if they moved on. Besides, Sara still had hopes that a drier climate would improve Vincent's condition.

Tom Whitson's offer to go with them had made up their minds. The big Cherokee had no wish to stay here now that Will was dead. They had been friends and partners for a long time, and even though the Cherokee Nation was the only home Tom had ever known, the thought of striking out for someplace new appealed to him.

"Cherokees ain't much for wanderin'," he had said when he told Sara and Vincent he wanted to go with them. "So I guess it must be the *yoneg* blood in me that's makin' my feet so itchy."

Sara had found a smile somewhere within herself as she put a hand on his shoulder. "We'll be glad to have you travel with us, Tom. Where would you like to go?"

"Anyplace but here." He sighed. "Anyplace but here."

Sara knew exactly what he meant, because she felt

the same way herself. There were too many memories. Everywhere she looked, she would be reminded of Will.

If Vincent thought anything about her reaction to Will's death, he hadn't mentioned it. Maybe he thought she was just upset by the violence that had destroyed their home. Maybe he knew about their affair and just didn't care anymore. Sara would try to puzzle that out later, once they were away from here.

She folded the letter and put it in the pocket of her dress. Vincent said, "Do you want to go back to Handley's Mill?"

"What for?" she asked. "My father is dead and buried. My mother hasn't known me for years. John's there, but he's going to have to find his own way. He always has." Sara shook her head and looked toward the west. "No, I think we should go on as we planned. There'll be a place somewhere that needs a doctor, a place where we can settle down and get on with our lives."

"A place where we can be happy," Vincent said.

Sara just smiled. She couldn't bring herself to be that optimistic.

But maybe he was right. When Will died, she had thought that she might as well be dead, too. Funny thing, though . . . the sun had come up the next morning. The world had kept turning, and the new life within her had continued to grow. She remembered what Will had said. *Life is what happens.* The squirrel never thought about it but was happy anyway.

"Remember, Sara," Vincent said quietly, "I love you."

She nodded. "I know."

Then she took the big hand that Tom held down to

her and climbed onto the seat next to him. Vincent made himself comfortable in the back of the wagon. Tom lifted the reins, slapped them down on the backs of the horses, and called out. The team strained against the harness.

The wagon rolled out of Tahlequah. Sara swayed a little on the seat as the vehicle bounced over the rutted road. In the pocket of her dress was the other letter John had sent to her, the letter her father had begun but never finished. She would read it later, she decided, once they had put some miles behind them.

For now, she lifted her chin, blinked away the tears that tried to form in her eyes, and watched to see where the road would take them.

TOP WESTERN TITLES FROM JOVE BOOKS!

__HIGH MOUNTAIN WINTER
by Frances Hurst   0-515-11825-7/$5.99

It was 1850, and a young nation looked westward to the promise of new land and a new life. But Maryla Stoner's destiny takes a different turn when her family dies on the journey west and Maryla must survive the high mountain winter...alone. Based on a true story.

__ME AND THE BOYS
by Ellen Recknor   0-515-11698-X/$5.99

Sixteen-year-old Gini Kincaid had hair of flame and a spirit to match. Running with outlaws, her name was on the tongues of righteous and criminal folk across the Southwest. And she had a mouth that got her into all kinds of trouble...

__THUNDER IN THE VALLEY
by Jim R. Woolard   0-515-11630-0/$4.99

Falsely accused of trading with Indians, Matthan Hannar barely escaped the hangman's noose. He ran for his life through the treacherous valley, eluding scalpers and surviving the wilderness. Now, for the sake of a woman, he was going back...where the noose was waiting for him.